At the End of the World, Turn Left

At the End of the World, Turn Left

Zhanna Slor

Copyright © 2021 by Zhanna Slor
Cover and jacket design by 2Faced Design

ISBN 978-1-951709-25-9
eISBN: 978-1-951709-54-9
Library of Congress Control Number: available upon request

First hardcover edition April 2021 by Agora Books
an imprint of Polis Books, LLC
44 Brookview Lane
Aberdeen, NJ 07747
www.PolisBooks.com

Dedicated to the memory of my mother, Edit Vaynberg, and my grandparents, Nikolai and Khaya Vaynberg.

FEBRUARY 2008

MASHA

CHAPTER ONE

The second I land in Milwaukee, I'm a different person. My whole body tenses, from my leather-booted feet to my long brown hair, crimped into stifled curls during the fourteen-hour flight from Israel. If my dad notices any of this, he doesn't mention it. He's smoking again, staring out the window. I haven't seen him with a cigarette in years, and for a second I can't help but wonder if I got in the right car. But there is no mistaking his dusty, maroon clunker in which I spent much of the nineties dreaming of other continents. Nor is my unsmiling Russian father difficult to distinguish from the other middle-aged men idling at the arrivals terminal.

"Hey," I say, sinking into the old sun-bleached passenger seat. I decide not to ask about the Marlboro Lights on the dash next to a Nirvana sticker I'd once pasted there, nor why the right mirror is still duct-taped on at a strange angle, like a misplaced limb. When it comes to my dad, it's better to wait until he offers information. Normally this drives me crazy, but I'm too tired to feel much of anything. I attempt a smile anyhow. "I appreciate your efforts to save money for my inheritance, but you might want to consider getting a car that's not held together by superglue?"

Papa starts driving onto the highway, Mitchell Airport a giant brown slab in the rearview mirror, along with my regular life; schwarma, Nescafé, sirens and underground bunkers. David's faded *Golani* t-shirt coiled around his tanned biceps, his gun never too far from his body,

9

or mine. I suddenly miss it in a way I hadn't noticed throughout my hastily planned flight. Gone is my semi-upbeat disposition, buoyed by three mini-bottles of wine and an endless stream of movies I'd watched on the plane. In its place a familiar, unsettling discomfort takes root.

Papa, more at home in this discomfort than not, is still mulling over my failed attempt at levity.

"If it ain't broke..." he finally replies, in a thick Russian accent that makes me momentarily homesick before finding its way into the humorous part of my brain.

I find myself stifling a laugh. "Papa, I don't think you understand that saying."

"Right. I just stupid old man."

"But it *is* broke..." I start. "Forget it." I don't bother trying to explain.

My dad's hands are so tight on the wheel it pains me to look at him. Maybe coming back was a bad idea. I generally try to avoid lending credence to his anxieties, which have always hung over us like humid air that never draws rain. I try to tell him: everyone's healthy, everyone's safe. Isn't that something? But in his mind, it's still 1980s Soviet Ukraine. No matter how much money we had growing up, it was never enough; no matter how safe, it was not safe enough. This is how we ended up in the middle of Wisconsin, the only Russian kids for hundreds of miles, not to mention the only Jews. Well, that, and my great-aunt Rachel happened to live in Wisconsin, and since she sponsored us to immigrate, we had to come here too. That didn't mean we had to *stay*.

"Papa!"

"What?"

I grab his phone out of his hand, stopping him from typing instead of looking at the road. I catch what I think is an email header from a law firm. Without looking at it again, I put the tiny machine into the cupholder with two fingers, as if touching it will spread some disease I don't want.

"People crash from doing this every second of the day," I explain. It's the first iPhone I've seen in real life, and something about it gives me the chills. Or maybe I've been spending too much time among the Israeli Orthodox.

"Maria Pavlova." My dad rolls his eyes, his use of my full name and patronymic inducing a slight cringe. No one ever calls me anything but Masha. "Forty years I driving."

"That was before Steve Jobs," I explain. I cover his phone with my hand so he can't retrieve it. No way I'm going to die on Highway 43 surrounded by dried-out empty fields and fireworks warehouses. "These things are dangerous. Trust me, in twenty years they'll call it a plague."

"Plague," my dad laughs. "Bozhe moy, you sound like your sister. It's 2008, Maria. Soon cars drive themselves. If you don't use all tools at disposal—"

"Then you're always going to be at a disadvantage, I know," I finish. "The thing you always forget is that tools can also be weapons."

"Oh, I don't forget." He shakes his head and lights another cigarette, his expression dark again. Watching him chain-smoke like that, I feel myself get worried for the first time since he called. Or maybe it's the familiarity of the drab Wisconsin roads, all that flat, dry land, punctuated only by strip malls and convenience stores. The sight of it produces an agitated feeling in my gut. Only then does it occur to me I could have said no to coming back. But my dad had been so riled up—it was Yom Kippur so, like most of Israel, our phones had been turned off for almost two days by the time he got through to me—that I'd automatically agreed to everything he said. There's a German adjective for this, fisselig, which means flustered to the point of incompetence as a result of another person's direction. If our phone call—admittedly, our entire relationship—could be summed up by one word, it would probably be that one.

That isn't entirely why I said yes—I said yes because my dad has never directly asked me to come home, not once. He is not the kind of person to request favors. It was a sign, him asking me to do this on Yom Kippur, the day of atonement. Even I couldn't ignore a sign so obvious. I'd done the unthinkable, in a Russian immigrant family: not only did I avoid becoming a doctor, lawyer, or engineer, I'd dropped out of college. And left the country on top of it. The country they had *chosen.* I can't explain exactly why, but once my eyes saw the landscape of Israel—its ancient, dazzling architecture sprinkled across endless hills, the overly friendly young parents and bustling cafés sprouting up on pieces of land so old it's impossible to fathom—it was inevitable. I was, to put it simply, *meant* to live in Israel. As immigrants themselves, you'd think my parents would understand this, but it had proved to be the opposite, if anything.

I turn to face Papa. "So. What's the plan?" I ask. Downtown flies past us, a measly constellation of skyscrapers split down the middle by the snake of the Milwaukee River.

"Huh?" he asks, his forehead lined with confusion.

"What do you mean, *huh?*" I ask, louder, equally confused. Papa blows out a cloud of smoke through the crack of the window, the rush of air making it suddenly loud. I can't get over how weird it is to see him smoke again. Like I've jumped through a time portal and I'm suddenly twelve, not twenty-five. Any minute now, I'll sprout acne and gain ten pounds of water weight. "You made me come all the way out here, and you have no plan?"

My dad inhales again before he speaks, his words coming out smoky. "What are you saying? Is that Hebrew?"

"Oh! Sorry. I didn't even notice," I sputter, switching back to English. I could probably go with Russian, but I am too jetlagged to attempt untangling the wild mess of grammar that my native language calls for. If we'd come from the Soviet Union a little later, say when I was thirteen as opposed to nine, I would probably have a native's perfect grasp of Russian. But my parents were really into the whole American Dream thing when I was growing up, and our Russian skills suffered as a result. They didn't know that by the time we could attain

12

it, the American Dream had morphed into something else entirely, and no one could pinpoint what it was anymore. Maybe that was the whole point. In America, the dream is whatever you think it is.

"Papachka," I start, trying to get to the heart of the matter quickly, the reason he'd asked—no, begged—me to return. Seeing him so frazzled over what is probably nothing is making this whole trip seem less like a friendly visit home and more like an intervention. "Have you considered that, uh…maybe Anastasia is just…mad at you? That she's not really… missing?"

"Maria, please. I may be old but I no idiot. I not heard from her in weeks," he roars, in English. "She started hanging around in that stupid Riverwest." Here he frowns at me like this is my fault. Which it probably is. I'd been the one to first show Anna Riverwest, an eclectic but semi-dangerous neighborhood of Milwaukee full of artists and musicians and, most importantly to my dad: a lot of crime. "I think she shacked up with guy."

"Her roommate? They're just friends. Get with the times already."

"No, not Anarchist."

I stifle a laugh. "I don't think he's an anarchist. He fixes bikes."

"Not him. A boyfriend," my dad explains.

"Oh. Well. It isn't a crime to have a boyfriend. She's an adult. She's allowed to do whatever she wants."

"This is what cops said, too." He shakes his head again, frustrated. "Gospodi, I wish I'd had boys."

"*Papa!*"

"When you last talk to her?"

"I think a few weeks ago, online," I say. "I gave up calling her a long time ago. You know how much she likes to answer the phone."

"Her phone is dead. I called AT&T and guy couldn't tell me something except phone is dead, which I already know," he says. "Durak."

"That doesn't prove much, except that she's nineteen," I explain. "Right now, the most rebellious thing a person can do is get off the grid."

"It just like what happened before," my dad responds, pointedly. "This why I ask you to come. You think it was easy for me?"

I sit on this for a moment, that old familiar uneasiness bubbling up inside me. Guilt. It coursed through every interaction I'd ever had in my family, even before I'd had reason to feel it; the unfortunate outcome of surviving when so many didn't, I'd supposed—pogroms, Hitler, Stalin, mass poverty, my family had escaped it all. How would I ever live up to that? All I'd managed to do was escape *them*.

"I don't want you to get your hopes up. I'm not sure I'm going to be able to find her," I tell my dad, quietly. "You should talk to the cops again if you're worried."

"You think I did not talk to cops again? They have better things to do than look for girl who no longer posts on Bookface account."

"It's called Facebook, Papa. And she wasn't on Facebook, she was on MySpace."

"Okay. My space," he parrots, as if speaking in an alien tongue. He exits the highway via Locust Ave., instead of continuing north to the suburbs, where he still chooses to live for some reason I will never understand. "I ask you to try. You used to live down here. You familiar with area. You know...young people."

"Not really. I've been gone a while. And I'm not so young anymore." I turn my head to the side, confused. A sign directing traffic towards UW-Milwaukee appears on the left. On the right, the standard string of rundown houses, baggy-clothed youth with paper-sack forties and cigarettes lingering in groups. My dad goes left. "Where are we going?" I ask. "I need to sleep, Papa. And I stink. People will think I'm homeless."

"This is better. You blend in," my dad says, with a hint of a smirk. It's the first relatively positive emotion he's expressed since I got in the car. Not that my father is a man of many positive emotions in general; Dostoevsky was right when he said, "The Russian soul is a dark place." Still, for a moment the knot in my stomach loosens, until I realize he's

14

serious. I turn to the back seat.

"What about my stuff? What about Mom? I haven't seen her since...I can't even remember. When was it that you came to Jerusalem for Totya Lana's funeral?"

"So you wait few more hours, big deal." He pauses for a moment, then exhales another long plume of smoke out the window, where the familiar landscape of Riverwest begins to pass us by. Center Street, Uptowner, Foundation's bamboo door and candlelit windows. A line of parked, multicolored road bikes. They shimmer in the bright, hot sun all the way down to Fuel Café, patios filled with aging hippies and crust punks in black-and-beige thrift store fare, all smoking cigarettes above some scraggly dogs. It's like seeing an old lover again; half adoration, half punch in the gut.

"*Seriously*, Papa? This really can't wait?" I ask, in Russian now.

"I've *been* waiting, Masha," my dad sighs. "You know this not good for me," he adds, tapping his chest. "With my condition."

"And you know this place isn't good for *me*," I say, looking back down at my hands, which are clenched. I unfold them onto my lap. I feel angry, then immediately after, like I could cry. I can't explain why exactly. What am I so scared of? This used to be my favorite place in the world. And Center Street is abuzz with activity—a leather-clad couple walking two spotted pit bulls in bandanas. A dreadlocked mom with a baby attached to her chest, a face-tattooed cyclist splashing past on a bright yellow tall bike.

It's exactly like I left it.

My dad, noticing all this too, shakes his head in confusion. This type of rebellion, more aesthetic than political, is inexplicable to a Soviet immigrant, where going against the grain could mean gulags or death.

"I told you not to move here, didn't I? You could have lived at home. Anastasia too. Nothing would be happening if you girls listened to me."

"We don't even know if anything *is* happening," I say, not taking the bait. "All I was saying is that..." I start. I swallow the lump in my throat. "It's, I don't know. It's really weird. For me to be here."

Papa drops his cigarette out the window and double-parks in front of the alley right past Fuel Café, where a purple-haired barista is throwing out a large bag of garbage. She turns and looks in our direction, squints, then drops the bag inside the dumpster.

"I could care less about weird. Your sister is gone," he says. He reaches across me to open the door, essentially kicking me out of the car. "You still young. You manage."

MASHA

CHAPTER TWO

Before I know what's happening, I'm back outside in a barely-there leather coat watching as my dad's car disappears down Fratney Street. For a moment I stand there, numbly, staring at his bumper—plastered with Bush/Cheney stickers, something you could probably get punched for around here these days—and forgetting what it is I am meant to do. Then I turn to find myself in front of Fuel Cafe's awning. Right. Fuel. A good place to start, if I'm really here to find Anna. Anna loves Fuel. Plus, I could definitely use some coffee.

Walking through the narrow, flyer-covered vestibule, I'm immediately bombarded with a vivid memory of her. My parents had gone to China for the week, so I stayed at the house and brought her to Fuel with me a few times. There was nothing unusual about the hours we'd spent. She doodled mugs and smoke rings in her sketchpad while I studied for my linguistics final: *A group of dragonflies is called a dazzle. Tsuris is a Yiddish word for grief and trouble, especially when caused by a son or daughter. Bamboozle derives from the French word, embabouiner, meaning "to make a baboon out of someone." To explode originally meant "to jeer a performer off the stage."*

To unhappen something means to make it look like it never took place.

This word made so much sense to me when I was in Israel, but now I can suddenly see what it's really referring to is an illusion. Unless you are capable of erasing your memory, it is impossible to succeed in unhappening an experience. Already, things are coming back to me that I'd somehow forgotten. How at some point, during our evening at

Fuel, I had caught Anna looking around the smoky room and smiling. She had been becoming rather stingy with her smiles (see: Dostoevsky), and it surprised me to catch one.

"What?" I had asked her.

"Oh, nothing," she'd said then. "I just like this place." She released a shy sort of shrug that reminded me for a moment that she was only fourteen. It was hard to remember sometimes, with all her painting skills and sharp remarks, that she was still basically a kid. I almost felt bad for being annoyed that I was stuck watching her. In retrospect, I realize now, that week had been a gift; it almost felt like maybe, if one of us had been more keen on trying, that we could have been friends again.

Now, back in Milwaukee, alone, every single thing is telling me that I missed an opportunity. As the eldest, wasn't it my responsibility to keep up with our relationship? Well, perhaps it's not too late just yet. I look around Fuel to see what's changed, and am relieved to find that except for the right wall, which used to be painted yellow and teal but is now covered in a floor-to-ceiling photo of young motorcyclists, nothing much has. There are still the same old, creaky wooden floors and tables, an ornate white ceiling that would be better fitted for an old downtown bank. The long gray radiator is steaming next to the windows, causing a slight fog. The stereo is playing The Cure's "Lovesong." After so many years of cheesy Israeli pop, it's a shock on my system to hear something familiar and agreeable to the ears. A good shock.

Someone clears their throat and I turn to follow the noise. It's the barista, the girl with purple hair and cheek piercings from the alley, who has finished with the customer in front of me. I move forward in line, ordering a large black coffee. I'm so tired I forget to force a smile, watching like a slobbering dog as the young girl pounds her fist over the decanter, allowing a long, hot stream of caffeine to pour into a large paper cup. I should probably explain: Israel has many great attributes, but the ubiquity of Nescafé is not one of them. I have dreams about American coffee more than I dream about my parents.

The barista puts down the cup and then, as I pick it up, her eyes narrow ever so slightly and glaze over. All she sees is the three other people in line she has to serve before she can have a cigarette break, the ones behind me who have spent the last five minutes debating the best places to dumpster-dive (*Trader Joe's in Shorewood!* I want to tell them, but decide against it). She is still looking at my hand when I realize what she wants: money.

"Sorry," I explain with a nervous shake of my head. "Jetlag brain." I put my giant canvas bag on the floor and open it to find a handful of loose cash my dad must have thrown in there when I wasn't looking. The barista's eyes widen before I can get the bag closed. With an apologetic smile, I hand over two one-dollar bills and leave the change, almost half of it, as a tip.

"Have a nice day," the girl says to my back, as an afterthought, once she's pocketed my tip. Within minutes, I'm back outside; I don't know why, except that I don't particularly like feeling young and self-conscious again, which is the only way I can feel while listening to The Cure. I take the lid off the coffee cup and inhale before whispering "Baruch atah Adonai, Eloheinu melech haolam, shehakol nih'yeh bid'varo." The blessing for coffee. As automatic to me now as lighting up a cigarette used to be; perhaps a replacement to it, if I'm being honest. Sometimes the only way to break a bad habit is to replace it with a better one (or a worse one).

I drink the coffee in a matter of minutes; it's a little burnt but still basically heaven, and by the end, I don't feel so sad or so cold either. I'm about to go back for a refill when something catches my eye. Not my eye, actually, but my nose. I know that smell.

"Rose?" I ask.

A young woman in bright red cowboy boots stops walking past me and turns, her long, pale face annoyed at first, then morphing into surprise. "Masha?" she asks. "Is that you?" Rose hugs me tight, nearly knocking the air right out of me and replacing it with a cloud of patchouli and sandalwood. For a moment it feels like no time has passed at all since we last spoke; like I'm still in college, living two blocks away, falling for men only after I'd slept with them a few times and they didn't want me anymore. Chasing annihilation like it was my job. I wonder now why I wanted to disappear so badly when all I had to do was leave. What is so intoxicating about self-destruction? Is it merely the freedom to be able to do it, or is there something else? In Israel, I never have this feeling.

"What are you doing here?" Rose grins, her large hazel eyes sparkling. I smile back, relieved. Rose knows no one well, but she knows everyone just a little bit. Back in the day, we'd go to parties, and in an hour she'd have met everyone there and remembered their names. It could be useful now, as it had been then. "Did someone die?"

"No!" I laugh, before feeling a superstitious chill and getting serious again. I remove a pack of cigarettes from my bag that I'd bought without thinking at duty-free, and give her one. Rose takes the offering, lights it. Her shoulders loosen right away, as if she can only ever be comfortable with a cigarette in her hand.

"But I thought you..." she starts, squeezing my hand now. "Never mind. I guess I thought you were never coming back here." She sits down, still holding my left hand. "Wow, I can't believe it's you. You look so good, girl."

She, on the other hand, looks like she needs to go back to rehab, but I don't want to be the one to tell her this. Otherwise she is generally the same, except that her hair is a new shade of pink. She's wearing shorts with tights underneath and a lacy tank top under a loosely draped Aztec-patterned shawl, a giant chest tattoo of wings still visible beneath. I'd almost forgotten all about that poor decision, and wince as I look at it. Not because she is basically barring herself from ever having a real job—I have no delusions Rose is capable of holding down such a job—but because it's so poorly done. The wings are flat and mechanical when they should be full of movement and freedom, like an actual bird. Instead, they look like they belong on a flag icon, a call to arms, like all the old hand-drawn posters she used to hang in the house that said "courage" or "resist," with images of boots with flowers on them.

Maybe it was the linguistics major in me, not enjoying seeing words so out of context, but I always hated those posters. I couldn't help but wonder: resist what, exactly? Sentences?

"I heard you were in the Middle East," Rose interjects before I can respond. "What's up with that?"

"Israel isn't *exactly* the Middle East. I mean it is, but—"

"Are you like, really religious now?" she interrupts, smirking.

"No," I say, quickly, before remembering that isn't true anymore. "I mean...I don't know. In Israel, it's more about the customs—holiday dinners and no phones on Shabbat, stuff like that. It's kinda nice." I leave out the part where I go to synagogue with David once a week, and celebrate every holiday with his family, and love Shabbat. I remember myself when I used to live here, and I know Rose would merely use this information against me. Already she lets out a small laugh.

"What about those crazy fanatics with the funny hats?"

"Well...I'm not sure I would really call them *fanatics*, Rose," I start, annoyed. In Korean, there is a word—dapjeongneo—for when someone asks you a question and has already decided the answer they want to hear from you and are waiting for you to say it. I know she wants us to make fun of the Hasids. But Rose hasn't talked to me in five years, years that were intensely transformative for me, so her expectations are going to be very off. "Remember the group of communists you used to hang out with? They seemed like fanatics to me."

Rose's shoulders deflate a little. "Wanting everyone to get their fair share is not *extreme*," she says flatly.

"Okay...and who decides what's fair? You?"

"Common sense decides! No one needs a billion dollars. Especially not when there are so many poor people suffering in the world. In this day and age, with how much money America has, we can all afford some more equality."

"Oh boy. Equality. Now that is a loaded word." I lean back on the bench and take a long, deep breath. This is not the conversation I want to be having, and yet, I can't help myself. "If you haven't noticed, nothing is equal in life, other than in mathematics. That *is* where the word originated, back in the 1400s. Latin. *Identical in amount or portion. Uniform in size or shape.*"

"Well, yeah, that's the problem, don't you think?"

"No. The problem is that 'equal' can't be applied to people, because people are never identical. Except twins, I guess, but even then, there are studies…" I pause. "It really reminds me of the story of Sodom and Gomorrah. Do you know it?"

"What?" Rose gasps. She drops her cigarette on the ground and grinds it down with her shoe. "No. You know I never read the *Bible.*" Rose spits out bible like it's a dirty word. In Riverwest, it *is* a dirty word. Here, the only religion is counter-culture—which, if anything, is merely an absence of culture, not a replacement with another. A vacuum that sucks in everything around it.

"Never mind," I say. I should probably have shut my mouth back when she mentioned crazy people in funny hats. If I start talking religion in Riverwest, I won't make it through the day. I imagine a crowd of torch-holding anarchists throwing me out onto the Humboldt Avenue bridge, where artsy Riverwest turns into the college-partying East Side. Even when I lived here, I barely talked to anyone about religion, or politics for that matter. Not because I disagreed, more because I didn't care. I didn't care about anything—that was the problem. It was what you found at the bottom of the vacuum. Nihilism sucked you in with its ideologies, but it kept you with its existential crisis, its replacement of meaning with parties and the everyday dramas of your neighbors. It's easy to get lost in these things for years, for decades even. A person could get lost forever, looking for something, when she doesn't know what it is she's looking for.

"Um, okay," Rose starts, as if she is talking to a crazy person. "Have

22

you thought about getting a snake?"

I turn to face her, my face morphed into confusion before I can stop it. "What? Why?"

"Well you need one, like, desperately. Your energy is really dark right now." She does not explain how a snake could change my energy from dark to light, not that it would make the sentiment more logical in my eyes. She simply scowls at me, then glances down at her wrist, where there is a large tattoo of a bass sticking out from under a thick plastic watch, and abruptly stands up. "Shit. I'm late for band practice," she says. "I really have to go. We're playing later at Bremen if you want to check it out! The band is kicking ass lately."

"Who? The Silver Plague?"

Rose scoffs, as if spitting out a bad egg. "No, The Langston Hughers. The Silver Plague was getting too famous. I had to quit that shit."

"Why?" I ask, puzzled. I know that famous in Milwaukee only means people in Milwaukee know who you are, not that you're touring or making money; nevertheless, it only makes her statement more puzzling to me.

"I don't know," she says, looking to the sky, her mouth set deep in contemplation before turning up a little at the edges, as if she is proud of the answer she's come up with. "Maybe I'm scared of success or something. Sellouts are so lame."

I open my mouth, then close it again.

"Anyway," says Rose, the smirk from her face gone. "You know I'm not one for deep thoughts. I'll leave that to people like you." She starts walking off, but I stand, blocking her exit on the sidewalk.

"Wait." It suddenly occurs to me why I'm here, and it's not to convince anyone about the deeper meaning of bible stories or discuss local music. "You ever see my sister around?"

Rose begins adjusting the large plaid knit wrap over her shoulders until it's essentially covering all of her skin, like a shield. A shield from me. "Uh, yeah, sometimes."

"Where?" I ask, stiffening.

Rose keeps looking down at the sidewalk, which is covered in cigarette butts and wet coffee sleeves, before stealing a glance in my direction.

"I don't know, just around."

"*Rose.*"

My old friend sighs. A flash of something dark—worried, maybe? Jealous?—passes through her, and I suddenly wonder if my dad isn't being paranoid at all. "I really don't remember," Rose says. She lights another cigarette from a pack in her shawl.

"Are you sure?"

Rose crosses her arms over her chest as if warming herself, but I know it's an instinctively defensive move. Against me. Probably all that Krav Maga I'd been learning in Israel making its presence known without my realizing it; fighting is all muscle memory, after all. Had I ever been so meek? It's hard for me to imagine. Still, I sit back down and try to relax my posture as much as I can. I practically slouch right out of my chair.

"You should check out Valhalla," she finally tells me. "That's where everyone her age goes."

I almost laugh. "Valhalla?"

"Plato's Cave?" she tries, her eyes bright and amused.

I shake my head.

"...The Blue House?"

"Oh. *The Blue House*," I say, remembering the blue-and-white duplex across the street from an abandoned basketball court. How could I forget the revolving door of punk houses in Riverwest? I used to spend half my free time at them. They were always changing location or name, but they were all the same: messy, overcrowded duplexes full of cigarette smoke and sticky-beer floors, and way too many people living there than could be legal. Local bands screaming from basements every other night, while bonfires burned high in the yard. The feeling of camaraderie enforced by vast amounts of alcohol and the fact you all lived in the same mile radius. At one point, it was the closest I'd ever come to some sort of religion. Only now that I've experienced true religion do I realize how immensely far away it was from one. The connection I'd felt hadn't been real; I never talked to any of those people again.

"Anything else you can tell me?" I pry. But Rose merely breaks eye contact and hugs me again—a light, casual-type of hug now, one reserved for strangers—then turns on her bright red cowboy-booted heels.

"No, sorry, Mash. Good luck, okay?"

Then she disappears down the street without another word, and I have no choice but to go, too.

MASHA

CHAPTER THREE

At the door of Valhalla, a tattooed, muscular man in plaid boxers squints at me, like I am a too-bright sun. Or like he hasn't seen the sun in a while, more likely. He lets out a noisy exhale, the cigarette hanging out of his mouth nearly falling to the floor.

"Whoa," he says, eyebrows thick with confusion. "Masha?"

I'm surprised too, admittedly, but I hide it better. "Hey, Liam. Can I come in?"

Liam steps back, still blinking profusely, and opens the door wider. I follow him inside, while three huge dogs circle and sniff me in a frenzy, then get bored and crash down onto the floor. Liam presses pause on a remote and points at the flat screen, where a bald man is standing out in a desert with no pants on. "Have you seen this show yet?" he asks. "*Breaking Bad?* It's the shit."

"No," I say, sitting down. "I don't really watch much TV, to be honest."

"Oh, bullshit," Liam says. "Everyone says that, and no one means it. Come on."

"Believe what you want," I shrug. I could explain how American TV takes forever to get to Israel, and even when it does you often have to pirate it. Pirating shows may be fine for most people, but when your boyfriend works for the government, you don't exactly want to do anything illegal, no matter how small. But what would be the point? More importantly, do I really need to defend myself to a guy who still

26

uses blankets as drapes?

Liam shakes his head, then starts packing a bowl into a massive red bong on the table, his long, curly black hair falling around his shoulders. He still doesn't ask me what I'm doing there. Like it's perfectly normal for me to show up out of the blue and sit down on his dog-hair infested couch. "Always such a hipster," he says with a smirk.

"Says the guy growing not one but two kombuchas." I nod my head in the direction of two large jars filled with a yellowish-green liquid. He turns and looks.

"Those are *not* mine," he explains.

"That's what all the hipsters say," I joke, letting out an uncomfortable laugh. "Well, that, and that they aren't hipsters."

Liam, still busy with the bong, allows himself a little chuckle. "Ha. Very astute, as usual."

Unaware of how to transition to the subject more naturally, I get to the point. "So, uh…have you seen my sister around, by chance?"

Liam is already taking a hit from the bong, so I have to wait a ridiculously long time for him to inhale and exhale. When he's finished, instead of answering, he looks up and asks me if I want some. I shake my head no.

"That's a first," he snorts. "You're not pregnant, are you?"

I roll my eyes. "Liam. My sister? Have you seen her? I heard she might be here."

"A lot of people hang out here." He shrugs and packs down the bowl again with the edge of a lighter. "Who's your sister?"

"Anna?" I say. I lean forward, sinking further into the couch. "Anastasia Gold."

He stops mid-bong hit, his eyes widening like he'd inhaled too much, before opening his mouth again. Smoke engulfs the already smoky room. "Anna's your *sister*?"

"She goes by my mom's maiden name," I explain before he can ask. "I honestly don't know why. She claims it sounds better. Maybe it's a feminist thing… Anyway, have you seen her?"

He takes a moment to let this sink in, then shrugs. "Not lately." He tries to sound casual but comes off slightly venomous. "I mean, I don't really know her, I've just seen her at shows."

"You don't seem happy about that," I say, curious.

"Like you're the paragon of happiness over here," he snaps, his mood souring. He pushes the bong away and lights a cigarette. Then, he finally looks at me. "What are you doing back, anyway? Aren't you too good for us common folk?"

"What? No. I'm only trying to find Anna."

"Well, I don't know where she is," he says, annoyed.

"Okay. Fine. If you hear anything..." I begin to stand up, but Liam comes over and stops me by sitting down. He smells like sweat and cigarettes and a hint of whiskey; it takes me a second to realize what the combination is, I've grown so accustomed to Israelis' over-generous use of colognes. In Riverwest, the closest people get to wearing perfume is using soap in the shower.

"So, are you back now, or what?" he asks, a squint in his eye.

"No, no, no. Just visiting." I move slightly farther down the couch, away from his half-dressed tattooed body and all those familiar pheromones. One of his dogs, a pitch-black lab with streaks of gray near his ears, jumps up onto the couch between us and starts sniffing me curiously. I pet his thick fur, feeling slighter better. I think I remember the dog from when he was a puppy; and he must remember me too, the way he is so happily licking my arm.

"Get down, Bingo," Liam barks at him. The dog whines and resettles on the floor.

"Where's your girlfriend?" I ask, sliding farther down the couch. "What's her name—Melanie?"

Liam shrugs. "In Chicago. On a date, I think," he says.

"Oh. You're still doing that open relationship thing?" I ask.

"I am..."

"But?"

"Lately, Mel's been...questioning the whole concept," he complains.

28

"It's frustrating. We broke up for a while, and I was seeing someone else, but now we're trying again."

"What's the point of open relationships, again?" I really can't remember, though I was the same when I'd first moved to Israel. David wouldn't have any of my wishy-washy stances on commitment. He wears a kippah and works in a top-secret unit of the IDF, I don't even know what country he is in half the time, but the hardest thing about our relationship was agreeing to be monogamous. Now, I am no longer sure exactly what I spent so much energy fighting him over. Riverwest has a way of seeping into all the crooks and nannies of your brain. But what works in one place, doesn't work in others.

"You've been living in the holy land for too long, girl," Liam says, shaking his head, amused. "You're no fun anymore."

"I've had a lot of time to think about things," I shrug.

Liam moves his hand slightly, so it's touching my shoulder. "What's going on with you? You seem...emotional," he says, watching me, as if genuinely concerned. "It's so not like you," he adds, with a nervous laugh, then takes his hand back.

I swallow, my mouth suddenly dry. His focused attention is unsettling. Not just because he isn't David. But because he's Liam. "Have you ever considered maybe you don't know me as well as you think?" I ask. "I mean, you always did most of the talking between the two of us."

Liam laughs, his whole body shaking with amusement. "Of course I did. Are you kidding me? You would never tell me anything." He hands me his cigarette, and I take a drag without even thinking about it, an intimacy that confuses me more than his close presence. It's a shock to the lungs and I try hard not to cough. Sometimes I forget how much I once loved mindaltering substances. I want to slap that version of myself in the face, and tell her to get it together. There are better ways to learn to live with yourself, and most don't leave you feeling worse the next day.

And all of them involve staying far, far away from Liam Knox.

"Masha?" he is asking me. "Hello?"

"Sorry." I shake my head. "That's not how I remember it," I mumble, handing back the cigarette. My head starts buzzing from it, and I stand up; I haven't had one in years, not since we were together. Sober and tired, all it does is give me a headache, turn things fuzzy at the edges.

"Oh yeah? How do you remember it?" Liam leans against the couch, arms wide, letting out a puff of smoke while half-smiling, something I've seen very few people pull off without looking foolish. But Liam never looks foolish. Every gesture he makes is confident yet relaxed, like he came out of the womb knowing exactly where to place his hands, stack his legs.

"Um..." I lean back against the wall for a moment. The dogs, the smoke, the trash, it's all getting to me. I am possibly even getting a contact high from his bong hits. My head feels fuzzy and disoriented, like when you're in a faraway place in a dream but don't remember how you got there.

Liam stands up and touches my shoulder again. "Hey. Are you okay?"

I nod. "Just a head rush." What am I still doing here? I ask myself. It's getting dark, and he already told me he doesn't know anything. I make a quick judgment, and even though it's rude, walk out of there without another word.

If I thought this hasty exit would in any way work, I clearly forgot who Liam is. Outside, he has already followed me out. "Take my number," he says, producing his phone out of his pocket, still looking concerned, which makes me concerned. "If you need help or something."

"I remember it," I say, so he puts the phone away. Then he stands there and grins, watching me, and I remember why I'd liked him so much to begin with: those eyes. No one had ever looked at me like that before. With such intensity, such focus. Now, I recognize it as a total player move, but then? I'd only ever dated one person before him, my high school boyfriend Nick, an older, melancholy musician that I'd met freshman year when I lived in Hartland, the third and most repulsive of the four suburbs my parents dragged us to post-immigration. He'd had a difficult childhood and I felt more friendship and empathy towards him than attraction. Not Liam. The second I met Liam I was a goner.

He moves forward on the steps, interrupting my thoughts. "I've missed you, you know."

I clear my throat. "You don't know how to miss someone, Liam," I mumble. "You just find someone to replace them."

Liam giggles again. "That's a good one, Masha. That's really good," he says. "You should have been a writer. I always thought that."

I relax a little, realizing maybe he's right, that I am remembering things wrong. When had I become so...serious? I used to be fun. I could still be fun, right? "Sorry," I say. "That was harsh. I didn't mean it."

"Yes, you did. But it's cool, man. I can be your punching bag for the day," he says. "I probably deserve it."

"Oh, you *definitely* deserve it," I say, smiling too, and feeling a little better about being such a grump. I put my coat back on, barely feel warmer. Then I gaze around Pierce Street, thinking about which direction I should go, what my next stop should be. It's nearly dark outside now, or the sky is so overcast it only feels like night. Automatically my body tenses with nerves, because I'm on the exact corner where my former best friend Emily and I once got mugged. We were lucky to get away unharmed, having lost only two flip phones and Emily's fifty-dollar bill, a Christmas gift from her grandma, though it didn't feel that way at the time. Because worse things happen in this neighborhood every day. Beatings, robberies, murders; all of it inevitable from living in one of the top five most segregated cities in America, just behind Detroit. It's the downfall of affordable rent, of cheap old buildings with creaking stairs and windows that breathe in every storm, of carpets molding under leaking radiators. That's the price of living between the cracks of the world.

That, and never being able to get out of them.

I hear Liam's voice again and turn around. He's standing right next to me now. "By the way, what are you doing over there in Israel?" he is asking. "Are you in school or something?"

"No, I'm not," I say. No one has asked me this since I arrived, and for a second it throws me off. But then I remember how much I love my life, when I'm not in Milwaukee, and I am suddenly very chatty. "It took a while to get settled because when I made Aliyah I had to learn Hebrew—"

"What the hell is making Aliyah? Isn't that a singer?"

"Oh, sorry. It means to immigrate to Israel. Anyway then I had to go into the army for a year, but now, I do a bit of translating, and I tutor people in English, mostly Russian immigrants…" I trail off when I notice Liam's eyes have grown wide.

"You? In the army?"

"I only worked in an office. I wasn't, like, shooting anyone." I did learn how to shoot in training, but I don't mention this part. Nor do I mention how surprisingly good I am at it. Everything in Israel came so naturally to me, as if I was always meant to be there. The language, the culture, the repetitive customs and rules of religion, all of it. All anxiety gone. And then David had come along, and I never wanted to leave again.

"What kind of…office?" he asks.

"Just a small base in the north, near the Golan Heights. It was for one of the secret units, so I can't really talk about anything I did there."

"What? Was it—" Liam says, then stops himself. "No, never mind. I mean, I definitely want to know, but I'm a pacifist…"

"Like I said, it doesn't matter if you want to know or not. I can't talk about it. Literally *can't*. I would be breaking the law. And not one of those dumb ones like *don't hang out at the beach after ten PM*, that America has so much of. As if that stops teenagers from having parties and sleeping with each other."

32

Liam doesn't go along with my segue, and continues talking as if I hadn't very recognizably changed the subject. "There's a lot of bullshit going on that country, Masha. The way—"

"Don't start with me, Liam. It's easy to be a pacifist when you're at peace," I interject. "You might feel differently if everyone in Canada and Mexico wanted you dead just because of your nose." Liam starts to say something in response, but I cut him off. "Or if everywhere you went people started ranting at you about how terrible America is, like it's your fault what the government is doing."

He deflates a little, because Liam may be many things, but he is not stupid. "Okay, I guess you're right."

"I know I am." I knew before coming back here that the mere fact that I'd gone to Israel would be like carrying around a neon sign attracting political arguments; something about the place makes people aggressively reactionary, and unlike other countries with less-than-ideal ways of governing, people also don't feel conflicted about being loud about their distaste. Growing up, it was always underneath the surface of things, that to be a Jew in Milwaukee you had to condemn Israel also. Part of why I'd been so reluctant to see the place when I was younger was because my peers spent a lot of time repeating anti-Israel talking points they'd read from headlines, and since my family was not part of the local Jewish community, I'd received no counter-education on the matter. This quiet anti-Semitism was so persistent and so fanatical that by the time I left college I didn't feel comfortable telling anyone I was a Jew. This is likely part of why friends from Riverwest were so surprised when I moved there.

I can tell Liam really wants to continue this conversation in that exact direction, so I try to change the subject again. Now that I've lived in Israel, I understand fully the biases and blind spots of the American media when it comes to the Middle East. But I didn't come here to be an ambassador for the Jewish homeland; I came here to find my sister.

"Look," I say to Liam. "You really didn't know she was my sister?"

Liam's thick black eyebrows knit together. He's thrown back, I can tell. "And what would you have me do? If I had known?"

I take a long breath. "I don't know. Look out for her, I guess."

"Come on, Masha. Don't you remember yourself at that age?" he asks, a wicked grin overcoming his face. "Because *I* do."

"I was such a mess. I don't even know why."

"It's pretty obvious. Your parents were so strict with you. And, well, moderation is a learned skill. Pretty cliché stuff, actually."

"Great. Now I'm a cliché."

Liam smiles again, like he made a great joke. "Well, whatever you were, *I* liked you," he says.

I pause, thinking. It isn't like Liam to be so evasive, or to give compliments. "Did you like Anna too?" I ask. In truth, I don't think there's any way Liam would go for my sister. Liam has a thing for lost girls, and Anastasia had always been so determined, so sure of what she wanted. Nothing at all like me. She'd been winning art contests since she was in grade school, and I was a year into college before I decided on my major, a double in Russian and Linguistics, which I didn't even finish. But his answers strike me as strange. Like he's leaving out an essential piece of information.

Or maybe I'm reading into things too much because all he does is smile again, cool as a cucumber. In fact, he even reaches over my shoulder, pulling on a strand of hair that has fallen loose from my ponytail and placing it behind my ear. "You know me, Masha. I like everyone."

Then, before I know it, he's kissing me.

34

MASHA

CHAPTER FOUR

Riverwest hasn't always been so rundown. It started off with high hopes, at least. In the early nineteenth century, it sprouted up as a summertime playground for wealthy Germans, before becoming a haven for working-class Polish immigrants, as mills, factories, and tanneries were built along the Milwaukee River in the 1890s. Polish immigrants referred to it then as Zagora—roughly translated as "land beyond the hill." Later, in the 1960s, it was home to Milwaukee's counterculture movement, around which time it also became more racially and economically diverse. Now it is more known for its crime than anything. If you tell someone you live in Riverwest, a look of concern is generally the first response.

And sure there is danger, and a shadow you can't name, but there is wonder too. Japanese has a word for this, Wabi-Sabi: finding beauty in imperfections.

In Riverwest, the sidewalks crash into each other like broken teeth. Homeless people wander the streets aimlessly, begging for change. There is a lot of trash—broken bottles thrown from roofs of drunken house parties, cigarette butts, sometimes even used condoms. But it's also surrounded by an immensity of color that could almost hurt to look at: an endless array of trees, multi-colored Polish flats, teal and pink and blue with wrap-around wooden porches.

In Riverwest, even the quiet is boiling over with danger, tension. It's nothing like the quiet of early morning in Tel Aviv, reading a book at a café on Sheinkin Boulevard, tourists still asleep in their hotel beds. Or even the quiet of the nearly empty cul-de-sac where my parents live, thirty miles north of here. You could cut it with a knife, and your hand would come out bloody. That's Riverwest quiet.

It's that quiet that I notice when Liam is kissing me. And it's the quiet that reminds me to push him away. It doesn't belong to me. None of it does. Not anymore.

I push myself backward, nearly falling against an iron railing. Liam sees my face and steps away with his hands raised.

"I'm with someone now," I tell him, when I finally can form words. It takes a second for me to process it; the kiss was so unexpected. Nothing unexpected had happened to me in a long time. Years ago, I'd have anticipated this sort of behavior, but now? People don't kiss you in the street in Israel. Well, maybe they do, but not where I live, not the people I know. There are synagogues where men and women don't even sit in the same *room*. Areas of Jerusalem where people will yell at a woman for walking there unescorted, or not wearing enough clothes. My first week there I got screamed at so much for accidentally walking in a tank top and shorts into Meah Sharim, an Ultra-Orthodox neighborhood off Jaffa Rd., that I never attempted to find the market again. I don't agree with this practice—if it's a hundred degrees out women should be allowed to wear shorts—but it's a normal occurrence in the holy land, something I've now gotten used to. It's easy to avoid these areas.

"Shit, Masha," Liam says. "Sorry. You didn't say anything."

I close my eyes for a second, thinking about David, and what he would say if he were ever to find out. I'd come here to atone, not create more things to atone for. And Liam was right, I hadn't said anything. Why hadn't I?

No, no, no, wait, I remind myself. I'd stopped it. I did nothing wrong. "I have to get out of here."

Liam looks at me incredulously. "This was always your problem,

Masha. No matter where you go, you can only think about leaving. Have you ever tried to just...I don't know, relax?"

"I have a life in Israel," I explain. "I like it there."

"Do you?" Liam asks. "Or are you confusing boredom for contentment? You used to do that too, but the other way around."

"*What?*"

Before I can process his question, the slam of a door makes us both jump. A dreadlocked Native American man in black Carhartt overalls wanders out to the porch, shoeless and coatless and smoking a joint the size of a cigar. He's wearing a torn beige Anti-Flag shirt, and his overalls are more hole than pants. One of Liam's revolving door of train-hoppers, I imagine. They'd been staying on his couches for a month or two at a time for as long as I could remember.

"Hey, Tao," Liam says with a nod, leaning against the railing. "Sup?"

Tao stops mid-toke, his forehead scrunched in recognition, like we know each other, which of course is impossible. And yet there is something familiar about him. It takes me a moment to realize what it is: his hat. It's black with a jagged red stripe across it; I recognize it from somewhere. "Whoa. Déjà-vu," he says, his voice slow and meandering. He is very high. Is he drunk, too? I can't help but wonder how this is possible. Train-hoppers don't have jobs, unless you count sitting outside Fuel Cafe playing the banjo or hitting a plastic bucket like a drum a job. Which some people around here genuinely do count, by the way.

I straighten up, trying to remember where I've seen that hat.

"This is Masha," Liam says to Tao, winking at me. "We're...old friends."

"Have we met before?" Tao asks.

"Definitely not," I say, backing away a little. Something about his energy makes me uncomfortable. Maybe it's because I haven't been around train-hoppers in a while, or maybe I'm not good with strangers sober. Tao seems perfectly relaxed though. He's probably very used to encountering strangers. Not sure what attracts them to Milwaukee, but every summer, these modern-day faux-gypsies flood into Riverwest, a sea of dreadlocks, homemade tattoos, patched-up overalls, tattered black or beige shirts. They play homemade instruments on the sidewalks, sneak in cans of beer to punk shows, dumpster-dive for food outside grocery stores. At first, they are interesting; their lives seem beautiful and free, they make you wish you weren't tied down with jobs, schools, lovers. But come September, you're sick of them. Sick of the smell and self-importance and mediocre singing, sick of tripping over the empty guitar cases littered with coins. You become glad it's getting cold soon, when, like the birds, they go south for winter, live in the parks of New Orleans or scatter across California, Georgia, Florida, and you can have your sidewalks back.

Tao looks up at the gray, darkening sky, snapping his fingers, which are tattooed all the way down to his elbows. "I don't know, man, I think we have," he says. And then I remember where I've seen that hat before. I stand up and retrieve my phone from a pocket, scrolling through for a picture of Anna. It takes me a while to get to one. But when I do, she is wearing *that exact hat*. Long black hair, eyebrow piercing, red-cheeked—from drinking, most likely. Her arm is around some tall, thin man whose head is cropped out. I'd snapped the picture from her MySpace months ago, back when she still posted photos online, because she looked so happy. I'd done so partly because it made me feel less guilty for being gone. Like, if Anna was happy, then it didn't matter that I hadn't visited and barely ever called. But of course, that's a stupid thing to think. The faces we show the world are rarely our true selves. True unhappiness? It's a personal matter. I'd already learned this the hard way once: if Anna was having problems, I'd never discover it from her Internet accounts. Probably not from a phone call, either, now that I'm thinking about it. Anna was always so private about what she was feeling. I can't remember if she ever cried in front of me once after the age of four. So maybe she is happy in this picture, but it's just as possible she isn't.

38

I swallow the lump in my throat and walk up the stairs, bringing the photo over. The air is thick and wet, like it's going to start snowing any second, but Tao doesn't even look cold. "Are you maybe thinking of this girl?" I ask, so close to him now I can smell the grease in his hair. "You're wearing her hat."

"Oh. Yeah!" He looks at the tiny, pixelated photo, then at me. "Shit, you look a lot like her. No wonder I was confused."

I take out my pack of Camel Lights again, offering him one, which he takes eagerly and without thanks, like he is used to people giving him things. He passes the joint to Liam, who either has a very high tolerance or is also going to be this spacey soon. I try not to cough from all the smoke now billowing around my head.

"Where did you find her hat?" I ask this in the most innocent voice I can muster. Which is maybe the wrong approach, since Tao inhales, then looks at me strangely, like he is suddenly suspicious.

"Why are you asking?"

"She's not in trouble or anything," I explain. "Did she give it to you? Where did you find it?"

"Uh," he looks down, and licks his lips. "I dunno, man. The hat? Coulda been anywhere."

"Maybe she left it here after a show," Liam suggests.

"Okay…" I look from Liam to Tao to Liam again, having the strong feeling they are leaving something out. Snow starts to fall then, out of nowhere, covering us all in thick white flakes. Typical Wisconsin weather. Right when you think it's warming up there's another blizzard. Tao doesn't move, or attempt to put on shoes. "Well, do you know where she is, by chance? Or who she's been hanging out with?"

Tao glances at me skeptically, then focuses on Liam, who shrugs. "I think she's with Tristan," Tao finally admits.

Liam's eyes grow large. "No shit?" His lips turn down into a disgusted pout.

"Who's Tristan?" I ask.

"Just some crusty asshole," Liam says. "Stayed here a couple of times and then I'd find shit missing the next day." He shakes his head. "Not cool, man."

"He's really tall," Tao adds, shaking his head and looking again towards the sky. "Like a space creature. He can reach *anything*."

"Does this Tristan guy have a last name?" I ask, frowning.

"You want his social security number too?" Tao jokes.

Liam laughs. "Last summer a guy came around calling himself Twigs the Clown."

Tao perks up and turns to us again. "Twigs was here?" he asks. "I love that guy."

"Do you know anything else about him?" I try. I don't have time to sit here and listen to them talk about a clown. "Anything at all?"

Liam and Tao exchange glances. "No," Liam says. "Why would we?"

"I don't know," I say, taking in a deep breath. "Just asking. Thanks." I turn on my heels and start walking away. At least I have a name now. A lead. That's enough for one visit. More than that, I can't be around Liam anymore. It's too confusing.

"Masha, wait," Liam says, catching up to me on the sidewalk. The snow is falling harder now, but none of it is sticking to the ground yet. It's actually quite beautiful. And somehow sad, too. "I'm glad you stopped here. Really."

"Why?" I ask.

"It's… good to see you doing so well."

I look at him skeptically.

"What? Come on I was joking before, you do seem happy. Tired, but happy," he says. "Which is all we can really hope for right?"

I shrug.

Liam steps forward to hug me. "You're shaking, girl."

"I am?"

"You're freezing," he says, holding me tighter. I let him stay there for a while, because he's right, I am cold, and because he smells so good. Or maybe because I could really use some human interaction right now, I don't know. I can't think straight when I don't get enough sleep, I turn into a quivering baby. Part of me wants to cry, and part of me wants to pass out, and neither one wants to keep walking in the cold. But I know I have to. This isn't my world anymore. I don't have time to get bogged down in nostalgia.

"Thanks," I say, shyly. *Wrong, wrong, wrong*, my brain keeps yelling. *You have a clear conscience now, don't mess it up.* After a moment, I wiggle out of his hug. "I really should go. It's about to really blizzard out here."

"You can come back inside if you want," Liam says. He puts his hands up in surrender. "I won't try anything, scouts' honor."

"I have to find Anna," I say. "Sorry. But thank you." Then I start walking as fast as I can down Center Street, feeling like I dodged a bullet. Before I can get away, Liam calls out my name again. I spin around, but don't head back.

"You should try Bremen Café. Or Foundation," he suggests, but doesn't explain why. I would have tried both those places anyway, but I thank him and continue forward. Speeding through the torrent of giant snowflakes, I can't help but wonder if Rose led me to Valhalla only to throw me off. She is perfectly aware of our history, after all. Liam claims he doesn't even know Anna. Maybe she was there at some point for a show, long enough to leave a hat, but this is nothing new for my sister. She is always leaving stuff everywhere. When we were kids, I would find her things in the most random places; a toothbrush in the freezer, a fountain pen under a cereal box. Once I discovered an entire box of photos she'd taken of a neighbor's dog in my winter boots. In *my* room. She had no idea how they got there; she was just like that.

Which begs the question: why would Rose send me to Liam's house? She couldn't have known that some random train-hopper would be walking around with information I needed. And maybe Anna is with this Tristan guy, but I am not sold on it. It doesn't sound like her to become so nihilistic. Train-hoppers live nowhere, and don't care about anyone or anything; Anna is the opposite of that. She's sensitive and fanatical. She wouldn't leave her room for a week once because her

41

friend's parakeet died. She wouldn't fit in with that crowd. They're not all bad, but many of them walk the line of criminality and drug addiction. They're definitely not artist types.

No, it doesn't sound like Anna to fall in with them. But I better ask around to make sure. I head towards Bremen Café, only a few blocks away from Liam's, because in Riverwest, everything is a few blocks away from everything. As the snow falls harder and harder, I pick up the pace. There are people out and about everywhere, biking down Center Street, going in and out of bars. You can hardly tell it's the middle of February, and a weeknight. Unlike suburban Wisconsin, where my parents reside practically in solitude, and hearing a car drive by makes you jump because it happens so rarely.

I'm about to slip on a patch of new snow when I catch myself on a patio table and realize I've managed to reach the door for Bremen Café. Not the door actually, but the crowd of smokers standing outside of it. I find my balance and push my way through them, to find more smoking inside. My glasses fog up from the heat, making the whole place appear like a blob of leather. I pocket them and head straight to the pool room in the back, but Anna isn't there, of course. That would be too easy. I don't see Rose either. There is, however, a group of train-hoppers hanging around playing pool. Maybe they will know something. I turn into the room, watching. Some heads are bobbing along; others are focused on the tables. No one even looks in my direction. I check my outfit—jeans, black leather coat, red beanie hat—and decide I can't appear *so* out of place here. But maybe there's something about my energy now that I can't see. Like I've sold out, or something. As if people can smell that I have a job and a lovely apartment and a healthy relationship. As if they can detect I go running on the beach every day.

Does being an adult have a smell?

Being existentially lost has a smell; the room is drowning in it. Like grease and beer and sourness. I breathe out of my mouth, get closer. Hakol le'tova, I remind myself. Everything happens for a reason.

42

There's probably a reason for all this too. I just may not understand what that is for a while.

My glance falls on a young girl who's wearing a relatively new t-shirt and is staring into space, bored. I head towards her first. "Hey, I like your shirt," I tell her pointing at it.

The girl finally looks in my direction, aggressively confused, septum piercing hanging crookedly from her nostrils. "You like Reverend Glasseye?" she asks, studded brows arched upwards, suspicious.

"I do. What's your favorite song? Mine is 'Sleep Sweet Countrymen'." She relaxes a little now that I've brought up a relatively unknown New Orleans band that is popular among train-hoppers but continues to eye me suspiciously while I take out my phone, its screen stuck on my sister's face. "Have you seen this girl?"

"Are you a narc or something?"

"No."

"A cop then?"

I shake my head again, for some reason embarrassed. I used to get confused for a train-hopper all the time, and now I look like a cop? Sure, my jeans are new, not bought for two dollars at Salvation Army, but it's not exactly like I am wearing a goddamn suit. My boots I've had for five years, at least. I never dye my hair or paint my nails; *I haven't completely changed.*

I stop this train of thought. Why am I trying to justify myself? I take in a deep breath, try to remember I am twenty-five years old, with a boyfriend who loves me. That I speak three languages and can wake up at eight a.m. without an alarm. This insecurity I once had, the one that allowed me to confuse being part of a subculture with being part of an actual family, belongs to another person I can hardly relate to, most days.

"I'm not a *narc*," I explain. "I'm her sister."

The girl looks to her right, where there is a redhead in suspenders and a stained striped shirt, with five piercings at least that I can count at first glance. He reminds me of an aggressive Doberman who has spent all day playing in the dirt. For a moment I wish I'd left my septum piercing in, not taken it out years back after getting too many strange looks in Jerusalem, where I'd lived before the kibbutz. Kids would quite literally point and laugh at me on the bus. David hated it. And what is a piercing anyway, if not a message to outsiders, another human version of butt-sniffing? In one country, it could mean anger or confidence, in another, it looks incredibly silly.

Things that work in some places do not work in others.

"Is she bothering you, Mary?" Doberman boy asks, stepping forward. Unquestionably the alpha male of the group. His black boots echo against the linoleum floor, and his glance is hard, like a wall.

"Nah, she's just looking for someone," Mary tells him, to my relief.

"I'm..." I struggle to think of an explanation that wouldn't silence them, then find myself babbling nervously. "Look, I don't live here, I'm in town for a few days and want to say hi. Someone told me she might be hanging around here."

"Maybe she doesn't want to be found," Mary says.

"Maybe I don't care," I explain, getting annoyed. I know that train-hoppers don't think much of outsiders, but it's not like I'm asking for their friendship or something. I put my phone back into my coat and look from Mary to the Doberman, but they're mute, wide-eyed. What am I doing still standing there, letting them push me around? I have three more bars to look through, and that's not including the ones farther out from Center Street. I am about to give up and head to the next dive when I smell Rose again. Turning, I see her behind the bar pouring out a line of shots. Her eyes grow large at the sight of me. Large, but duller than before, like some spark has gone. "You came!" she says, looking behind her to a large clock above the beer cooler. "You're really early."

I don't tell her I have no intention of watching her play. "Can you come outside with me for a sec?"

She looks around the bar, which is surrounded by several patrons holding out wallets. "You got another cigarette?" she asks. I nod. Rose whispers something to the other guy bartending, who seems annoyed but also resigned to this sort of behavior from Rose. His glasses shimmer from the bar lights, but for a moment it looks like he is watching me with some recognition. I wonder if I know him from somewhere. Then he waves Rose off, and she follows me outside without putting her coat on.

"Do you know a guy named Tristan? Probably a train-hopper, newish to town?" I ask Rose, once we get outside. We stand under the awning to avoid getting wet. Snow is now swirling in small little tornadoes around the orange glow of streetlamps up and down Bremen St., making me shiver in my shitty coat. Why didn't anyone remind me to bring something warmer?

"Sure. Tall. Sticky fingers," Rose says, waving her fingers around. She lights the cigarette and exhales happily. "Why? You looking for drugs or something?"

My stomach drops into my chest. I remember how sparkling her eyes had looked earlier in the day, and figure she must have had experience getting drugs from this guy. Which means he could be an addict, or that Anna could be. "No, no. I heard he might be with Anna."

Rose's large hazel eyes grow even more. But her face doesn't quite match her expression. "No shit?"

"Do you know where he's staying?" I ask.

"Nah. Could be anywhere. I'm sure she's fine," Rose says. She puts a hand over mine when she sees my face. "Anna isn't stupid enough to get into that shit."

I frown. I am no longer sure of that at all. "And you never saw them together?"

Rose directs her gaze away from me and towards the ground, which is littered with cigarette butts. "Okay, you got me. I did see them at Bremen once or twice. I didn't think they were dating though."

"Why didn't you tell me?"

She shrugs. "I don't know. I guess I didn't want to worry you."

45

I can't decide if she is telling me the truth or not. Maybe she has her own reasons for keeping it from me, but it isn't like she is going to explain them if she hasn't already. Is it jealousy? Maybe she liked Tristan and he wasn't interested in her? "Then why did you tell me to go to Valhalla to look for her?" I ask, still perplexed.

"That's where all the crusties go," she says, nonchalantly. "She wasn't there?"

"No."

"What about Liam? Did he say anything?" she asks.

Then it hits me. I have to stop myself from rolling my eyes. Her reticence has something to do with Liam. Of course. Did she send me there to spy on him?

"Nothing nice," I grunt. "Or useful. Not that I would expect more from him."

Rose watches me intently when I deliver this bit of news, then licks her lips. "Mash, you look beat," she says. Heavy bass combinations start vibrating through the windows; a band has taken over the stage, tuning their instruments. "Maybe you should just go to sleep. Whatever the deal is, it can wait until tomorrow." She then does something to surprise me: she takes out a giant loop of keys from the pocket of her jeans. "Here. Meet me at my house. Take a shower, sleep, whatever. I'll be back around eleven." Then she pauses, and looks to Bremen, then back at me with a smile. "Well, unless the night goes well. Did you see that banjo player? *Mmm.*"

At the mere thought of a bed, I feel so tired my eyes begin to close. The long day is really getting to me. I have a hard time sleeping on planes, so I barely napped coming here. "You still on Center and Weil? In the upstairs unit?"

"You mean your old house?" she laughs. "Yeah. Bob hasn't raised the rent once, because of..." she stops, swallows. "Because of what happened."

I nod, pushing away memories of the place. I'd really loved it there, until I didn't. "I'll go take a nap then, I guess," I sigh.

46

"My brother lives in your old room, and my friend Vince is in... the other room, but they went to Chicago yesterday, so you'll have the place to yourself," she says. "He's a rapper now, did I tell you that? My brother, I mean. He's so fucking good, too. I know you hate rap but you'd like this, Mash." Then Rose looks past me, towards the front entrance, where three more people are entering the bar. "Better get back in there," she says. "Money doesn't grow on trees, like everyone loves to tell me."

I watch her leave and am about to do the same, when someone grabs my shoulder and pulls me back.

OCTOBER 2007

ANNA

CHAPTER FIVE

I could tell you that when I first got the message, the one that changed everything, I was sitting there at my desk trying to do homework. But this just isn't true. Yes, I was sitting at my desk, and yes, I had my computer open to an Intro to Website Design assignment. But really, I was staring at the screen, listening to Regina Spektor and thinking about this cute drummer I'd been seeing and why I hadn't heard from him that night. There, I said it. Lame, I know.

I like to think that had I known our lives were about to get turned upside down, I'd have done something more...memorable. But I probably wouldn't have. What memorable thing could I possibly be doing anyway, living in Milwaukee? A sophomore in college, I basically live in a bubble, all BYOB basement shows and coffee shop homework marathons. If it were up to me, I'd be painting giant canvasses in some warehouse loft in Brooklyn or waiting tables in Paris, but alas, because I'm the good sister, the one who didn't drop out of school and leave the country, here I am, having to live out my parents' dreams instead of my own. Which is to say: I never do *anything* memorable.

This is unfortunately (or fortunately?) about to change.

At first, the message seems like nothing. Like spam. It's 2007, and I'm on MySpace, so a message from some girl named Zoya *would* more than likely be junk mail. There's not even a profile picture up on her account. Normally I would delete it without thinking twice, but I don't, only because it's in Russian. That's my native language, shared with many delightful historical figures, such as Joseph Stalin—who starved and murdered more people than Hitler—and Ivan the Terrible, so bad they put it in his name— and don't even get me started on this Putin fellow. Because I know nothing about him other than he is also quite bad. Did I mention history and politics are not my strong subjects? I can memorize dates and names for a test, but they're usually gone a month later. Apparently, my brain would prefer to use that space for other, more useful information, such as every line of dialogue uttered by Kate Winslet in *Eternal Sunshine of the Spotless Mind*. If my high school Social Studies teacher Mr. Blankovich didn't like me so much, I'm not sure I would have been able to keep my 4.0 GPA. All I know is that the USSR was pretty bad, so here we are, in the Cheese State, far more likely to run into a cow than an undercover KGB officer.

Anyway. Jokes aside, I quite like the sound of Russian. Also, it's a strange letter, so right away my curiosity is peaked. Above all else, I am a lover of strange things. If you don't believe me, you should look inside my closet.

"Dear Anastasia Pavlova," the message starts. *"Please forgive me for contacting you like this. I've known about you for a long time, but you don't know about me. It would just be interesting for me to talk to you. If you are able, please message me back. Thanks!"*

Well that's a ridiculous message to send a person, is my first thought.

My second thought is that it is probably spam after all.

But, no, that doesn't quite make sense, for two reasons: first, the girl, Zoya, is from our hometown: Chernovtsy, Ukraine. Chernovtsy, just over the border near Poland and Moldova, is not a very large or famous city; its population is a third of Milwaukee's. Almost no one has even heard of it, so that would be a strange coincidence for a spammer.

My third thought is more complex: What if she is some long-lost relative? My grandma is the youngest of seven or eight siblings, all born in Chernovtsy. Although none have lived there since the 90s' Ukrainian Jewish exodus, and hardly any are still alive, it's definitely possible I have cousins I don't know about, and probably a few that have entirely slipped my mind. How else would she know my patronymic? I haven't used it on any documents since we moved here, and one would have to know my dad to guess it. (I mean, do you blame me? It brings to mind a dog, if you've had any sort of classes in psychology and have read about classical conditioning.)

Which is all to say that I should probably just ask my dad. Either he will laugh it off or tell me she's some long-lost distant relative. In either case I can dismiss the whole thing right away. It takes me about five minutes to find my phone, as it turns out I left it under the trash can. When I do find it, I call him right away.

"Are you okay? Did something happen?" my dad asks, picking up on the second ring.

"Does something have to happen for me to call you?" I ask, innocently. I move the phone away from my face and light a cigarette. Logically I know he can't see me, but it still sometimes feels that way, and he would *kill* me if he knew I smoked.

"You're not coming Friday, is that it?"

"No... I'm coming," I reply, trying to remember what it is I am coming to. Is it someone's birthday? Anniversary? It's always someone's birthday or anniversary. Russians really like to party, and they will find any excuse for it. I've been to one-year-olds' birthday celebrations that could rival a wedding.

My dad clears his throat, and responds to me in Russian, which means he must really be busy, or at least very tired. "Anastasia, what is it? I'm swamped here."

"Do I have a cousin or aunt or something named Zoya Oleynik?" I ask. As I have him here on the phone, the whole idea feels ridiculous. I take a quick drag on my cigarette, and stand to blow it out the window. It hovers in the thick autumn air before lifting up over Center Street.

"No you don't," he says. "Not on my side anyway."

"I figured. She just messaged me, that's why I asked."

My dad clears his throat. "What did she say?"

"It was kind of weird, she didn't really say anything, just that she knows about me and wants to talk."

There is a moment of silence on the phone that I will later find far too long. Liars pause like that. Well, bad liars do. I have since learned to notice these things.

"Hello? Dad?" I ask.

"Just ignore it," my dad says finally. "I get messages all the time from Ukraine. They think we're rich because we live in America."

"Does her name sound familiar at all?" I ask, to be sure. "Do you—"

This time, before I can even finish getting these questions out, my dad interrupts. "Just forget about it. It's nonsense. If you respond she'll only ask for money, trust me."

"Okay…"

"Don't talk to this woman. Please."

This is when I start to wonder: Why does he care so much if I talk to her? The tiniest feeling of *something isn't right here* starts growing in the back of my brain. I don't follow this feeling to its source, or investigate it further, but it's definitely planted there for later scrutiny, like a seed.

"Okay, Anastasia?" he says. "I know you hate to listen to me, but I mean it."

"Okay, okay," I tell him.

Then he hangs up.

Immediately my heart starts racing. I can't pinpoint why— excitement? Fear? The pull of history? Whatever it is, I start pacing in the middle of the living room, around all my old paintings and my roommate Margot's plants and the cool, bitter breath of Autumn, seeping in through the windows. I stick my head out and inhale, hoping that will do the trick. There's this smell that only exists in Milwaukee in October. The thin smoky jet of laundry after the rain. Wet leaves half-drying, half getting wet again. Open PBR cans, cigarettes, leather. A mix of youth and nostalgia, of losing something as you're living it.

The feeling, both terrifying and comforting, that life would always be exactly like this.

It's this feeling I'm trying to focus on as I go outside and smoke three cigarettes in a row, before sitting back down at my computer and turning Regina Spektor on again. I forward to the song "Après Moi," the most theatrical melody of the album. A little melancholy can be beautiful, and it distracts me from the impulse I have to answer this woman right away. It takes a while, but I manage to return to myself eventually. By the time I finish my homework assignment, I am feeling relatively normal again. But maybe I'm a masochist because right as I have finally forgotten about the message, I return to MySpace and look once more at my inbox.

This time, reading it again, I'm really sure it's nothing but an Internet con. So she knows my patronymic; it can't be that hard to find out. She would only have to research my dad's name. And my hometown is listed in my profile, so that would be easy to investigate, too. My dad is right: the woman—if she is, even, a woman—only wants money. I've always been told I have a trusting face, maybe broadcasting it on the Internet is only begging for negative attention. I have the urge to delete all the profile pictures that I've ever posted and select one of the side-angle self-portraits I painted instead, which I do in a rapid haze, until there's no more documentation of my face left online at all. Now only someone who really knows me in person will be able to recognize it, which is how it should be anyway. I should have never gotten on this website in the first place. It turns people into lazy voyeurs, fulfilling their need to socialize in a way that only leaves them wanting more, like a sugary treat you know you shouldn't have because it won't fill you up and it's bad for you, too. I debate deleting my account entirely, but I don't.

Finally, feeling very grownup and accomplished, I close the message and move on with the rest of my day.

ANNA

_____

CHAPTER SIX

As much as I try to forget about the message, I find myself staring at it again and again over the next few days. On Friday, after I get back from my Russian literature class and empty my heavy bag of its Turgenev and Dostoevsky—why on earth did I think this would be an easy elective because I'm Russian?—I sit at my desk and look at that message again for a long time. I keep re-reading the line *It would just be interesting for me to talk to you.* I can't help but wonder: what does she want to talk to me about? Why would it be interesting? The only thing I can come up with is that she is somehow related to us. But I have no way to prove a relation without replying. And I'm not sure I'm prepared for the consequences of actually communicating with this person. Eventually, I am forced to stop thinking about it, because the door to my room slams open. I crane my head back to see my roommate and best friend, Margot, heading straight to my bed.

"There you are!" Margot says. Without thinking, I minimize the chat window, as if she caught me watching porn or something. And maybe this would be equally as embarrassing, if it's really a scam that I've opened myself up to. "I've been looking all over for you."

Margot collapses on my bed, taking off her backpack—my backpack, that, like many things, she has acquired from my closet— and numerous layers of wool sweaters and bright scarves. The sight of her fills me with relief. With my best friend's face there in front of me, I can put the MySpace message out of my mind. It's hard to believe

I found her on Craigslist, but I did. After high school, neither of us wanted to pay the outrageous sums of money UWM was requesting for a tiny dorm room, so we found this giant duplex instead, and spent the first school year studying and drinking and filling the upstairs to capacity with weirdos. It's only two blocks from campus, so there's the downside of having to live next to many drunken former football players and homecoming queens that view school as an excuse to party on their parents' dime and have casual sex every other day. I'm not a prude or anything, but jeez, the conversations I've overheard while walking through the Union to get to Prospect Avenue. They would make anyone blush. They're nothing like the conversations in our house, which do reach the topics of physical love on occasion but are mostly about feelings, or hours-long analysis about whether or not modern art has ruined art. (Which it totally has.)

"Did you call me?" asks Margot, who doesn't agree with me about anything regarding art. The uglier something is the more she likes it. It's not totally surprising, if you've seen her paintings. Why would you want to admit the odds are stacked against you? It's hard enough to be a successful artist when you *have* talent.

I glance at my phone and open it. I can't remember calling her. All that I see listed there is several missed calls from an unknown number and one from my mom.

"No. I don't think so. But I *was* hoping to see you."

"I know. I felt it. That's why I came home," Margot says. She leans back against the wall, in her plaid shirt and striped skirt and brown beanie we got together on a road trip to Chicago, and makes herself comfortable on my bed, where she will probably stay for the next few hours. She does this often, because her own room is such a jungle you can barely walk from one end to the other. I don't mind it. The less time I spend alone, the better. I did enough soul-searching in high school, thank you very much. "What are you doing? Why is Abby running around the house naked?"

"Do you want the logical explanation or the one she gave me?" I ask.

"I think we're gonna have to kick her out," Margot says, not answering.

"And the revolving door continues," I groan.

Margot reaches into her bag and haphazardly takes out a small purple glass pipe we once named Sylvia Plath and packs it with weed. I momentarily consider telling her about the strange message from Zoya but don't. I'm not sure why; five minutes ago it's all I wanted to do. Margot and I usually talk about everything. But something about the strange missive makes me quiet.

"She keeps coming home at four a.m., and blasting country music like no one is trying to sleep," Margot says, then taps the green nugget down into the bowl. A lighter surfaces out of her bag and she uses it to take a hit. As she lets out the smoke, she adds, "Then when I ask her to turn it down, she moves the knob back and forth until I leave. Not to mention all the homeless people she brings around. Can I wake up one morning and not find a stranger on our couch?"

"Actually, most of them are just hippies, not homeless people..." I don't add that I also like seeing people in our house in the morning; it makes me feel like we are at the center of something. The center of what, I don't know, but I like it anyway.

"—And why is she running around the house naked?" Margot interrupts.

"Oh. She thinks she has scabies," I explain. "She's going to burn all her clothes in the yard."

Margot hands me the pipe, and I take a drag. "Jesus," she says.

"I don't know about kicking her out, though. I like Abby. She's fun," I say, letting out the smoke. I hand the pipe back.

Margot takes another hit before answering me. "I knew you would say that. Have you ever stopped to think if you are actually ever having this *fun* you're so obsessed with?"

I frown, because obviously I *do* have fun; if anything, a little too much. Lately, since we both got accepted to the Honors Department,

Margot has been getting frustrated that she has to work harder to get an A, and can't go out with me anymore most nights. She would never admit this to me, but she also doesn't know how to be subtle, so she might as well have. Not that I care about grades. Who would ever look at them again? A finished degree is all you really need these days, and that's only if you want a regular job teaching or in an office. If you don't, you may as well skip the financial burden of school altogether. I would have done this myself if not for the *extreme* parental pressure to go.

"Let's just talk to her about it," I say. Now that I'm feeling more relaxed—likely from the pot—I turn my body to face her. She's knee-deep in her Art History 101 textbook. Correction: *my* Art History textbook from the first semester of freshman year, when I still thought I might major in painting. Just *try* telling a Russian immigrant that bit of news. "She's probably only worried about scabies because Riley and Jackie had it at their house and she is secretly having sex with Riley. I mean, not so secretly, because it's fairly obvious. In fact, this whole charade is probably to announce it to the world."

"So we can add home-wrecker to her list of wonderful attributes." Margot rolls her eyes, then grabs the pipe and the lighter, which says Gemini on it, and puts it on my windowsill. "Fine. I guess you better hope she doesn't burn our entire house down," she sighs with defeat.

"...It's literally the worst disease in the world!" I hear Abby scream from the other room.

"Should we tell her about cancer? Or AIDS?" I ask, which makes Margot laugh.

As if she knows we are talking about her, Abby opens the door and barges into my room, still naked and holding a giant garbage bag. "Okay, I got all my stuff. I found some gasoline. I have a lighter. I need your clothes now."

"Uh, *no*," Margot says. She turns the page of her art history book from Lucien Freud's grotesque impressionism to Francis Bacon's even-more grotesque surrealism. I get a brief surge of excitement, like I always do when I see art to aspire toward, followed by a pit in my stomach, remembering that's not what I do anymore.

"Margot!" Abby screams, distracting me again from my roller coaster of emotions. It's hard to think deeply when a naked eighteen-year-old girl is standing in your periphery vision, even if you are straight. "Come *on*."

"Do you want to borrow something to wear?" I ask, getting more concerned about her nudity now that it's in my face. I've seen most of my friends naked, but it's usually at a distance, in some body of water. Up close it's more uncomfortable. Plus, her body is too perfect; stick thin down to her hips, where she curves out into an hourglass shape before thinning out again at the legs. Perfect, semi-tanned skin, not a blemish or pimple to be seen. I will never be that thin or have blemish-free skin; my hormones are too wacky. Looking at her—or, trying not to look at her—is starting to make me feel as grotesque as Freud's portraits.

But Margot, who is just as thin from playing competitive soccer all of her life, is only annoyed, not jealous. "Abby, you don't have scabies," Margot sighs without looking up. "Just take a shower for once."

"You definitely can't burn my clothes," I tell her, trying to diffuse the tension. "I don't even have enough money for groceries, let alone a new wardrobe. This shirt is like five years old."

"That's my shirt," Margot says, glancing up at my top, a dark gray v-neck with a tiny pocket. "I got it last year at Salvation Army."

"Oh," I say. "Well, in that case, it's probably more than five years old."

"It's the only way to get rid of it! Our whole house is probably infected," Abby whines. She looks back and forth between us with skepticism. "I can't believe you guys aren't more supportive." Her lower lip, which is cartoonishly larger than the top one, so much that you could always see a stretch of cigarette-stained teeth, droops down like a permanent pout. But her eyes, they are wild with excitement. Or no, that's probably Adderall. We've been ingesting a lot of that stuff lately. Half the dollar bills in my wallet are still covered with orange powder at the tips, which has made for some uncomfortable interactions with the baristas at Fuel.

"Fine, don't believe me," Abby sulks. "You'll see soon enough when you wake up itchier than you've ever been in your *life*." Then she walks off without closing the door.

I get up to close it, then Margot finally looks up from her book. She and I exchange wide-eyed glances.

"God, some people are really hard to live with," Margot says.

"Isn't it funny how the people who complain about you not being supportive enough are the ones who totally disappear when you need something?" I ask. "*One* time I called Abby to pick me up from school when there was a blizzard, and she didn't even answer her phone. For the rest of the week."

"Yeah, it's hilarious," Margot says flatly. Then she goes back to her textbook, now onto Andy Warhol, the beginning of the end. When art becomes a question instead of an answer. Personally, I would prefer the latter; isn't life confusing enough without every person trying to decide if something is transcending its own nature? A toilet is a toilet. A chair is a chair. If you think the majority of people can distinguish whether a photo or an object is successful based on the artist's intentions, then you've never been to a DMV. "You know that you don't have to be friends with everyone who asks you to hang out, right? You're not in high school anymore."

I ignore her. I do know that. Don't I? Sure, a part of me will always be that girl eating alone in the art room—or, okay, the girls' bathroom on days before the art room became an option. But that's why I spend all my time when I'm not here in Riverwest. Riverwest is like ten blocks of people who ate lunch in their school bathrooms.

"Of course I know that. Abby has good qualities, too," I reply, unequivocally.

"Like what?" Margot scoffs, not looking up. She is far more interested in her book now that actual skill has been replaced by a cartoonish attempt at existential thought. Andy Warhol. Jackson Pollack. Ugh. I mean, sure, paint a can of soup, but can't you at least make it look good? "Besides her ability to find every hippie in a two-mile radius?"

"She's sweet. She has a good heart," I shrug. "I think she just legit has ADD." Absentmindedly, I glance back at my MySpace messages. Nothing new, as I expected. That note from Zoya is like a pulsating neon sign in my mind. I know this woman is probably only interested in my nonexistent funds, but I can't help wondering if there's something else to it. I also find myself slightly jealous of her: she's in Chernovtsy, the place I've been missing since I began missing things. I know this doesn't make sense, I was only three when we moved and I've spent almost my whole life in Wisconsin. But sometimes being from Ukraine is the only thing that feels real to me. Even before she messaged, I was thinking about trying to go back there, maybe studying abroad or something.

"If she had ADD, then Adderall would calm her down, not make her even more restless," Margot explains. "Not that I'm a doctor or anything."

Before I can argue, there's a knock on the door.

"Yes?" I say.

A pair of tattooed hands, which read *Hard Rain* across eight knuckles, push the door open. Our other roommate August sticks his head in, followed by the rest of his body: his long, copper-colored hair curly and matted, a dimpled grin, ropy muscles bursting out of a tight beige shirt. August looks so much like Elijah Wood's Frodo we've gone as Hobbits for two Halloweens in a row. "Anna! I've been calling you! Your dad is downstairs."

I look again at my phone but don't see any missed calls. He leans into the room more, followed by a pleasant musty smell combined with bicycle grease from the shop where he works, or possibly one of the fixed gear bikes he's repairing at home. "He seems really annoyed. He *hates* me, Anna."

"He doesn't hate you. He doesn't even know you," I explain. "He just doesn't like that you're not the same gender as me."

"Come on, Anna. Dude is scary. Wasn't he in the KGB?"

"No, he had *friends* in the KGB."

"Whatever. I'm not going back out there until he's gone."

"All right. I'm coming, I'm coming," I tell him.

"Has Abby started herself on fire yet?" Margot asks him with a laugh.

"Not yet," he answers, shaking his head. "I told that crazy chica to stop snorting so much shit up her nose, but she never listens to me."

"That's not limited to you," Margot grunts. "I don't think she listens to anyone."

"I heard that, you fuckers!" Abby's voice yells from the other room.

I smile at August, then turn back towards the computer. No new messages. And why would there be? I never responded to Zoya and all my friends are currently within ten feet of me. Satisfied, I close Zoya's message and log out of MySpace.

ANNA

CHAPTER SEVEN

August is right; my dad is annoyed. Not that he tells me why. He doesn't say a word the entire drive, which is fine, I guess, because it's not as if I particularly *want* to talk to him. When he's not actively telling me to get my life together and be more responsible, he's thinking it silently. I guess it's not enough I stopped painting so I could get this generic college degree, I have to be totally miserable while doing it.

A mere five blocks later my dad pulls into the parking lot of my grandparents' subsidized apartment complex and double parks. Without looking up he asks, "Can you get them? Try to make it quick." He starts typing something on his phone, a new "smart" one that is almost a computer. He's like a little kid with a new video game, the way he hovers over that thing. I don't know why but it's embarrassing. I mean, who does he need to email so urgently anyway? With the exception of CIA agents, who does anyone need to email that urgently? Maybe he is a CIA agent? That sure would make me like him more.

"Quick?" I ask him, with exaggerated shock. "Have you met your parents?"

"I said try."

"*There is no try, only do,*" I say in a gravelly voice, then laugh. It forces my dad to look up and attempt a smile, but only for a second. Immediately after, he starts typing again. It makes me a little sad. We watched that entire movie series together, and now his phone is more interesting to him than me.

At least my dedushka is happy to see me. He is always happy to see me. Sometimes I visit just for a hit of his unconditional love to get out of a bad mood. "What brings *you* here?" he asks when I get upstairs. Confusion wrinkles the brows behind his thick, clear glasses, then quickly turns to excitement. "It's so late."

"What? It's only five. We go to that party at Marik's," I explain in broken Russian. "Why you aren't wearing clothes?"

Instead of answering my grandpa happily pulls me into the apartment, where the television is blasting Russian news. He struggles with the remote, pressing at least five or ten buttons that I can tell even from here do not control the sound, if it's the right remote at all. I walk over and press the power button on top.

"So. What's new in Putin-land?" I ask, jokingly, when it's quiet.

My grandpa—a man who has survived a concentration camp, the Russian army, and entire decades of near starvation—shrugs now in the face of Russia. "Oh, who cares? It's not our problem anymore," Dedushka says. *Then why are you always watching the Russian news?* I want to ask, but don't. He looks behind him toward the open doorway to their bedroom, a small barrier of wooden beads hanging over the tiny hallway.

"Mila! Anastasia is here!" He tells me to sit down—"sadeece, sadeece"—and points at the couch. But for the last decade and a half, the couch has been covered entirely by various old, itchy rugs they'd, like nearly everything inside, brought with them from Ukraine. I do not particularly enjoy sitting on twenty-five-year-old rugs, especially when they are being used as couch covers. Instead, I choose a chair by the small dining room table, the granite top cluttered with white doilies and crystal bowls also brought over from Ukraine. I drop my winter hat and coat on top of a pile of unopened mail, a stack of photos that came from one of my cousins. Because she has so many siblings, my grandma has many nieces and nephews, and they are all starting to have children, a fact she never lets me forget for a moment, even though I'm barely nineteen and very single.

My grandpa, his bald forehead now perspiring from sweat, yells for a second time, "Mila, Anastasia's here!"

"Dedushka, we have to go. Why aren't you ready?"

My grandma finally waddles out in a paisley robe, looking half-asleep and smelling like old unwashed clothes. She sits down on the rug-covered couch and immediately asks me when I'm going to get married. Her thin white hair is matted, as if she just woke up, which can't be true, at five PM. "I want grandchildren!" she says, melodramatically.

"You *have* grandchildren," I say, pointing to myself.

"I'm old! I'm going to die soon!" my grandma says.

"You're not going to *die* soon," I say in English. My babushka has a penchant for languages, knew five of them before moving here, and now she's the only one in the family above fifty who can technically understand me though most of the time she chooses not to. "I'm not going to start having babies with random people because you have a headache or whatever."

"Did I say random people? You should *only marry a Russian Jew,*" Babushka continues to lament. This part she emphasizes as if she hasn't been telling me the same thing my entire life. I still can't understand why it's so important to her. They may have a mezuzah next to their door now, but we don't even celebrate Hanukkah. I find the concept of religion very creepy. Who needs more orders, let alone from made-up things who live in the sky? I have enough people telling me what to do, thank you very much. Unless it's coming from Leonardo DiCaprio, and the order is to kiss him, I prefer to make my own decisions about whom to date.

"Leave her be!" my grandpa says, sitting down on the couch beside her.

"Did we move to America just to marry Russian Jews?" I ask, switching back to Russian, which gets better and better as it approaches a subject that it is so familiar with. "Why didn't we stay in Chernovtsy, then?"

My grandpa starts to laugh but then stops himself when he sees my grandma's face. She continues along in her speech, now on the part where everyone hates the Jews. It's some version of this rant every time I see her. "Everyone. They all want us dead. Believe me, I know."

"For the millionth time: this is America," I sigh.

"It's all the same everywhere," my grandma continues, shaking her head. "Oh, you'll see one day, Anastasia. Just because no one is trying to kill us now doesn't mean they won't again." She stands, looking suddenly agitated, but doesn't go to her room. Or take any clothes out of her closet. I am starting to see why my dad sent me up here instead of going himself. "Not that it matters to me. I already have one foot in the grave...but for you..."

"Mila!" my grandpa yells. "Enough!"

"It's okay, Dedushka," I sigh. "She's allowed to have her own opinions." It's true, but I have wondered how their opinions could diverge so much on the same issue. Is my grandmother more stubborn, or does she merely have a better memory? My grandpa escaped a concentration camp on his own two feet, after watching his entire family die. Baba Mila spent most of the war hiding in a farmer's shed. Not that it's so much better to sleep on a pile of hay and wait anxiously to be caught, but you'd think of the two of them, my grandpa would be more pessimistic. The only reason for the disparity I've come up with is that maybe some people choose to hold on to their traumas while others throw them out like a worn-out coat. Maybe you can decide between it making you weaker or making you stronger. Or maybe the decision gets made without your input at all, and you have to live with that. The most traumatic thing that ever happened to me was moving to America, which is nothing in comparison. I don't even remember it. Just the shadow of a feeling I can never put my finger on.

Babushka turns back to me, ignoring her husband of over fifty years. "Have you spoken to your uncle Pyotr lately? I'm supposed to be buried right next to my brother Nikolai, and he's trying to take the spot from right under my nose. My own nephew!"

"That can't possibly be true, Babushka," I say. I stand up, and look towards her bedroom door, hoping she will get the hint. When she doesn't, I take off my coat and place it on the chair. It's close to eighty degrees in their apartment, so I might as well not pass out from heat exhaustion.

"It is true. You don't care. You've forgotten all about us."

"I didn't forget," I interject.

"Yes, you did. You've forgotten us old people. You've forgotten Russia," she complains. "Good luck to you, devotchka. It won't work. It's in your soul forever, it doesn't matter where you go. You may be in America now, but you cannot merely cut off your roots and continue to walk." She looks away into nothingness then starts shaking her head in disbelief. I don't entirely disagree with her on this point, so I stay silent. "In Russia, I was so happy. I had my whole life ahead of me. Now I just sit around waiting for death."

The way she emphasizes the word death—smerta—makes me start laughing, I don't know why; it's not like I haven't heard it before. I've heard it all before. I simply never realized how funny it is. I laugh so hard tears rush from my eyes. Only then do I remember I'm still a little high.

"Oh, she's laughing at me now!" Grandma Mila says, staring straight ahead. "Ha-ha-ha. Ha-ha-ha. I'm funny to her."

"What a funny shootka, Baba," I say, laughing even harder.

"I'm a joke now?" she asks, slowly, looking at my grandpa.

"No, Babushka, I said you *made* a joke. It was funny."

"I'm a joke, she says."

"That's not what I said."

My grandpa claps his hands together. "Mila, come on. Let's get dressed."

"Yes . . . I was happy in Russia," she continues. "Even with Stalin, and the war, and all the lines." She sits back down, swaying forward and backward, almost as if the last conversation didn't even happen.

"Are you really missing Stalin, Babushka?" I've heard this all before, but I never fully considered what she was saying.

68

"Of course she isn't," my grandpa says, gruffly, no longer looking at either of us.

"We all thought he was a great man," Baba Mila is saying, a hint of pride in her eyes.

"But you know that he *wasn't*, right?" I ask, incredulous. I may suck at history, but they lived through this. Shouldn't they remember?

"You wouldn't understand," she says, with a brief, disapproving glance at my unwashed hair and ripped jeans. "You weren't there. *You* never had to wait in line for bread."

"Mila," my grandpa snaps. "Enough already!"

"You're not happy here?" I press on. Sometimes I don't know what she wants from me, except maybe to go back in time and be my age again. I'm sure it doesn't help that they never leave their apartment and have nothing to do now that we don't need them anymore. "You'd rather have Stalin?"

"*Phoo*. I'm not talking about Stalin," Baba Mila grunts, even though she was indeed just talking about him. "You're too young. You wouldn't understand."

"Understand what?"

"When I was your age, I didn't believe the old people either . . ." she says.

"Who did you know in the USSR that was eighty?" I'm no history buff, but I know it's very unlikely she knew many people above sixty; not in her time anyway. Most who survived the war still died young from so many years of starvation and stress; and in our family, hardly anyone survived the war.

Babushka shakes her head. "Now I have one foot in the grave..."

"Mila!" my grandpa yells.

"What! We're not newlyweds anymore, skipping down the beach!" she says.

Dedushka starts to laugh. "Ha! You, skipping down the beach? That's something I'd like to see."

I look at my grandpa. "Dedushka, are you not happy here?" I ask,

69

suddenly really wanting to know.

He waves a hand in my direction, as if to say how can we be happy sitting around in this small, stinky apartment all day? But this blasé reaction doesn't match what he says, which is, "Of course we are. Don't listen to your grandma when she's in this kind of mood." Then he chuckles a little. "Stalin. Now that's a name you don't hear much anymore."

"You don't..." I search my brain for the right Russian vocabulary. "Prefer another city? Not here?"

"Where else would we go?" he asks, grinning again.

"Back to Ukraine?" I ask, even though this is a dumb question. I know that there is no going back to Ukraine, not the one we left anyway. That place no longer exists. The Soviet Union is gone. For as long as I could remember, home was a street I could never reach, other than in my dreams.

"Back to Ukraine, she says! And what would we do there, Annushka?" Now my grandpa is the one who starts laughing. "Sell a basket of apples on the street to tourists? Live on the street? This is what happens to old people who are alone. They're like the stray dogs running around downtown, except those dogs are better fed." Dedushka shakes his head, the laugh gone from his voice. "We had this conversation too many times. When you were little."

"Da?"

"Every day, when I would walk you to school, you would ask: Dedushka, can we go home today? I want to go back to our apartment on Ruska Street, I miss the swings and the cats and our neighbors, Alla and Nella. I said, Devotchka, this is our home now. There's nowhere to go back to." Dedushka sighs and claps his hands on his knees. "You were a very sad little girl."

"Dedushka, you're thinking of Masha," I tell him. "I was only a baby when we were on Ruska Street."

My grandpa blinks then turns his head towards the ceiling. "Da, da. Pravda. You're right. It was your sister," he says. "You've always been more angry than sad. More... American."

"Me? Angry? *American?*"

"I will tell you what I told her then: there are good things and bad things about living anywhere," my grandpa says. "As long as you have your people, why should it matter if you stay on one tiny piece of it over another tiny piece of it?"

"Try telling that to Hitler," my grandma laughs, and actually, it's pretty funny, so we all start laughing. But then the phone starts ringing, and my grandpa ushers Baba Mila into the bedroom, and the moment has passed. "Go on already!" he tells Babushka, then saunters to the kitchen wall and picks up the phone. It rings five or six times by the time he gets there. "Yes, yes, we are almost ready," he says, which is a straight-up lie. "She doesn't have to wait here, Pavel, we're not *children.*"

He looks at me then and hangs up the phone.

"What?" I ask.

Dedushka starts leading me towards the door. "Go, go, you're only making things worse," he says, practically pushing me out. "We'll be down soon."

"Dedushka, he can wait two minutes," I say, but he keeps pushing me until my hand is on the knob. "Don't you need help?"

"Who's here? Pavel?" my grandma asks, coming out of the bedroom, still in her robe. "Why doesn't he come up here? He's avoiding us."

"He was here yesterday, what are you saying?" my grandpa asks. "Go back to the room and get ready! You'll see him in the car!"

"There's something very strange about him the last few weeks," my grandma says, shaking her head. "Maybe I was a bad mother... Certainly, I did something wrong that he treats me this way."

"Oh, enough already," Dedushka Sasha says. He's starting to really get mad, I can tell. I feel sort of bad for him. All he's ever wanted was for everyone to be happy but no one even wants to be happy. They want to feel alive.

"What do you mean he's acting strange?" I ask my grandma in English. "How has he been strange?"

71

"Sneaking around here, all quiet and serious," my grandma says. "Like when he used to get a bad grade and didn't want to tell us." Here she looks at me. "Your father was not a very good student, you know. It's really a miracle he's done so well, if you think about it."

"Mila!" Dedushka Sasha cries. "Bozhe moy! Are you a saint, and didn't tell me? He's perfectly normal!"

My grandma shrugs at us like we're idiots. "Well, what do I know? I'm just an old useless lady, like everyone keeps telling me."

"Who told you that?" I ask, almost laughing again. People are always getting mad at Baba Mila, but I doubt anyone said this to her. She is cantankerous, but she's no fool. My dad always told me how he couldn't get away with the smallest indiscretion when he was a child, because she always seemed to know what he was up to before he did. This is part of the problem with being an only child for so long: too many eyes watching you. She and Dedushka Sasha had wanted more kids, but after my dad, she had nothing but miscarriages. She used to call him her little miracle. Then she called him her little joker. Not because he was especially funny, but because he was always getting in trouble for talking too much in school. Her idea of him as a class clown made it better somehow. As a result, to combat this notion, my dad has since been far too devoted, always prepared and preparing to save them and us. Always so serious. If he jokes at all it's after several rounds of shots and I never get the joke. I never get any Russian jokes. I think there must be an inverse correlation of how separate you are from a culture with how much your sense of humor can align with it.

"Go, Annushka," my grandpa says. "She doesn't know what she's saying."

"I know perfectly well what I'm saying!" my grandma yells. "Just like I know perfectly well that Mikhail is trying to steal my grave right out from under my nose!"

I look at my grandpa with sympathy. "I thought you said it was Pyotr," I tell her quietly.

My grandpa, who is sitting back down again, leans forward, claps his hands even harder on his knees, and says, "Enough, Milachka. That's enough."

"Why, Sasha? What did I say?" she asks, looking more confused than ever.

"It's fine, Babushka. You didn't say anything wrong," I explain, but still, I put my hand back on the doorknob. Before I open the door, I turn around to ask her one last thing. "Hey, Babushka. Do you have any nieces or great-nieces named Zoya?"

My grandma takes maybe two seconds to think this over before she starts shaking her head. "No, I would remember such a poor choice in names."

I can't decide if I feel relieved or not, knowing this for sure, but I don't have time to worry on it much because my grandpa starts pushing me out the door.

"Lyudmila," Dedushka says. "Let her go! Get dressed for God's sake!"

I hear him screaming this all the way out the door and down the hall, which smells like burnt eggplant. It could be coming from anywhere, Russian immigrants make up most of the building's residents and they all love to burn eggplant. Half this floor used to be full of my grandma's siblings, but some level of dementia has taken nearly all of them. It doesn't look like she will escape this fate either. How terrifying it must be to become lost in your memories when you have memories of Stalin and Nazis holding guns to your head. I bet no one ever thought about that after making it out alive and starting to rebuild their lives from scratch. Will my grandpa be forced to watch his sister die in his arms again at the camps? Will he relive being shot at by SS soldiers while he climbs the broken fence and runs through the fields of Poland? He barely talks about that time in his life, and I don't blame him. He and my grandma probably assumed all those terrible years were behind them. That the past stayed in the past.

Maybe my dad thought the same thing. But he was wrong. They were all wrong.

ANNA

CHAPTER EIGHT

Walking back to the car, I start to get sad. Seeing my grandparents always makes me sad, all cooped up in that stuffy apartment building, unable to get around on their own. And guilty, too. Couldn't my parents have insisted they learn more English, or how to drive a car, or do anything at all besides babysit us? They probably feel so useless now, or at the very least bored out of their minds. I try to visit often, now that I live only five blocks away, but I am handicapped by my poor vocabulary and never stay long.

If I studied abroad for a semester, though? I'd pick it up in no time. And the more I think about it, the more I can't stop thinking about it.

"No luck?" my dad asks when I get in the car, where he is blasting AM 620, a.k.a. the channel where Republicans scream a lot. They're even louder today, angry, talking about the upcoming election. John McCain is not leading in the polls, and people are mad. I'm simultaneously glad and don't care. Everyone already knows who they are voting for. They knew before it all started. Now it's all about telling each other they are wrong and evil people for agreeing with the other guy.

Yeah, I'm staying out of that, thank you very much.

"They're still changing," I explain. I lean back into the chair and rest my legs on the dashboard. Then I notice my converse shoes have torn at the seam and put them back on the floor before my dad has another fit about how he didn't move here from the Soviet Union so that I could wear ripped clothes. "Sorry. I tried."

"Hmm," my dad mutters, not looking up.

After a long silence, I search my brain for what I can talk about so that it is no longer Republican pundits screaming in my ears. "Babushka said you've been acting weird the last few months," I say, casually. I let out a long, exaggerated yawn. "Is everything okay? You and Mom…?"

My dad sighs and reaches toward the knob of the radio, turning it down. "Babushka also says your cousin Yulia is stealing all her bedsheets," he says.

"She didn't mention that to me…"

"She's sick, Anastasia," my dad says. "You know that."

"I guess."

I want to say more, but my dad looks so lost in thought that he might as well have put a brick wall between him and the passenger seat. Furthermore, he won't look up from his phone, and keeps furiously typing away. His expression reminds me of the nights when I was little, and he used to check if Masha and I were asleep in our room, how angry he was to see us still awake, playing games or giggling about something. Once he even locked us in separate closets as punishment. Now, when I think about it, I wonder why he did that. Didn't he want us to be friends? Later, when we were older and had our own rooms, he never had to do this again, but mostly because we were no longer interested in talking all night long. Sometimes I miss those nights, even though at the time it felt so unjust. Having to share a space will make anyone closer, even if you don't like the person. They become as necessary to you as your bed or desk or clothes, if only because of their constant presence. It's probably why even though my grandparents on both sides didn't always get along, they still treated one another like family. And why I've always felt so close to them. Some of my earliest memories include walking to school with my grandpa, or playing card games with them for hours while our parents were at work. I spent far more time with my grandparents the first five years we lived here than

I did my parents or Masha, who was older and made friends easily.

"Who are you emailing anyway?" I finally ask. I cannot fathom being able to email someone from my phone, let alone needing to so urgently. "Is it work?"

"It's nothing," Dad says, but he stops typing on the phone. I turn my focus to the floor of the car, at the wrinkled, coffee-covered pieces of paper. An empty bag of Fritos. This is also strange for my dad; usually his car is spotless.

A door slams shut outside, and I see my grandparents finally meandering towards us. My dad slips out of the driver's seat, and goes to the back of the car, clearing it of papers and folders. He leaves his phone in the cupholder, and I glean what appears to be a long email exchange with a lawyer. The header says from the Law Offices of something or another. I catch something about a living will, and a question about inheritance. Why would he be asking about that? I can't get a better look, because soon my grandma is guided into the backseat, a tirade of complaints following her. "...He's not my brother," she spits.

"Mama, come on. How can you say that?" my dad asks, coming back around to his seat.

"A brother comes over once in a while. A brother at least sits down for tea."

"Maybe Marcus doesn't like tea," he offers with a forced smile.

"Marcus is her brother?" I ask of the quiet, elderly man I'd seen on occasion in their building, who is now standing outside waiting near a bus. "I thought they were friends or something."

My dad moves to the other side of the car to help my grandpa into his seat, then answers me: "Anastasia, how can you possibly think that after all this time?"

I shrug. "He never comes to anything. He seemed familiar to me but that's it."

"That's what happens when you always fight with your siblings. You can live on the same floor and never speak," he says. "That's why

I always tried to encourage you and your sister to be friends."

"That's not how I remember it," I snort, thinking again of the separated closets. If anything, we became friendly *despite* his efforts. Until she up and left me, of course. Since then, it's been basically crickets. I'm self-aware enough to realize my obsession with the email from Zoya has something to do with this; an urge for more family, when the rest of mine is either gone or doesn't speak the same language or, in the case of my dad, totally disinterested in talking to me. He doesn't even pretend to wonder what I mean; he simply gets back into the driver's seat and pulls the car out of the parking lot, turning onto Farwell Avenue.

I'm taking off my coat again when my grandma clears her throat. Her breath smells fishy and I have to cover my nose with a shirt sleeve.

"Pavel," my grandma starts. "Don't you know someone in Ukraine named Zoya?"

My heart plummets. Considering she has on occasion forgotten which grandchild I am, or who the president is, I hadn't expected my grandma to remember that I said anything. I barely remember that I said anything; it's already so far out in the back of my mind. Now, all I can do is hope she doesn't call me out.

"I do not," he says tightly. If he is worried, he is good at not showing it. I squeeze my nails into my palms and wait anxiously to see where this conversation will end. I don't expect him to admit much, but maybe it will throw him off his game. Deep down, I suspect the message couldn't have been random. Plus, why would he be talking to a lawyer? Could the two things be connected?

"Are you sure?" my grandma asks. She stares ahead, deep in thought. I watch my dad's face. If I'm not mistaken, he looks a little sweatier. This seems like an overreaction for what he claims to be a spammer, but what do I know? It is getting pretty hot in the car. I open the window a little to get some air.

"Yes." My dad glances in my direction, then turns back to watch the road. "Why do you ask?" he says. I wonder if we are both thinking the same thing: did Zoya find a way to contact my grandma too? If so, I must admit the girl is thorough.

"Oh," Babushka shrugs. She thumbs a crumb from her chin and then folds her hands across her lap. "I don't remember."

Inwardly, I breathe a sigh of relief. My dad, on the other hand, grips the wheel with an intensity that was definitely not there before. Then he turns the radio back on and doesn't speak for the rest of the drive.

ANNA

_____

CHAPTER NINE

Later, I'm standing on the balcony of my uncle Marik's house with my fourth glass of wine when someone comes outside to smoke. For a moment I think it's my dad, wanting to confront me about my grandma's question, but it's only Marik.

"Privet, Annushka," he says, starting his cigarette with a shiny gold lighter. "How are you?"

"Horosho," I respond. Uncle Marik is really my dad's cousin but in our family everyone's just an uncle or aunt. It took me until I was quite old to work this out; when I was young, I assumed my parents had tons of siblings, but they're both only children. Marik is married to one of Baba Mila's nieces, my great-aunt Rachel's daughter Marina. He owns a painting and remodeling company and is super rich, judging from the location of this brand-new riverfront condo, replete with string lights and perfectly assembled patio furniture that is very clearly not from IKEA. I can't begin to imagine what any of it costs. All I ever do, when it comes to money, is think about how to not spend it. "How are you?"

"Good, good," he mumbles back, about as bored with my question as I am asking it. Below us, a few tiny boats buzz down the Menomonee River, transforming the water into icy white streaks. Beyond the river is an unimpressive constellation of skyscrapers; further on, lights of factories burn yellow. "Life is good."

I watch as Marik takes another long drag of his cigarette. Maybe it's the four glasses of wine, but for a second he no longer looks like my uncle—a tall, muscled man in his late forties, always dressed in outrageous silk suits and pointy leather shoes at family functions—and instead seems like some old-timey Russian gangster. I wonder if this is how others see him: like a person to be frightened of. I really have no idea what he did for work before we immigrated, besides spend three years in the Russian army. It's possible someone mentioned it before, but if so, I no longer remember. This happens to me a lot; the way I didn't realize I was losing my native tongue until years after it was already happening, I somehow managed to misplace everyone's histories too. I wonder how much farther I can stray before it all disappears entirely, forever. Is heritage a lighthouse, blinking in the night, always prepared and preparing you for an eventual return? Or is it an unmapped land, a place that, if you leave, you may never find your way back to? Look at any immigrant family once it's had a generation or two of kids. Histories fade into anecdotes; foreign words are buried along with elderly grandparents. Every year that passes we are closer and closer to losing everything that makes us what we are. It's the shadow that lingers behind every American dream. The one you don't even realize is there because you never see it.

But I see it. I see it all the time, like a sixth sense, a different kind of ghost.

"Marik, what did you do in the Soviet Union?" I ask aloud. Because why the hell not? "For work, I mean?"

Marik glances at me in his periphery, then looks back out onto the river warily. "Oh. This and that."

"That sounds shady," I respond. "Were you in the KGB?"

Marik lets out a surprised chuckle. "No, no, not the KGB."

"Were you in the mob?" I ask, knowing of course that if he was, he would never tell me. Not that I could picture him in the mob. He's too nice. His kids are such squares they don't drink the wine set out on our table at family functions.

Marik turns to look at me, suddenly serious. "What is this about?"

I shrug. I should probably just shut my mouth, but I'm a little drunk. It's hard not to get drunk around my family; at nineteen, it's hard not to get drunk, period. It just seems to be the thing everyone is always doing. "Just wondering," I explain.

"It isn't interesting. I didn't have a real job, Annushka, not like I do here." He exhales a long line of smoke, looking like an angry bull. "I had a lot of friends, though. I helped when I could."

"Oh," I say. I know without asking that this is as much information as I'll get out of him on the topic, though now I am even more curious than I was when I originally asked. Like an itch that only gets itchier when you scratch it: this is the summary of my familial relationships. In general, it's better not to scratch at all. "Did you ever work with my dad?"

Marik nods indifferently. "Sure."

We're both quiet again, as another boat swims by, slicing a line through the pitch-black water. Marik is almost done with his cigarette. It is possible he is rushing it so as to get away from me quicker, but maybe that's my imagination. It has often felt to me like no one in my family really wants to talk to me. That they don't really know how. And it's not only the language barrier, there's something else too. I inch closer to Marik, inhaling his smoke, which is as close as I am going to get right now to a cigarette. He mistakes my interest as disgust, and switches the hand he's holding it with so that it is farther away from my nose.

I decide to ask him one more question. "Did he ever work with anyone named Zoya Oleskin?"

His head snaps to attention. "What?" he asks me. I repeat my question.

For a moment my uncle's face goes blank. He's probably thinking about all the bread lines and bribed police officers he's left behind. The divided apartments that smelled like cats, working on the collective farms in summer, friends mysteriously disappearing. I've heard about these things, but it's like listening to a tape that's a copy of a copy of a copy; you can barely make out the words, so your imagination fills in the rest. God knows I've tried, anyway.

Marik clears his throat, without giving anything away. "Annushka, that was so long ago. What are you getting at?"

"Oh, nothing," I say, searching my brain for what I can use to cover up this blunder. The only way out of this trainwreck is to turn and crash it in another direction. Good thing I have several tricks in my arsenal to vex family members. "You know what I've been thinking about a lot lately?"

Marik sighs. "What's that, Pochemushka?" my uncle responds in Russian. Pochemushka is a slang, cutesy term that comes from the word pochemu: why. I probably deserve to be called one today, but it still irks me, as it is generally used in a sort of a derogatory way.

"Going back to Ukraine," I say. It's an easy target because it's also true.

Marik turns to look at me, and his entire body is trembling with laughter. "Why?" he asks in Russian. "What did you forget there?"

ANNA

CHAPTER TEN

Back inside my uncle's condo, I'm gratefully packing three Tupperware containers full of leftovers (a very exciting development when you're living mostly on instant oatmeal packets), when Marik sees me and relays to everyone what I told him on the porch. He starts laughing again. He thinks it's the funniest thing.

My dad is quiet, and my mother is furious. "Are you crazy?" she asks me when we're back in the car. The mix of her perfume and my grandmother's immediately makes my stomach uneasy, on top of the fact that sitting in a car always feels to me like being trapped in a moving death cage. And did I mention the wine? There was a fifth cup consumed inside, while I was waiting for my mom to finish showing off her purple studded purse from Japan to my aunts. "Everyone is killing themselves to leave that country, and you want to go *back*?"

"Just to visit! I want to see what it's like," I say. I don't blame Marik for saying anything, but I do regret opening my mouth. I know my parents might see my desire to return to Ukraine as a personal insult to their decision to move. But it's really not. I get why they came; but I also don't understand this means I can never go back. Or why I have to forever be in their debt, when it was their decision, not mine. Sometimes I wonder if all kids feel so indebted to their ancestors, or it's only immigrants. Or if the debt is merely on a different level; for most people, it is only the act of being born and raised that they owe. With immigrants, one adds moving to a new country and having to start a person's life all over again. And, on top of that, if you are Eastern European and Jewish, like we are, the weight of everything your grandparents survived is compounded on it too; if they hadn't escaped the Nazis, there would be no parents, no me. Every step I take I am dragging a thousand ghosts behind me. My great-grandpa, Baba Mila's father, was an artist too; a musician who played four or five instruments, when he wasn't running the Jewish orphanage in town. Then the Nazis came, and there was no more music.

"Do you know what they would do to you if they found out you were American? Or if they found out you were born there and left?" Mom asks.

"They kidnap tourists all the time," my dad adds. "For ransom money."

"Right. I'm sure they still do that now, and it's not all over the Internet somehow." I lean back into the seat and close my eyes, trying to keep a wine headache at bay.

"What's happening?" my grandpa asks, sliding into the car next to me, still smelling precisely like he did all those years he lived with us in our first tiny American apartments, like bad breath and Soviet-era industrial soap. I don't know where he finds the stuff; I hope he never stops. Like many things from Ukraine: it's terrible, but it's home. "Why are you fighting?"

"It's nothing," my dad tells him.

"Shto?" my grandma asks.

"It's nothing, he said," my grandpa relays. I open my eyes again and, in the dark, see him taking her hand in his. "Vco horosho."

"Why can't you people speak Russian?" Babushka complains in Russian for the millionth time, even though, as previously mentioned, she does understand English. "Would that really be so hard?"

"Da," I say.

"How can it be hard to speak your native language?" Baba Mila continues. "I still remember Romanian, and I'm an old lady."

I've never heard my grandmother speak a word of her native

Romanian, but it doesn't matter; her comment only serves my point on a golden platter. "See, this is what I'm talking about," I tell my parents. Maybe it wasn't the best time to bring it up, but now that I have, I might as well see it through. I have been fantasizing about going there ever since I saw the study abroad list at our Honors Department orientation back in September. "It's ridiculous that I barely remember how to speak Russian. I saw Russia *and* Ukraine on the list of places to study abroad. It can't be that unsafe if they let college students go there."

"We'll talk about you studying abroad, but you're not going to Ukraine by yourself. Or Russia," my dad says. Then he looks at my mom with an expression I am all too familiar with, because of my curfew-breaking, punk-loving sister: one of total vexation, like what did they do to deserve such an incendiary child. My mother has the exact same look on her face. As if I'm telling them I want to go on an unsupervised African safari, or drop out of school and join the circus, not simply travel abroad like a million other college students have done.

"Your sister speaks perfect Russian," my grandma complains.

"My sister lives in Israel, where half the population is Russian," I explain, a little bit stung. My entire life she has always compared me to older cousins who have had more successes, because duh, they are *older*; this is the first time she's pitted me against Masha, though. I have always gotten better grades than her, plus I stayed in the country, so there was never any need to. "We live *here*. If you guys wanted us to speak Russian so much maybe someone should have taught me better."

Of course, I can't blame her for being annoyed. I'm annoyed at myself. This is part of why I have spent years fantasizing about a return home. So many Russian immigrants got the Brooklyn Bridge, the Manhattan skyline lit up by an endless stream of lights, they'd gotten the Russian dolls and pilmeni of Brighton Beach, they got Holocaust survivors playing chess in the parks of Queens, but not us. The only Soviet immigrants I'd met in Milwaukee were directly related to me, and most of them lived in the same government-subsidized apartment building as my grandparents and their siblings. New York transplants got to keep their culture and inherit the new world at the same time. We, on the other hand, had to choose.

And what had my family chosen? *Wisconsin.*

The car comes to an abrupt stop. I turn to see we're back at my grandparents' apartment building.

"Oh, we're home already," my grandma Mila says, looking at me with a surprised laugh. She laughs at everything lately, I don't know why. It's like a nervous tic or something; I don't think I've ever seen her sincerely amused by something in my entire life. She says something to me in Yiddish, then laughs again. My heart surges with love and sadness in equal parts.

"What's that Babushka?" I ask her, helping her out of the car. Her white, fluffy hair is somewhat matted on one side of her head, and her eyes appear tiny without her glasses on, possibly a side effect of her glaucoma. This is probably not nice to say, but I always thought she looked a little bit like a hobbit. A cute Hobbit, but still a Hobbit. She even has enough whiskers on her chin to qualify as a small beard.

"She doesn't speak Yiddish!" my grandpa yells in Russian from the other side. "Bozhe moy!"

"It's okay, Dedushka, you don't need to yell," I tell him as I help them to the door. I find the two of them so adorable when I see how much they still adore each other, especially when I am tipsy. They hold hands all the way through the vestibule and across the doorway and into the elevator, where they disappear from view. Part of me wishes to follow them, to bask once more in their uncomplicated affection instead of returning to the car. But it's late, and they need to go to bed—so do I.

"Anyway, Anastasia. I'm not trying to be mean. I've looked into going back to visit Chernovtsy a few times," my dad says, immediately jumping back into our conversation after I've finished helping my grandparents inside. He starts driving towards my house, which makes me relax a little. "They don't let you rent cars without drivers, and they charge a crazy amount of money. You can fly into Poland and rent a car there to drive to Ukraine, but that's also expensive. The visas are complicated to get. It's a mess," he says. "You're better off going to Paris or Berlin. Even Poland or Moldova are easier. Anywhere but Ukraine."

"But I don't want to go to Poland or Moldova or Paris," I explain.

"Or Israel," my mom interjects. "Birthright is free, and it's two weeks long! And you can see your sister."

"Isn't it basically a dating service?" I ask my mom. "I heard it's really for Jewish parents to have their kids meet other Jewish kids without actually setting them up. No thanks."

"Don't be ridiculous," she tells me. "You're too young for that anyway."

"And I also heard they brainwash everyone into becoming Zionists."

My mother gasps at this. "Where are you hearing things like that? In school?"

I shrug. "No, just…friends."

"It sounds like you're friends with anti-Semites! That's what anti-Semites would say," my mother exclaims, so aghast she's reverted to her native tongue without realizing. Which I find a bit dramatic, if you ask me. I don't really spend much time considering Israel or anti-Semitism, though, at least not in the present tense. It's not like anyone has ever criticized my cultural origins to my face or anything. "Pavel, did you hear this?" she asks him, but my dad stays weirdly silent. So she turns back to me, her naturally pale face even paler. "They made this trip so kids like you can understand."

"Understand what?" I say. "Religion? Religion is silly. No guy is sitting up in the clouds watching all of us and judging us. The Bible is a bunch of stories with a lot of plot holes."

"Huh. So you know better than thousands of people who came before you, that's what you're saying?" my dad asks, chiming in.

"No…" Boy do I wish I had a rewind button. I would go back to

87

that balcony and never open my mouth. Maybe I would go back to my apartment and never leave in the first place. I can't help but wonder why they are speaking Russian again if they hate it there so much. How can you hate a thing and be mad at someone for wanting it, but also use it constantly? It's so…hypocritical.

"Jewish people here for thousands of years," my dad says, returning to his choppy English. "Other cultures—the Romans, the Babylonians—they larger and more successful, they vanished," he says. "Why you think Jews still around? It's not easy…2,000 years of exile. The Spanish Inquisition, pogroms, Holocaust. Being kicked of every place in the world."

"In the years after the Berlin Wall fell, eighty percent of the Jewish community left Ukraine," my mom chimes in, also in English; hers is ten times better than my dad's because she worked so long in customer service. "They lost a million in the Holocaust, then another half million because of Gorbachev. At last count, it was something like 80,000 Jews left. In less than a hundred years, Jews were forced out of Ukraine almost entirely, either by gas chamber or anti-Semitic policies."

"And we still here," my dad continues. "Just think about. Without stories, we have nothing. We a chapter in history book. You don't think you have something to learn from that?"

"Sure. People can believe in very crazy ideas no matter what the century."

"Judaism not just an idea. It self-corrects. Rabbis adapt rules," my dad continues. "That's what makes it great."

"If it's so great why have I never seen you go to a synagogue?" I ask, rolling my eyes. I stretch my legs out over the now-vacant backseat, where it still somehow smells like my grandpa.

"We almost moved to Israel, you know," my mom says. She turns around to face me again, but I keep my glance on the road, which is getting closer and closer to my house. We pass a brick apartment building, followed by an endless array of vast duplexes with matching balconies.

"We were a week away from moving when we got our visas from America. Everything was packed and ready to go," my mom is saying now.

"I know."

"If you really knew—if you *understood* why—you wouldn't want to go back to Ukraine. Ever."

Before you go thinking I'm a total ignoramus, let's get one thing clear: I understand that the USSR was no picnic. But it was not all prison either. There were upsides, too: camaraderie among the oppressed, tight-knit family units, off-the-grid survival skills. The fact that you knew where you were, where you belonged. I've never had that. In emigrating from the Soviet Union, whatever we all gained in safety, we lost in an assortment of smaller, equally important things. Cultural heritage, community, a high-stakes life.

And then there's this: struggle isn't all bad. Struggle makes your lungs remember air, makes your eyes remember there are stars.

What makes us remember anything now?

"It's been sixteen years. It's not the same anymore. We went to St. Petersburg on that cruise. And Estonia," I try. "And it was fine!"

"That's different," my mom says. "It was only for a day, and we were there."

"I don't understand why you would even want to go to Russia again. You were miserable on that cruise," my dad says.

"I was miserable because I was fourteen, not because we were in Russia."

"It's not how you imagine it," my dad adds. "I promise. Everyone who could leave it left. You think that many people leave a place because it's so wonderful?"

"I know it's not *wonderful*," I say. "Cuba isn't exactly heaven, and people still go there."

"Bozhe moy," my mom says, placing two fingers on her temple. And if I'm not mistaken, she looks a little teary-eyed. This makes me feel bad—my mom is not a crier—but it doesn't make me stop. It's too late now to stop.

"Cuba?" my dad asks, his voice now an octave higher. "What are they teaching you at that school…"

With a dramatic sigh, my dad turns the car left with one hand, and allows the other to clasp my mom's, as if to remind me they're a team, and I'm the interloper. For a moment, I feel some empathy for Masha, who had to bear the brunt of their disagreements growing up. The three of them were always fighting. They fought so much that by the time I became a teenager, I decided that I would keep my opinions to myself, even if it meant making a few sacrifices. I didn't think I could take it. If this car ride is any indication, I was absolutely right.

"Anastasia," my mom says. "They didn't want us there, don't you understand?"

"I don't really need your permission. I'm nineteen. If I want to go, I can go."

"Maybe. But you *do* need our money," she says. "Or have you found a way to fly to Eastern Europe on your own?"

She has me there. It's the only reason I even bother arguing with them about going or not. I spent all my savings from summer jobs on coffee and cigarettes, and I'm still not done with a four-foot painting commission of Le Père Jacques's "The Woodgatherer" I was slowly working on for my former high school guidance counselor last year and no longer even bother trying to finish. There is also, of course, the daily distraction of drugs and parties and schoolwork. How I get anything done at all is nothing short of remarkable.

"No. But I could get a job." It makes sense they can't relate to my incessant pull toward all things Ukraine. They went through hell to get here. This displacement is something they will never understand. They did have a home, once. Now they have a new home. To them, it is simple: they were there, and now they are here. People they knew then are dead or in jail. The worst thing that could happen now to the people they know is that they become lazy, or Democrats.

It probably goes without saying I avoid talking to them about politics, too.

"You and this Ukraine obsession…" my mom sighs, still rubbing the sides of her head with two fingers. "I thought you were done with it years ago."

I, too, put my fingers to the sides of my forehead and rub them. When I look up again, I see we have finally stopped in front of my house. Feeling brave for one final moment, I say: "I wasn't done, I was just done telling you about it."

"Anastasia, there is a lot you don't know about life. And about people," my mom says. "We left that horrible place so you wouldn't have to."

"But don't you ever wonder…?" I start, but I don't finish the sentence.

"What," my mom says, flatly.

"Have you ever considered maybe you don't know everything?" I finally snap.

"Anastasia!" my dad interjects. "Don't talk to your mother that way."

I unbuckle my seat belt. I need to get out of the car, now. "Never mind," I tell her. She seems to feel bad suddenly because her body language changes. It's like she suddenly remembers I'm an adult and can choose whether or not to call her. Or maybe she's remembering what happened with her other daughter when they disagreed too much.

"School is more important, honey. Why do you need to go to Ukraine?" she coaxes.

"Because I want to," I say, knowing I sound like a petulant toddler but unable to help myself. "Isn't that enough?"

"You don't know what you want," is all my dad says. "You're a child."

I look out again at my apartment, where I can see Margot working on a terrible abstract painting of a dog for an upcoming art show at the school's gallery. A part of me wishes so desperately to be a part of that culture, hanging my oil portraits in line beside all the mediocre watercolor landscapes and mixed-media collages, drinking wine and eating cheese until I am ready to pass out. Everyone in the art department gets to do it and most of them have the talent of a shoe. Or maybe I'm simply jealous that they have the ability to try, and I don't. But why shouldn't I, too, have this chance? Because my parents told me I can't? Maybe it's the wine, or maybe it's the conversation we've had, but a little door starts to open in my heart then. And inside that door is a small voice that is telling me *your parents don't know everything*, and it's telling me *if you don't want the same things, then maybe you shouldn't do what they say*. That should seem obvious, the realization our parents don't always know what's best for us—but it's harder to see when your parents have made so many sacrifices for you and behave like perfect robots.

"Actually, Dad, I'm not a child," I say finally.

As I leave the car, and watch them drive off towards Highway 43, I'm awash in a feeling more familiar to me than love, or kinship, or even sorrow: an angry, guilty hopelessness.

If I had to name the feeling, it would be this: *Family*.

ANNA

CHAPTER ELEVEN

I drag myself upstairs and open the door into the kitchen, where August is at the table drinking coffee and smoking a hand-rolled cigarette while simultaneously rolling another one. The window is open to the crisp, cool autumn air, and it smells like one of our neighbors is having a bonfire. I love that smell. Immediately, I feel more at ease than I have all night.

"Hey," I tell August, with a nod. I let out a long breath of air and look for where to sit; the chairs are all semi-occupied. A polka-dot road bike leans against one, and a large backpack is open on the other. It's full of yogurts, bagels, and some bottles of wine. Probably he came home straight after dumpster diving. "Trader Joe's again?"

"Yep," August says. "And Einstein's must have had a very slow day." When he doesn't move, or offer me some of his haul, which he sometimes does, I begin to ransack the nearly empty cabinets for snacks, in order to soak up the alcohol and have at least *some* chance of sleeping later. Drinking too much gives me insomnia, for whatever inexplicable reason. And maybe I could get past the difficulty of falling asleep in a normal setting, but then every little noise wakes me up too, and my roommates are not quiet people. So I find a bag of pretzels and some cheese, and am about to head to my room to eat it, but then August starts talking.

"Hey, Anna! Sit with me," he says. He takes his overflowing bag and sets it on the floor. I sit down. He hands me the new cigarette, and passes his lighter over too once I sit.

"Oh my god, thank you. It's like you read my mind."

August giggles. "Your mind isn't hard to read, Anna. It's usually one of three things. Speaking of, whatever happened to Mr. Short, Dark, and Handsome?" He tips his cigarette into the ashtray, knocks the ash off in a way where half of it ends up on our antique wooden table, then brings it back up to his lips to take another drag. "Haven't seen him around lately."

"Oh, I don't know. Probably got back together with that ex he's always obsessing about," I say, then place my hand over August's mouth. "Do not say I told you so!" but it's too late, he says it at the same time as I do.

"Fine, fine, you were right," I admit. August pinches my cheek. "I'm not cut out to be the other woman."

"At least we won't have to go to anymore metal shows," he says, lightheartedly. "I didn't want to tell you when you were fucking, but his music is awful."

"Oh, I know," I laugh. "I could tell from your face."

"Could you?" he says. "I thought I was doing such a good job hiding it."

"Not everyone can be Bob Dylan, August."

"Sure, but can't they at least be Bob Seger?"

"Who's Bob Seger?"

August drops his head and shakes it. "Oh boy. Why do I even bother playing you music? You still don't know the difference between indie folk and progressive rock." He stands up, puts his cigarette out, and shoves the Drum baggie into his pocket. "Hey, can you keep an eye on my bike for a while?" he asks.

"Which one? That one?"

"Yeah, I sold the other ones," August says with a hint of a smile. "I'm leaving town for a bit. I can leave you the lock for it too, if you want to use it."

"Sure!" I agree. We are almost the same height so his bike would fit me perfectly, and it's much faster than the old Trek hybrid I'd been borrowing from my parents' house. I could go all kinds of places with August's bike. "Where are you headed?"

"Gonna hop a train with my friend Rod. We'll head south and see where we end up."

"Oh, that's so cool," I say. "Rod...the one with all the face tattoos?"

"Yeah," August says. "I haven't done the train thing in a while, and I'm feeling antsy. This fucking weather, man."

"Yeah, I don't blame you. Although, I really like this weather. I'm a weirdo, I guess."

"You want to come with?" he asks, then lifts his polka-dot road bike onto his shoulder as if it weighs nothing

"Train-hopping?" I ask, dumbfounded. At times, I've fantasized about going myself, jumping on a train as it starts moving, feeling the wind dancing around the steel car, and hearing nothing but a roar for six, seven hours. Going anywhere and nowhere, with no one to answer to. But I don't think I have the courage for that level of misbehaving, the kind that involves leaving everything behind. Or any kind of misbehaving, when it comes down to it.

"I don't think so, but thanks," I tell August, breaking eye contact. I pick my snacks up from the table and open the door for him so he can get out easier carrying the bike on his shoulder. "Maybe another time. When will you be back, you think?"

"I don't know. Couple weeks? I would rather not plan it too much." I fight an urge to hug him goodbye. All of our late-night wine drinking spent talking about our failed romantic dramas had really brought us closer the last few months, and I'm sad to see him go. But I don't want to come off as cheesy, so I settle for a more casual goodbye.

"Well, have fun, I'll miss you," I say.

"Aw, I'll miss you too, Anna," he says, then comes over and gives me a one-handed hug anyway. He smells like sweat and patchouli and platonic friendship. Relationships at nineteen are strange; sometimes they feel like train wrecks, the way you can bond so easily and so intensely. How someone you met only a few months ago now feels impossibly necessary to your daily existence. Sometimes I wonder if it's just luck or if this is how life is for normal people; or, worst of all, if this is a fleeting occurrence that only lasts as long as young adulthood lasts. In any case I return the hug and then carry my snacks back to my room before August can see my eyes are tearing up. I blink them away and light another cigarette, and after a few drags, I've calmed myself down enough to turn on my computer.

I don't like change. It's only a trip, I know, but something about it makes my heart beat faster and my stomach turn. Of course, it doesn't help that minutes ago I had possibly the biggest argument with my parents I've ever had. That the more I think about my future—two and a half more years of college, followed by working at some office nine-to-five, then marrying a Russian Jew my family would approve of and having kids—the more I feel like jumping off the Locust Street Bridge.

So maybe this will explain why I did what I did next, because this is the mindset I am in when I find another message from Zoya. The second message from her is on Facebook and sounds more urgent. I read it three times in a row to make sure I understand correctly. But even after the third time through, plus an internet browser's translation, I'm still not so sure that I do.

"*Dear Anastasia Pavlova*," it says. "*I didn't want to tell you this way, but I have no choice now. I am your sister on your dad's side. I would really like to speak with you, if you are able. Please write back as soon as possible.*"

Because I read Zoya's second message in an entirely different mood than her first, I do not ignore it this time. I do not delete it. Had I been anyone else, I would never have done what I was about to do, and nothing that transpired would have ever happened. My life would be normal—at least as normal as it could ever be for someone who does not want a normal life.

But I can only be myself; the girl who once asked so many questions my teachers had to limit me to three a day. The girl who, at age eight, begged the Russian hairdresser to cut off all her hair to see what it would look like (it looked very, very bad). The girl who turned into a woman who eventually learned it was easier not to ask questions.

Maybe that girl never died; she only went away into hiding. Until now. Like Howard Zinn has said, "Dissent is the highest form of patriotism."

Of course I was going to answer her.

And so, without thinking any more about it, I write, "Do you speak English?"

FEBRUARY 2008

MASHA

CHAPTER TWELVE

Outside on Bremen Street, I swivel around, my fists up, ready to use one of the many Krav Maga defensive moves I'd learned in Israel over the years, but then I see whose hand is on my shoulder and stop cold.

"Oh my God," I say, dropping my hands. "Emily."

My old best friend squeezes me with all her might, then releases her grip and looks me up and down. "Masha! I can't believe it's you. I thought I was seeing things." She looks at my hand and frowns. "Are you smoking again?"

I shake my head. I hadn't even realized I was holding Rose's cigarette. "This isn't mine."

Emily continues to watch me, then glances back at the door. She gestures behind her. "Want to go inside and talk? It's freezing. Is that a leather coat you're wearing? What are you doing out here?"

"Actually, I can't, I really have to..."

"Nonsense, woman," she says, taking Rose's cigarette, stealing a drag, then throwing it on the ground. "I'm sure you have five minutes for an old friend, right?" Then before I can protest, she is pushing me inside and buying me a drink. The bar is even more crowded now; bodies are stacked right on top of each other like sardines bathing in patchouli. A three-piece band is on stage; a stand-up bass, a gypsy guitar, and a banjo, all sticking out from the heads of plaid shirts and frayed jeans.

It's a strange sensation, sitting down at a table with a drink; I don't really go to bars much in Israel. A beer can cost eight dollars, twelve if you're in Tel Aviv. Plus, David is out of town so much that when he's home he doesn't really like to leave the house. I could go without him, but I only have a handful of friends, mostly David's family members, who are all young, busy parents.

"First question: Have you ever heard of the Internet? You know, Riverwest *does* have it," Emily says. "Even if everyone chooses not to accept that it's the twenty-first century." She slams her beer on the wobbly table, making it spill all over, then takes off her down coat to reveal a blue-and-red plaid flannel shirt. For the first time since I arrived in Milwaukee, I am amused. At least some things never change. I don't know if I've ever seen Emily wearing anything but flannel. She's from Kentucky and grew up training horses. The way Emily used to mention their names, it took me months to understand she was talking about animals and not siblings. She'd moved to Wisconsin the first year of high school, where we'd met in an English class and bonded over a mutual adoration for *Franny and Zooey*, then quickly become inseparable. As soon as we turned eighteen, we found a place together in Riverwest because it was so cheap. We didn't know that it would eventually drive us apart. That sometimes, saving some money isn't worth the cost.

"Hey, it keeps that DVD rental place in business," I joke.

Emily frowns. "Masha."

I shrug. "There's internet in Israel, too," I say. I look around in discomfort, and notice there are several people here with iPhones, looking down at bright screens in the middle of tables surrounded by friends. It really is a plague, I think. "It's not very good, but it works."

"I guess I thought you were mad at me or something," Emily says, so quietly I can barely hear her. Her long, stiff hair falls out of her hat like a pile of loose cords, much like her short-lived dreadlocks did the summer before college, when we went backpacking through Europe together, inseparable. Getting lost in Prague and eating gelato in Venice, somehow never getting tired of each other. Who knew that one event could derail our entire history together so easily?

"Why would I be mad at you?"

"I don't know," Emily says, shaking her head. "For how I handled things back then, I guess."

I take a long sip of my drink. I can feel myself getting dizzy again, and look down to steady myself, when I notice I am holding onto the table so tightly my fingers are white. I drop them to my side. "Emily, let's just not."

"I just...I feel bad about how everything went down," Emily says.

"It's okay," I say. The band starts playing what I believe to be an Elliott Smith cover—or maybe they're only trying to sound like him—and half the crowd is listening while the other half is trying to scream over the noise. Which means I, too, have to raise my voice.

"No, it's not," Emily says. "I know it's why we're not friends anymore."

"We're not friends anymore because I live on another continent," I explain. I finish the vodka soda she bought me and stand up from the chair, Rose's bed calling out to me. I put a hand over my mouth, stifling a yawn. "Emily, I really have to go. I'm so tired."

Emily grabs my hand and doesn't let me go. "You can't avoid it forever, you know."

I take my hand back and turn to leave, feeling myself start to get angry. "It's still a free country. Or did that change while I was gone?" I tell her. A new song comes on, a cover of The Decemberists' "The Chimbley Sweep." Emily seems to soften, as do I—we are both remembering, or perhaps trying not to remember, listening to this album over and over one warm summer day between semesters. Back when things were still so simple. Back when I used to think that friendships were easier to maintain than family relationships. Now I think they're both pretty hard, but it's way easier when you have a common interest, like Judaism. Even before I'd believed any of it, the bond was palpable right away. It's what eventually sold me; the connection, the camaraderie. So you have to put aside logic and even science once in a while; it's not like either of those things were ever my strong suit. I'd always preferred abstract ideas over math, poetry over physics.

"Sorry. We don't have to talk about it," Emily corrects. The music continues to blast through the speakers, giving me a headache, because I guess on top of everything else, I am now old and lame. I feel myself sliding off the seat, to the edge, where I always end up no matter how long I've been sitting somewhere.

Maybe Liam was right. Maybe I am always looking for a way out.

"What brings you to town anyway?"

Right as she is asking me this I ask, "Have you seen my sister around?"

We both let out an uncomfortable giggle. Despite our voices crashing into each other, we both seem to have heard what the other has said. "No. Not since you left actually. Why?" she asks, the question sinking in. Emily looks generally surprised. "Did something happen?"

"No, but we haven't heard from her in a while. You know how my dad gets."

Emily watches me with concern. "Is that why you're here?"

I sigh, and it turns into another yawn. I'm officially too tired to make something up. "Sort of."

"Shit," she says. Then she lets out a short breath. "Well, actually that's better than I thought. I assumed someone died." She sees my face, then mumbles, "I mean, I hope Anna is okay, of course. But if she's anything like us at nineteen... she could have gone anywhere."

"That's exactly what worries me."

Emily leans back and finally wipes up some of her spilled drink with a napkin. "You know, Masha, I think about you all the time."

"I think about you too," I concede. At the moment it even feels true. I'd forgotten—or chosen to forget—how much I used to like being with Emily. Something about her energy screams *Love me*, and really, you want to. She isn't particularly gorgeous, with a sizable round German nose and giant, nearly bulging, eyes—but she is confident, her energy so upbeat it brings yours up too. I worry she's about to start rehashing the past again when we're interrupted by a Chinese girl pulling up a stool and sitting down next to us.

"Emily, I have to tell you something crazy!" she says.

"Hi, you're back! How was your parents' house?" Emily brightens. "This is my roommate, Wang," she tells me. "Wang, this is my old friend, Masha."

Wang's eyes go wide. "Masha?" she looks at me, sticking out a hand. "I hear so much about you! I inherit your bed, too, yes?"

"Huānyíng guānglín!" I say, taking her hand and shaking it. Or, try to say, at least. I only managed to learn a few phrases in Cantonese before giving up. Okay, not really a few, just this one. Cantonese is really hard.

Wang grins and returns the greeting, even though I've probably butchered the phrase—directly translated, it means "I meet you with joy." It also connotes the image of daylight streaming in through a door. It's a way to say hello in China.

"*Wow.* Emily did not mention you know Chinese. You much impress." Wang takes a long drink from her beer and looks at Emily, then me.

"Oh, I don't know Chinese," I explain, stifling another yawn. "It's such an interesting language but way too hard for me."

"This is funny, because Chinese part of what I want to tell Emily," she says. She looks at Emily again, wide-eyed. "We almost get robbed!"

"What do you mean?" she asks, grabbing Wang's hand. "Are you okay?"

Wang nods aggressively. "Okay, so there is ad on Craigslist? It ask for Chinese lessons in exchange for housecleaning, yes?" Wang says. "So, without knowing, my sister and me both responded? This girl, young girl, comes over, to see house, a week or two ago. Only, girl never called about lesson." She takes a long drink of her beer. "But my sister, Ling, girl email back for lesson. When Ling go meet girl for lesson today, she come back home and all expensive things *gone.*"

"For real?" Emily asks, her mouth gaping open.

"That is so elaborate for Riverwest," I say, stifling a yawn. Usually, people are held up at gunpoint, or wake up to a missing computer. A Craigslist scheme involves some intelligence behind it, perhaps even a team.

Emily finishes her beer and slams it down, wiping her mouth with a hand. "What the *hell*," she says. "Good thing we literally have nothing of value in the house." To me, she adds, proudly, "We don't even have a TV."

"Who does anymore? Especially around here." I fail to stifle another yawn. Drinking vodka was probably a bad idea. I can hardly keep my eyes open now. "This is why I never understood why anyone would bother to rob people in Riverwest. Unless you consider kombucha a valuable item, no one has anything. And yet, it seems to happen constantly."

"That's not totally true," Emily says. "A lot of people have really nice bikes. And remember when you were dating the guy with the projector? What was his name?"

"*Antonio*," I say, cringing. "The filmmaker who never made even one film."

Emily frowns. "Yeah. That guy," she says. "I wonder where he is now."

"Last I heard he moved to LA and works on the set of some sitcom."

"He was a dick, but that projector was awesome," Emily reminisces. "Remember all those movie nights we used to have?"

"Yeah. Those were fun." I don't know why, the vodka maybe, but despite how aggressively I've been fighting it off, I'm suddenly nostalgic and sad. "It's too bad he had to go and date June while we were all living together," I say, shaking my head. "God, open relationships are stupid."

Emily's face goes slack with surprise. Then she looks down and starts tearing apart her wet napkin into little pieces, and I get even sadder. I realize I haven't said June's name aloud in…well, years. Not only have I not said her name, but I've also tried my very best not to

106

think about my former roommate, the reason I'd left town in the first place. People tell you that you can't escape your memories, but it's not true, you can. You decide to close the door, and the door stays closed. You merely have to be vigilant, like with any exercise routine.

"Yeah. That was not a healthy pair," Emily starts, slowly. "Not that you were a better one. Or what's-his-name, the one before Antonio, the tattooed guy?"

I cringe, a jolt of guilt flooding me as I remember what happened earlier in the day. "Liam."

"Yeah, he was kind of a loser too, no offense. I hope your taste in men has improved over in Israel."

I feign a chuckle. "Everyone kind of has their shit together there. Most of my friends have kids already. Must be those years in the army or something."

"I cannot even imagine having kids, good God," she says. "Maybe in ten years. Or never, I don't know. I deal with them enough at work."

An awkward silence ensues, and I know I am supposed to ask her about her work, but I already heard she's a kindergarten teacher and I'm too tired to make small talk about it. What is there to say? We are no longer in each other's lives. Catching up is rather pointless. In another circumstance, I would want to know everything about her new life, but in this reality, we are practically strangers now. I try to head out again, but Emily stops me by reaching out for my hand.

"Masha..." Emily starts.

Before she can finish the sentence, I turn to Wang, who has been quietly sitting there with her hands in her lap. I feel kind of bad she got stuck in the middle of our long-overdue reunion, but it's all I can do to keep my stomach contents down. I'd cracked the door open, and I now I have to shut it again.

"So what are you going to do?" I ask her, to get Emily off my back. "Did you go to the police?"

I admit, too, that I am a little intrigued by this scam. It certainly doesn't lack in creativity.

"We did. I just come from police. They made sketch already because this not first time Chinese family complain. Want to see?" she asks, then whips out a folded-up piece of paper from her backpack. I lean over and look at the photocopied drawing. The girl is dark-haired, with big bright eyes and two face piercings and a dimple in her chin. She has a tiny row of earrings and a bandana around her hair. Despite all that, her eyes are kind, soft. They don't quite match the outfit. There's something familiar about them that makes my heart jump into high alarm.

I take the paper out of Wang's hands and look at it more closely. The slender nose, the smattering of freckles. I know that face.

It looks remarkably like the photo I've been showing around all day.

MASHA

CHAPTER THIRTEEN

"You look like you've seen a ghost," Emily is saying when I finally start breathing normally again. She and Wang are both staring at me.

"Do you know her?" Wang asks, all the jest gone from her voice. "She stole precious things. Family heirlooms, not only money."

I swallow, then make eye contact with Wang, clearing my face of whatever it's doing. "No, no, I don't know her. I felt faint for a second," I explain. I stand up again and put my coat on. "I think it's the jetlag. I couldn't sleep on the plane. And I haven't eaten. I'm sorry guys; I really don't feel well, I better go."

"Masha," Emily says, starting to follow me out the door. I keep walking, but she pulls my arm back, and I nearly fall into one of the outdoor patio tables I'm so faint.

"Crap," I say, rubbing my knee. I look out onto Bremen St., dimly lit, empty and dark now, snow still dropping like sheets. "Crap, crap, crap."

Emily puts her hands on my shoulders, her forehead creased with concern, or anger, or both. Instantly, my reflexes want to elbow my way out of the situation, as I'd learned in Krav Maga. I have to fight against this urge. Emily isn't attacking me; there's no reason for my heart rate to be as sky high as it is. The inventors of Krav Maga were 1930s Russian Jews, sick and tired of seeing their people get killed in anti-Semitic attacks, not anxious girls who would rather avoid confrontations with former best friends. Slowly, I pick up and remove her hands, then step backward.

"Yes, Emily?" I ask. It's not clear what she wants from me, why she came outside. Doesn't she understand that I'm tired? That I've already done more in a day than I ever thought was possible? When I woke up this morning—yesterday technically—I had a pair of muscular, sweaty arms holding me tight, and a pretty comfortable life. Now, I feel as if I'm falling down the abyss, with nothing at all to hold onto on my way down.

Emily inhales sharply. "That's Anna, isn't it?" she asks.

"No!" This question takes me by surprise. I thought maybe she wanted to talk about why I lied about the drawing or why we aren't friends anymore, but I should have known better. She was reading me, like she used to before. Like I am some misbehaving kid in her class.

Or maybe she'd seen the resemblance as clearly as I did.

"Masha. Come on. It is," she says. "I won't say anything to Wang, but..."

"Emily, it could be anyone. All those train-hoppers look the same."

"Train-hoppers? I thought she was just hanging around all those anarchists. She's doing *that* now?" Emily asks, eyebrows raised. Then she crosses her arms over her chest, rubbing them for heat. The snow has stopped, but it's now freezing out, the wind turning from a slight discomfort into a bone-chilling cold—Wisconsin at its best.

"I don't know for sure. I just heard things," I shrug, also crossing my arms over my chest, shivering. A few years in the desert and you can completely disregard winter, apparently. How had I lived through so many decades of this cold and then forgotten to pack a real coat? To warm myself, I start hopping on one foot and then the other. I don't even care how stupid it looks.

"This isn't on you, Masha," Emily is saying. "You weren't here. How could you know?"

Of course it's not my fault, I think, before a second thought follows: unless maybe it is? "It's not her." I reach into my bag and take out the cigarettes I'd hidden there. This one, I light myself. Maybe this was the real reason I'd purchased them at the airport, and I've been in denial all day. In case I needed one, not only to barter for information. "It was good to see you, Emily."

I step around her and start walking as fast as I can throw the snow.

But Emily is nearly as stubborn as I am, and she isn't letting me get away so quickly. She keeps up with me as I speed-walk all the way down Bremen Street.

"Masha," she says. "Just stop for a second."

"I can't stop, Emily. It's freezing. And I need to get some sleep. I'm a zombie right now. My brain isn't working." Truthfully, it is working overtime, but I don't want her to know that. Wondering what's worse—that Anna is possibly a liar *and* a thief, or that I am *also* lying. Lying is supposed to be a thing of the past, like all the drugs and sleeping around I'd done during that brief time of flailing around in the abyss of adulthood. Lying is the old Masha. One day in Milwaukee is already turning me into a bad Jew. A bad *person*.

I will have a lot to make up for next Yom Kippur.

"If that's Anna—I mean, isn't that why you're here? To find her?" Emily asks, catching up again. "You can message the email from the Craigslist ad."

"If that's Anna—which it's not—I would have already thought of that, Emily," I explain. I walk even faster now, my breath hovering in the air like smoke. I can't help but miss Israel again, my cozy little apartment, half-hidden behind a Washingtonian tree and a giant Israeli flag, surrounded by neighbors I know and feel like friends. And David. I haven't been gone twenty-four hours, and his absence is almost like a severed arm. I know if he had been able to come with me, not only would I have already found Anna by now, I would be happier too. I have no way to contact him, either, being that he is off in some random country, doing God knows what, and as usual, I have to wait for him to call me, then drop whatever it is I am doing. He could be in America for all I know. He could even be here, and I would have no direct way of finding that out until I ran into him in the street.

This is pretty unlikely though. What business would Israel have in Milwaukee? Milwaukee certainly wants nothing to do with *them*. Everyone here thinks of the country as a political pawn, not a place full of interesting and diverse people of all sorts of religious and political leanings. It's easy to dismiss something when it doesn't have a face.

"God, when did you get into such good shape?" Emily asks, panting. "I could barely get you to go on a hike with me when we were in school."

"Running helps with my anxiety," I explain.

"Yeah, I have yoga for that," she says, following me as I turn right down Center Street. Its name sure is accurate. Everywhere I go I always end up on this street to get there. "Isn't that funny? We used to smoke weed and write those silly poems when we got anxious. Well, honestly, I still smoke a lot of weed. But I stopped with all the other stuff."

"I barely even drink now," I agree. "That drink you bought me was the first one I've had in weeks. Months maybe. I think I'm drunk."

"Really? You? But you love drinking," she says, shock apparent all over her face which is pink and stiff from cold. "We used to call you the shot Nazi."

"You know, it's just occurring to me how inappropriate that nickname was," I point out.

Emily pauses, thinks about that. "Yeah I guess you're right. I only meant that... I don't know. We're so...adult now."

I stop, turning to face her, the snow crashing into my hair and then melting. "I don't feel so much like an adult today, Emily," I admit. "Or most days. I feel like someone pretending to know what they're doing."

Emily frowns. "That's basically what an adult *is*, Masha," she says, shaking her head. "You think anyone knows what the hell they're doing?" Then, out of nowhere, she reaches out and hugs me, and I let her. No one ever touches me in Israel, other than David. Now I'm getting hugs all over the place. I must really look like the mess I feel.

Emily lets go, and I feel her head turning. "This is where you were going?"

I follow her gaze to the second level of a large white duplex with a green patio on its side, filled with mismatched chairs, empty wine bottles holding melted candles, and a large glass tube that is likely a bong. Below, an empty storefront that is in the process of becoming an art gallery, the fourth or fifth one in Riverwest. "Yeah, this is me. For tonight anyway." I head toward Rose's front door, which is not in front but on the side of the house under some more green awning. Snow is swirling again all around it, making it look like a snow globe.

"Is that a good idea?" Emily asks.

"No, probably not," I say. "But I don't have a lot of options. And I'm already here, and it's really damn cold in this country." I get the keys out of my coat pocket and find the gold one meant for this door. "Bye, Emily. It was great to see you."

Emily stands there, watching me, hesitating. "Masha. I have to get something off my chest."

I exhale deeply, waiting for the other shoe to drop.

"I'm sorry," she says. "It was wrong of me—of us—to blame you for what happened."

I stare at her, blinking. It's not what I was expecting to come out of her mouth. But she'd hit the nail on the head and I'm not about to dispute it. "Okay?" I try to sound indifferent, but my voice betrays how I really feel, which is grateful. This one sentence starts to melt the ice that has formed around my chest when it comes to my past life, my former friends, Riverwest. Maybe one action alone doesn't define a person after all. Maybe people are allowed to make mistakes and learn from them.

Emily sticks her hands deep into her pockets, her face red all the way down to her neck. "Call me if you need anything. I mean it." She starts walking away before I can respond, and for the first time since I left, I find myself truly missing my former best friend. I even consider taking her up on her offer to call her, when this is all over.

I turn and let myself into Rose's apartment. I head straight into her room, which looks like it hasn't changed at all since I last saw it, only been rearranged. There are hand-woven quilts and tie-dye shirts and those ridiculous posters with one word taking up the whole page. Incense piled into dust, celebrity magazines on the floor, clothes scattered about in an antique trunk and over Rose's bed. I take a pile of sweaters and move them into the chest, lying down over the tie-dye bedspread in a daze, when my foot hits something hard.

A laptop. Yes. That means I don't have to wait until tomorrow to send that email. Emily is right that emailing the ad is the best way to check if it's Anna behind the scheme. Maybe it will be that easy; I'll request a visit, and she will come here, and this can all be over. The crime, and the search for her. Maybe she is just *waiting* for someone to catch her. If it's Anastasia at all. What if we had both been projecting? Wouldn't that be the ideal outcome?

I open the computer, which isn't password-protected because it's only a step away from being in a recycling bin, and I search Craigslist for "Chinese." An ad for lessons in exchange for house cleaning comes up almost immediately, like Wang said. I try several other languages too, out of curiosity, but nothing else comes up. They are particularly targeting the Chinese community, for some reason.

In the bar where it lists an automated email address, I copy paste and open another browser window for Gmail, where I create a new address under the name WÉI_WÚ_WÉI, a Chinese term that has several meanings. Roughly translated it means movement without action; less like passiveness and more like Pascal's theory that "rivers are roads that take us where we want to go." To me, it has always meant having a little faith.

"Hi," I start writing in a new email window. "I'm a grad student at UWM. I know fluent Mandarin, and your ad sounds perfect for what I need. I'm about to leave town for the rest of the week, and was hoping you could meet me tomorrow before I leave? Thanks." I Google translate 'thank you' in Mandarin and paste it on the bottom. Then I click send and crash back down on the bed, falling asleep the moment I close my eyes.

MASHA

_____

CHAPTER FOURTEEN

I wake up to my phone buzzing repeatedly from my pocket. It's unclear how much time has passed, but it feels like possibly the middle of the night. Until, that is, I look towards the quilt-covered window and see a strip of sunlight attempting to break in. So maybe not the middle of the night. Early morning? If it is, I don't know how I'm still so tired. I could sleep another ten hours. My eyes feel glued shut with rubber bands.

"Masha?" asks my dad's voice. "I tried calling you more than few times. Vco horosho?"

I sit up, wiping the sleep from my eyes. "Sorry. I fell asleep."

"Where?"

"I ran into Rose, and she gave me her keys. To my old place. I ran into a lot of people actually. I forgot Milwaukee is basically a small town of drunks." I look around the room, which is empty, then go into the living room to see if anyone is there. No one is. The clock on the oven says eight a.m.

"Did you find something? About Anastasia?" my dad asks. I remember the email and head back to Rose's room to use her laptop.

"I'm working on a lead," I say, while Gmail finishes loading. One new email. I clear my throat. "I'd rather not get into it until I know more." With my heart in my throat, I click to open it. "Okay?"

In the email response, it says "How's ten?"

I write back that ten works fine, then give Rose's address. She won't mind—I hope. Rose has never owned anything of value besides that bass, and she didn't come home, so most likely she took it with her to whatever house she'd ended up sleeping at. Even her computer is a hand-me-down off-brand laptop that couldn't have cost more than a couple of hundred dollars new. She still has enough handmade scarves to clothe a small school of children, and judging from the piles of cash and coins littered about, probably has never opened a bank account. There's a word in Yiddish that perfectly describes her: Luftmensch. It refers to someone who is a bit of a dreamer; accurately translated, it means an "air person." The problem with Rose is that she has a different dream every other day. She devours things—jobs, plans, identities—and spits them back out so quickly it's like they never happened. I lost track of how many college programs she'd enrolled in and then dropped out of, how many restaurant aprons and name tags she's acquired, now haphazardly strewn about the floor. She also never learned how to clean. I have to fight the urge to rearrange and organize her room. But, holding the phone to my ear, I only allow myself to gather all her cash and hide it in a drawer.

"Hello? Maria?"

"Yes, Papa."

"I said, do you need me to come pick you up?"

"No. I mean, not yet."

My dad pauses, then asks, in Russian, "What aren't you telling me?"

There are lots of untranslatable words that describe my dad. Shlimazl: Yiddish for a chronically unlucky person. Or Won, a Korean word for the reluctance on a person's part to let go of an illusion. The fact that he still thinks either of my or Anna's lives could be in his control requires more stubbornness and reluctance than I can imagine.

"Trust me, Papa. You don't want to know."

"Bozhe moy." With a sigh, he hangs up the phone. My screen alerts me to four missed calls from him during the night and a text from Rose: *I crashed at a friend's*, her message says—code for she went home with a guy she is casually seeing. *At work till 5, help yourself to anything in the fridge.*

Relief floods over me; I am starving, and I get very grumpy when I don't eat. On top of that, I'm still groggy from the long flight. I get up to explore what's in the kitchen.

Groggy is another fun word, etymologically. It originated in the eighteenth century with a British sailor nicknamed Old Grog, on account of his weatherproof coat, made from a material called "grogram," a mixture of silk and wool. In 1740 he declared that his sailors start drinking their rum diluted with water; this drink became known as Grog. The feeling experienced when drinking too much of this, they called "groggy." So really, it originated as another word for drunk, but now people use it more for waking up under the weather or having jetlag. Despite only consuming one vodka-soda last night, then sleeping for nearly eleven hours, I happen to feel all of these things.

Coffee, I think then. Where is the coffee? I ask the kitchen. I dig through Rose's old pine cabinets and find a bag of Fuel Café beans, grind them up, and pour the grounds into a French press sitting on the counter. If I was Orthodox, like some of David's family is, I'd have to do my morning prayers now. But I've found it more than enough to merely take a moment to breathe and appreciate the morning, the fact that I've lived to see another day. Many people went to sleep last night and didn't wake up. We shouldn't take these things for granted.

While I wait for water to boil, I check the fridge, my stomach growling in anticipation. But I am disappointed to find that though I am welcome to help myself to anything, all that lives inside the fridge is a jar of Vegenaise and a very old apple. I close the fridge and look through the cupboards again. Not even a box of cereal. Plenty of ketchup packets and Splenda, but no food.

I sigh and settle for the old apple, cutting the bruised parts off. It almost doesn't even seem worth mumbling through the prayer for food, but I do it anyway. I'll have to get breakfast after this whole thing is over.

It's strange, being here. My old house, my old dishes; it's almost like jumping into a time portal. It even smells the same; like American Spirits and sandalwood incense. I'm surprised to feel no angst, or flashback of any kind. In fact, the feeling of dread that has hung over me since my arrival has begun to dissipate. Maybe it's because I got some sleep. Or that I may have already found exactly what I was looking for, which means I can go home. Sure, I hope to be wrong. The thought of my sister as a conniving thief makes me sick to my stomach. But it's better than her going missing, isn't it? In this neighborhood, there are far worse things that could happen to a person than to be caught stealing. As long as Anastasia is safe and unharmed, I could forgive her this mistake.

Once I drink a cup of coffee and finish the apple, I'm digging through a crate of old shoes, looking for some gym clothes—I'd feel ten times better if I could get a run in later—when the doorbell starts ringing. Already I have my suspicions it won't be Anastasia. She's never been early for anything, and it's not ten a.m. yet.

It's also possible I was only projecting when I saw that police photo. Similarly possible is that Liam's friend was wrong about her getting involved with a sketchy thief, or that Rose was wrong about his addictions. Maybe I was too quick to assume how easily Anastasia could turn to drugs for some sort of solace. It's not like addiction runs in the family, besides maybe smoking. Sure they like to drink at parties. (What can you expect from a language with more than ten words for hungover and even more for drinking, but no present-tense word for "to be?") But my grandparents have been alive a pretty long time, all things considered. Anna barely even snuck a taste of wine at our house, when it would have been easy to do so. She was a kid then, but still. She couldn't have changed that much, right?

By the time I open the door, I've worked myself up into such a state I don't know what I will say if it's Anastasia standing there. But it doesn't matter. Because it's not her face at the door; it's a man's.

MASHA

CHAPTER FIFTEEN

Tristan—if this is Tristan—is old. He's older than me, for sure; maybe closer to thirty than twenty. I'm surprised by this; I don't know why. He is also tall, like everyone mentioned; but what they failed to mention was that his hair is bright blue, and so long it passes his shoulders. He also has blue eyes and is skinny enough to be a model, if not for the acne pockets around the chin and cheeks, along with a pretty effective above-it-all attitude. If he's supposed to be pretending to be a student, he is doing a pretty poor job of it. His jeans aren't torn to shreds or Carharrts, like all the crust punks in Riverwest, but they're still pretty faded. Plus, he's got tiny wrinkles near his eyes; challenging to detect, typically, but it's so bright out I can see them. Probably because under all that blue dye he's a redhead. Freckles pool in dark circles around his nose and forehead.

Tristan clears his throat. He looks equally as confused to see my face there. "You're not Chinese," he says.

"And you're not a woman," I say.

He narrows his eyes at me. "What made you think I was?"

I pause, thinking. There's no great way to answer that question. And if this is Tristan, and not some random person, he might have some information to help me, so I can't go scaring him off right away. I hadn't even considered the option of someone else showing up, and I expend a lot of effort trying not to panic. I remind myself this isn't my house, these aren't my things, that none of it is of any value anyway.

"Are you coming in?" I ask, eventually. I try to relax my body language into a laissez-faire sluggishness instead of standing up straight like I usually do these days.

He hesitates, looking around the street, then at me; I can tell that in his mind, he is labeling me as a non-threat. I start up the stairs, and not long after, I hear his steps following mine. Once we're inside, I reach into my pack of cigarettes and offer him one. He looks a little thrown back but takes it anyway. "Oh, thanks."

"So. You want me to show you around? For the...uh, cleaning thing?" I ask, then without a response start the tour. I want to get it over with. Quickly, I show him the messy kitchen, its windows framed with large, overflowing plants; the living room's assorted secondhand couches. Even Rose's bike, a purple Schwinn with a metal basket, both its wheels flat, isn't worth anything. It's almost sad. Rose is a couple years older than me. At twenty-seven, you want to be able to afford a few valuable things, don't you? Otherwise, what's the point of working at all?

It's clear Tristan is realizing this too, half-checked out before the tour is even over. "Cool, thanks," he says, heading toward the door. "I'll email you about dates and stuff later. I have somewhere to be." Is this really how they play it? Or does Anna usually do this part and Tristan is just really bad at it? It seems easy to figure out something isn't it right. Although, I suppose a new immigrant would never imagine what kind of nonsense crime people in Milwaukee are capable of. If I still lived here, I would probably not let any strangers into my house ever. I guess that's what happens as you get older. Not only do you become less trusting, but you also acquire things you'd rather not lose. You procure more locks, both real and metaphorical. More reasons to keep people out than invite them in. But you also, hopefully, gain *some* confidence? Once you look around and discover that almost no one knows what they're doing, that they're all figuring it out as they go, the world becomes a slightly easier place to navigate—especially if you happen to truly be good at something. This knowledge has made me far more brazen than I once was. My high school self would be too scared of looking like a fool to ever try any martial arts. Now, I can't imagine how helpless I'd feel without it. How powerless. I wonder if this feeling is what changed Anna so much; maybe stealing made her feel powerful, at least for a moment. Knowledge and intelligence could be used as a tool almost as much as a body. But where had her moral compass gone? If I could convince her to join me in Israel, I know for sure she wouldn't be acting this way. But every time I'd tried, she laughed me off like I was some crazy person in a cult. It wasn't long before she stopped responding to my messages at all; as if my new religious beliefs could somehow rub off on her, thousands of miles away in Milwaukee.

Tristan walks slowly back to the door. For the first time I notice he's walking with a slight limp. "What happened to your leg?" I ask.

He turns around. His eyes dart away from mine, narrowing sheepishly at the floor. "Oh. Dog bite," he shrugs. "Had to get a lot of stitches, and it got infected... it's whatever." He takes a long drag of the cigarette, then takes another look around the apartment and asks, "Isn't this where that girl—"

"No, it's not," I interrupt.

He looks back down the hall, towards the bedrooms. The first one once belonged to me; there's a window that opens out to the roof, and I used to go out there to drink and watch people walk from bar to bar. Sometimes Emily and I would take these giant hula hoops up there to spin two or three at a time, and we'd throw them to each other like circus people. And June. June was also there, of course. It was always the three of us, even though I'd erased her out of my memory of those years.

"No, it is," Tristan is saying. "I'm just putting it together. Yeah. I was around that summer, I remember the news. I remember that odd-shaped balcony. It's the place where that girl hung herself from her bedroom doorknob."

My stomach falls, like I've been dropped from the highest point of a rollercoaster without warning. I swallow, hard. "It isn't."

"I wonder if she haunts the place," Tristan says, rubbing his chin.

I clench my fists until my nails are digging into my skin.

"That was so fucked up," Tristan is saying. Backpfeifengesicht is also a good word I wish we had in English. It's German for a face badly in need of a fist. Looks like gibberish but somehow isn't. "Didn't it take her roommates three days to find her body?"

"Shut up," I say, furious now and unable to control myself. "Where did you even hear that?"

Tristan looks taken aback, as if confused why his questions would cause such an emotional reaction. "I told you. The news. I have a lot of free time during the day."

I unclench my fists, inhale another deep breath.

It had taken three days to find June because the door was shut. And every time we tried to knock or check inside, we couldn't get the door open.

Because it was so heavy and didn't move.

Because, we would find out, her body was against it.

"What exactly are you learning Chinese for?" I ask. This interaction is not going the way I intended, and I need to change course. Immediately.

Tristan leans against the wall near the stove and takes another drag of his cigarette. "Just for fun."

"No one learns Chinese for fun," I say, watching him. I move to stand in front of the door, blocking his exit. In Portuguese, there's a term, Saudade, for the feeling of longing for something or someone that you love which is lost. It carries with it the repressed knowledge that the object of longing may never return; a bittersweet, empty feeling of something or someone that is missing. It's this feeling that comes over me now, like a wave. I have to close my eyes to push it away.

When I open my eyes again, the expression of a trapped bird has overcome Tristan's face, before being obscured by an aggressive impassiveness. "Sure they do. Not everyone can afford to go to college."

He surprises me by saying something in Cantonese. Something I don't understand because I don't actually know Cantonese.

I feel suddenly exhausted. What am I *doing*? This is a job for someone competent, not a Russian tutor who only made it halfway through a linguistics degree. There's a term in Estonian, Ei Viitsi, which means a feeling of such intense laziness you don't want to go anywhere or do anything. I've gone from energized to Ei Viitsi in less than thirty seconds. I'm not a cop. I'm someone who has seen too many detective movies. I should tell my dad to talk to the cops once more and leave me out of it. I *should* go home. "Can you please drop the act?" I ask, rubbing my eyes with two fingers.

"What act?"

I lean against the door, giving him space.

"You're Tristan, right?" I ask. But his face is unchanged. If he is Tristan, he's not admitting it. "I'm not going to tell on you," I add. "I just want to see Anna."

Tristan's head snaps to mine. "What?"

"Yeah. Anna," I say. "She's the mastermind behind this little scheme, right?"

Tristan looks past me again, blinking. "I don't know what you're talking about."

"Everyone looks to the left when they're lying. Easy tell," I say.

"That's not true. The only real indicator of a lie is a microexpression. You're better off looking at eyebrows than eye direction." Tristan takes a long drag from the cigarette, then looks down at the floor. "And I don't know what you're talking about, lady. If you don't want to do this, fine…"

"I'm not the police," I say. I point down at myself, my dirty black skinny jeans and David's extra IDF shirt I always sleep in, my unwashed hair. "If that's not obvious."

Tristan takes another long drag from the cigarette, watching me. He seems nervous now, and begins slowly backing away towards the kitchen door. "I really don't know what you're talking about."

123

I watch his eyebrows, but they don't move. Still, I know he's lying.

"Wait here for one second," I tell him. I cross the checkered laminate floor to the kitchen drawers, looking through them until I find a marker and an old Center St. Daze flyer with a white back. I write down my temporary number along with the message, in Russian, "*Call me ASAP - M.*" "Give this to Anastasia. Okay? No harm in that."

He looks down at it, then at me, his eyebrows furrowing, for a brief second, then straightening again. Is this the micro-expression he mentioned? Because what I saw there was confusion, for sure. Then something clicks in his head, and his shoulders relax for the first time. He puts the note in his back pocket.

"You should really talk to a therapist, lady," he says. He turns back for a moment, and I'm pretty sure he winks at me. "Or your dad," he adds, quietly. Then Tristan opens the door and disappears speedily down the hallway.

MASHA

CHAPTER SIXTEEN

I take another one of the cigarettes and head out to the porch to smoke it. The interaction with Tristan has frazzled me to the core. I feel lost and triumphant at the same time, somehow. Was he trying to tell me to talk to my dad about Anna? Or did he think I was crazy and that I needed to talk to someone related to me? I'd spoken to my dad plenty. It's my mom that I need to reach. But every time I call, her cell goes straight to voicemail, because this not answering the phone thing is some kind of genetic plague. Why did any of us even bother to get phones in the first place? I cannot help but wonder. We either hate them or cannot live without them or both.

Emily was probably right. I shouldn't have stayed in an apartment with so many ghosts. Everywhere I look, I see June's face, her giant eyelashes, the little mole on her cheek. I knew she was depressed. But I had no idea how much. I thought she was like everyone else in Riverwest, a standard mixture of high school angst with a dash of rebellion more superficial than not. She was a poet, so it wasn't exactly unusual. She was a great poet actually. I still remember some of her poems, but especially the one that she wrote and printed on our tack board right before she died:

Love is a siren song.

Chasing a shadow in dim
alleyways

125

for every night to lose its
darkness.

"You're beautiful," they say
and tomorrow
push another tiny brunette against a
pale wall.

At the time, I thought she had written it about Liam, who I'd been dating for several months. He was a common topic of conversation in our house then. It was a wild animal, what we had; one day it was eating you alive, the next licking your wounds. It took me a while to learn that wasn't what a relationship was supposed to be. I think June would have learned that too, had she stuck around. She had a thing for lost causes. I guess I did too, as we did briefly end up dating the same guy. Antonio. The beginning of the end. In a way it was my fault, for bringing him in the house. Of course I didn't know at the time what would happen, that after he was done confusing me for two months, he would meet his match in emotional imprisonment.

Later, after the funeral and the wake and weeks of confusion, I looked at that poem again and I wondered: am I the other tiny brunette? Was the poem a message to me? Right before June died, after some fight with Liam, I'd hooked up with Antonio again; some silly drunken thing that meant nothing, I'd been over the guy for months. It's easy to get over someone when you let them live with you for free and then they start dating your roommate. Especially when they're bipolar and spend much of their time yelling at you. The problem was that Antonio was hot. And I was drinking too much at the time. No one went the committed route in Riverwest, so I didn't have a clue that Antonio was cheating on her.

Sometimes I wonder if Antonio felt at all responsible—at times I definitely felt responsible, how could I not, when all my friends saw it that way? But I was pretty sure he wasn't capable of taking responsibility for anything, let alone a person's need to harm herself. I don't really blame him, personally. Only a romance novel is about a romance, and our lives are not romance novels. In fact, they aren't like novels at all. If anything, a life is a room filled with scattered pages. Sure, you could try to deconstruct and organize, but what's the point? Discovering something isn't the same as changing it. A feeling can be written about, can be painted, can be sung. The question is what to do about that feeling before it consumes you. How to stop having such feelings in the first place. This was never something June could figure out; any tiny little thing that went wrong would consume her for weeks on end. It wasn't our fault, what happened, logically I know this. She was a troubled person from the start. She always said writing poetry was her therapy. I'd believed her because it was this way for me too. But she should probably have *actually* gone to treatment as well, instead of spending weeks on end re-watching episodes of *Buffy the Vampire Slayer* on the computer and drinking by herself when she got depressed.

You can't get out of that deep a hole alone; that was one of the main metaphorical points I'd retrieved from watching season six with her. Buffy, I had to admit, was not only a great distraction but a pretty good motivation tool. Buffy was why I'd had the idea to try martial arts in the first place. Kickboxing, originally. Then Krav Maga once I got to Israel and learned enough Hebrew to follow directions. Somehow all the show did to June was make her more lethargic. It was like she didn't want to get better. The only reason I could come up with when I occasionally tried to come up with a reason beyond laziness, was that part of her must have craved the sorrow, so ubiquitous it came to feel like a friend. To her, sadness was like a drug. And for whatever reason, June didn't want to stop being sad. I never did find out why. As much time as she'd spent writing her feelings into words, she did not leave a suicide note. Just that poem.

I wipe my eyes, realizing they're wet. As I said, I never think about June. There's a reason for that. Weirdly, this is followed by an unquenchable need to talk to my mom, so I take out my phone and try calling her again for the third or fourth time since my arrival. In a few hours, the sun would fall, and it would be Shabbat, which meant I could no longer use my phone. If we are ever going to talk it has to be now.

A throat clearing, then a fuzzy "Hello?"

"Mama?"

"Masha? Is that you?"

I let out a sigh of relief. "Finally. I was starting to get worried," I breathe. "I tried calling you a few times."

"About what?" my mom asks, in Russian. Her voice sounds distant, muffled even. Like after she's had too much wine, or woken up from a late nap. "Is everything OK? Whose phone number is this?"

"Yeah, it's fine, I just... I haven't talked to you since I got here and it feels weird—"

"Got here? Where?"

"Milwaukee," I say, slowly. "Are you telling me that you didn't know that?"

A pause from the other end of the phone. "I'm in New Jersey."

A long breath of air escapes my mouth unexpectedly, and I have to close it before it turns into a cry. How extremely strange. My dad had definitely left that out when summoning me here. I had been so looking forward to seeing her. "What are you doing in New Jersey?"

"Oh...it's a long story."

"Can I hear this story?"

"Have you talked to your sister?"

"No, that's kind of—" I pause, suddenly unsure if my mom even knows Anastasia is missing. There seems to be a lot of miscommunication going on here, and I don't want to make things worse. And why hadn't my dad mentioned to me that she was out of town?

"Talk to her, please," Mama says.

If only I could, I want to say aloud, but don't. "Where are you exactly?" I ask.

She clears her throat again. "I'm visiting Svetlana. I've been here for a little while. How long are you staying?"

I swallow. "Um. I'm not sure," I say. "I'm kinda bummed. I mean, I know I've been hard to reach lately, but...Anyway, Papa didn't tell me you were out of town."

More silence. Something is wrong, I can feel it. She sounds...what, sad? Distant? I can't quite put my finger on it. My mother is usually a very severe person. This woman seems emotional. How strange of her to travel to New Jersey in the middle of the week, too. Maybe Tristan was right after all, and the clue I needed has been under my nose this whole time. My dad is obviously keeping *something* from me. "Is Sveta okay?"

"Mashinka, I'm so sorry, but I have to go. Can I call you back later?" She pauses for a moment, then adds, "It's so good to hear your voice, honey. I'll call you back soon."

And before I could finish saying "It's Shabbat today," my mom drops the call.

I call her back, but it goes straight to voicemail. So I leave one. "Mom, in case you forgot, it's Friday, which means in three hours I'm turning off this phone and you won't be able to get a hold of me. Please call me tomorrow night if that happens. Also, I hope everything is okay! I miss you. Bye."

I hang up the phone, which blinks at me in orange, a sign of low battery. I don't even bother getting my charger. I am all out of words. All I can think is:

What.

The.

Hell.

MASHA

CHAPTER SEVENTEEN

When I get into my dad's car an hour later, he looks peeved. My shoes are soaked, and my muscles are sore from spending the time between calling him and his arrival walking around the slushy streets of Riverwest. There's a Parisian word for this sort of aimless ambling—flâner. It refers to the art of leisurely strolling the streets of Paris without any goal or destination simply for the pleasure of soaking up the city's beauty. These aimless pedestrians are known as "flâneurs." I'm not sure what you'd call a person who does this in Riverwest—besides, perhaps, careless—but it did not help. I'm still as in shock as I was before, only colder.

"I was in the middle of cooking," my dad is saying in Russian. There's more, but I'm too spacey to listen. "What was so urgent that you had to come home right this second? You find Anna?"

I put a hand on the gear shift and don't let him move it out of park. "Why is Mama in New Jersey?" I ask in Russian.

My dad sucks in some air between his teeth. "Oh." I think he is about to deny it, make up some excuse to appease me, but instead he digs into his pocket and lights a cigarette. Then he moves my hand away and begins driving, heading west down Center Street then turning right on Fratney. We pass an array of multi-colored Polish flats with wraparound porches and balconies. I've been inside at least seven of them, though I'm not sure any would still have the same residents. Although, I'd assumed that about Liam too, and had been wrong. Maybe Milwaukee really is quicksand, just like I'd always thought.

"That's, uh...long story."

"Can someone please tell me this long story?"

"There are things... that have been going on here the last few months."

"I can see that," I tell him. "Don't you think you might have mentioned that to me before I came here? Shto sloochelas?"

My dad turns his head toward the window, then itches his neck with his cigarette hand.

"Papa?" I start. "Does it have anything to do with the fact that you're smoking again?"

For whatever reason, Papua New Guinea is full of languages with untranslatable words. My favorite one is Mokita, a Kivila word for *the truth everyone knows but agrees not to talk about*. It makes me wonder. What would Anastasia tell me if I found her? Here I'd thought this whole ordeal was about her disappearing, but it's not, not really. There's something else. Something that has to do with my parents, with my mom being in New Jersey. If that's the case, perhaps I should let her be.

"Papa! Talk to me, or I'm getting on a plane home right now."

Finally, Papa sinks into the seat, unstiffening. Then he takes a deep breath. "Well. Actually, your mom...uh, she needed break. She went to see your aunt," he explains in English now.

"Yeah. I got that part. What did she need a break *from*?"

"From me."

"Don't you think that would have been important information to give me before I got here?" I ask. "No wonder Anna just up and disappeared." No wonder she has resorted to *stealing*, I think. It could have been worse; when the world falls out from under you, it takes a lot of will power not to grab onto the first thing you catch on your way down—and she's young and sensitive and newly involved with this blue-haired thief. I think of the French term, l'appel du vide: literally translated to "the call of the void"; contextually used to describe the instinctive urge to jump from high places. Or low places, depending

131

on how you look at it. I know from experience that the call of the void comes easier than you might imagine. One little change can send anyone reeling, if they're not standing on solid ground.

"Look. Masha. It doesn't change facts. She gone and I'm not finding her."

"It does, though. Obviously, something happened, and she decided to leave for a reason. It's not just your general nineteen-year-old angst, which you have quite purposely lead me to believe," I say. I pause, and inhale a deep smoky breath, before coughing. My dad opens the window, despite being on the highway, so that I almost have to scream my next question. "So what on earth did you do to make Mama leave?"

My dad licks his lips, which are chapped to the point of peeling, and glances over at me before his eyes turn back to the dashboard again. I can't explain precisely what I catch there in his glance; it looks like guilt, but if it is, there are too many other things crowding it out. It must have been pretty bad if my dad feels guilty. He's not someone who says sorry often, if ever. No matter the outcomes, he always thinks he's right. Maybe I imagined it anyway; after that split second, it's gone. He takes the next highway exit, and the car quiets a little.

"Did your sister ever mentioned woman named Zoya?" he finally asks me.

I think about this. The name sounds familiar, I'd met a few in Israel—one a Russian model, one an elderly widow—but I don't recall hearing the name from Anna. We haven't talked in weeks, months maybe, and when we did, it wasn't about any specific person. I'm pretty sure I would remember that. "No? But we kept missing each other the last few months. The time difference…Well, it's mostly my fault. I was so busy. I should have made it a priority to talk to her."

Before I can ask what any of that has to do with my mom flying to New Jersey or Anna going who-knows-where, my dad turns into a cul-de-sac of identical condos and pulls into the driveway of a plain orange brick house with a simple gray roof. Once more I can't help but wonder why on earth they chose to move here, of all places. It's even worse than the house in Hartland. At least there, we had tons of neighbors, with big houses that all looked sort of different. And trees. Rosebushes. Dogs playing in yards. Here, it's so…. Quiet. Empty. The middle of nowhere, basically. It reminds me of a saying in Hebrew: B'sof Ha'olam Smolla. At the end of the world, turn left. It's slang for the middle of nowhere, so it definitely applies to suburban Wisconsin, but I think there's another level of looking at it that is less literal, a layer of unintended meaning. Metaphorically speaking, it could entail starting a new life; which, there's no doubt about it, all the members of my family have done at least once, if not more. Even I've done it. Maybe Anna is just following in our footsteps.

"Did you find out if Anna is dating guy?" my dad says, finally, in lieu of an explanation. "You know how young girls are. Remember Nick? He made you…what is word? Goth."

"He did not make me goth," I say, stifling a laugh. "First of all, it was punk, and secondly, no one made me do anything. I liked it and Nick just happened to be around." I pivot toward the real issue. "So… who is Zoya?"

My dad ignores me and continues along. "She's very impressionable. If she's gone, she's with the guy." He turns off the car but continues to sit there, silently, while AM 620 plays around us, staring ahead into the garage; several large packages of bottled water, shovels hanging from hooks, bikes and toolboxes that haven't been used in years.

"But why did you mention—" I start, but am interrupted by my phone ringing. Hoping it's my mom, or David—or maybe even Anna—I don't hesitate in answering.

"Hello? David?"

Usually, an unknown number means David. But if it is David, he would be saying something. I think I can hear breathing on the other end of the line, but no words. In that case, it's probably not David. I open the passenger-side door and cover my mouth with a hand when I get out. I whisper, "Anna?"

But I never learn who it is that's calling. Whoever it is drops the receiver, and when I try calling back I only get an error, like the number doesn't really exist. The only time that ever happens is when David calls me from internet cafés in Europe. The program he uses automatically creates a fake number in order to connect via phone line and not Wi-Fi. If it was David on the other end, and he had encountered technical difficulties, then he would call back. There's no reason to worry, or panic. And yet, my stomach begins turning in knots. Maybe my dad is right and Anna is with Tristan, like I originally thought. But maybe there's something else going on altogether. What if she's in trouble? Or worse?

"Who was it?" my dad asks, getting out of the car too. He goes to the backseat and removes my bags, dropping them on the cement floor beside some dusty work boots. "Was it Anna?"

"I think I've answered enough questions for today," I say, in barely a whisper. The conversation we had has drained me of all energy required to talk, or move, or do anything. "It's your turn."

"Hmm," is all my dad says before taking my bags inside. I know asking him a third time won't help, because if he doesn't want to tell me something, he won't tell me. So I go inside too, and head straight for the shower. I spend an enormous amount of time in there, closing my eyes and letting the hot water run over me. I stay so long my skin turns bright red and prunish and yet I still don't move. I'm too tired. I think I'm possibly more tired than I've ever been in my life. I'm so tired I don't even know what to think anymore, and possibly I finally understand why it took so long for the human race to come up with all the complicated words they have for emotions. They were too exhausted to feel guilt, shame, nostalgic; or at least too tired to know what it was. You can follow the complexity of emotion arising at the same time as more and more color words became part of the vocabulary; in ancient Biblical times, there were mostly only words for dark and light. Now we have the entire rainbow. We have cultures crossing and vocabulary continually shifting, languages dying (Latin) or emerging (texting). Some languages, like Russian, have so many variations of color words that they use several different words for blue, while others, like the Dani language, spoken in Papua New Guinea, have only two color words: one used for darker, cooler colors, one for all the lighter, warmer tones. Which makes you wonder: if you don't have the words for something, can you still see it? Can you still feel something if you don't know what it is you're feeling?

In some ways, I might have to admit you cannot. But this is the beauty of our global culture: if there's not a word for what you want to say in your language, then most likely, you can find it elsewhere. In this moment, for example. I can channel the Germans; I am the epitome of Lebensmüde, which, roughly translated, means weary of life. Part of me wants to go back to sleep, but I know I won't be able to sleep in this house. It's too weird; the energy is all off. And it's not only because there's nothing to look at outside besides a vast array of flat, dry land with trees planted in perfect little rows. Houses so far apart you will never see your neighbors. It's too quiet. It's the exact opposite of Israel, where everyone is on top of each other, and it's impossible to ever feel alone. In Israel it's never quiet. Here, I can hear every single creak in the floorboard, every sneeze and cough from another room.

Once I'm dry and dressed again, I feel like a new person. I take a walk around the house, looking at how my mom has rearranged everything she moved from our previous house in Hartland. Even though she has the same hand-painted vases and custom mirrors and Kandinsky prints, it all looks so different here in the vast emptiness of the wide-open single-floor design. I can't really pinpoint why. But something is staler. Maybe it's the actual building, or maybe it's just that no one is here but us.

Finally, after several tours around the house and finding nothing of interest, I go to Anna's room. I'd figured they would turn it into a guest room or an extra office or something by now, but it looks like no one's been in here since she moved out. It's still totally filled with her stuff. There are piles of old canvases and art supplies and textbooks, even some old dolls. Her bed is there, unmade, like she could return at any moment, and the closet is full of clothes, thrift-store items, full of holes and stains.

Next, my glance falls on Anna's desk, adorned with more paintbrushes than I can count and a small tabletop easel held together by duct tape and two lamps. And a computer that looks as though it's been hastily dropped off, not even plugged in.

Then it hits me. That's *my* computer. The one I gave her before I left. Surely, as her only computer, she had taken it to school with her? Which means she must have brought it here along with all her art supplies before she left town. That's why there's so much stuff in her room. Wherever she was living before she disappeared, she is no longer living there, that's for sure. Which means everything she owns is basically in that room.

I plug the computer in and wait for it boot up, hoping she hasn't changed the password, and ideally, that some of her logins are saved. If I could get into her emails or maybe her MySpace account, there might be a chance of finding some kind of clue. A nineteen-year-old girl, in this day and age? Her whole life would be on this computer.

I'm so used to laptops that for a moment I think the computer might be dead. Apparently it's just slow, because eventually it starts to make a very loud whirring noise and text begins to appear on the screen. There's not even a password required to login and the house Wi-Fi automatically connects, so in seconds I'm all set to go. I open an internet browser and open MySpace. A message prompts me to update the browser, which I decline. I write in Anna's screen name, then wait to see if the password bar is populated automatically. But no, it remains blank. Crap.

I try the same password I used to use, buffy1983. I get an error in red: incorrect password. I try another version, with her birth year instead of mine. No go. It makes sense, I suppose. Anna was never as big of a fan of *Buffy the Vampire Slayer* as I was. What is Anna into? I can hardly remember; it's been so long since we had any sort of innocuous conversation about TV or anything really. I look around the room for clues. There's a Salvador Dalí calendar hanging on the wall above the desk; I try combinations of Dalí with our birth years or her favorite number, 23; at least, what I remember her favorite number being in school. A stack of DVDs on the floor ignites five more minutes of password combinations; characters from *Lord of the Rings* and *Harry Potter* and *X-Men*. I'm about to give up when I have the idea to try my own name. Masha23, I type.

Bingo! I'm in.

Before I have a chance to feel guilty that she would use my name as a password—a black hole of guilt that I do not have the time to fall into—I open her profile to see if she is friends with anyone named Zoya. She is, indeed. I go to the page, but there's only the barest minimum of information on there, no pictures or anything like that. I could try talking to her on the chat sidebar, but what would I say? Have you seen my sister? If only I could read their previous messages....on Facebook, the messages automatically save themselves on the server. Not on MySpace, though.

Without thinking too much about it, as I doubt it will get us anywhere, I open a chat with Zoya and write *Hi*. I leave it open while I move to Facebook. As far as I know, my sister never joined this platform. But I never really use any of these websites. I always preferred good old-fashioned phone calls or email. So what do I know?

Apparently, nothing. Facebook's login page loads, and lo and behold, Anna's email address is typed into the login bar. I try the same password I used for MySpace, and now I've logged into her Facebook, too. Facebook congratulates me for reactivating my account. Because she had only deactivated her account and not deleted it, all her info is still available.

I move straight to the messages and find a conversation with "Facebook User" at the top. This is easy to do as there is only one other person she was messaging on here anyway, someone named Ashley who was trying to reconnect from high school, who Anna had ignored. Whoever it was she was talking to on here, she deleted her account. Her name is gone, but the conversation is still there. Getting excited now, I scroll all the way up to the top.

The best way to understand something, I have always thought, is to start at the beginning.

MASHA

CHAPTER EIGHTEEN

<<ANNA>>	Hi! Do you speak English?
<<FACEBOOK USER>>	Yes, but badly. Do you speak Russian?
<<ANNA>>	Yes, but badly.
<<FACEBOOK USER>>	Haha. We can try to use Google, yes? Did you understand my message?
<<ANNA>>	Yes. I did. I talked to my dad about it.
<<FACEBOOK USER>>	And what did he say?
<<ANNA>>	He said I don't have any cousins named Zoya.
<<FACEBOOK USER>>	Naturally he would say that. I'm not your cousin. I am your sister.
<<ANNA>>	Sister, like my dad is your father or my dad is your uncle?

Here I stop for a moment. It's definitely Zoya, but her messages are all in Russian, whereas Anna's are in English. In Russian, "sistra" can mean either sister or cousin, depending on who is using it. So I can understand Anna's confusion, though I am pretty sure I already know the answer. My stomach clenches in anticipation, or possibly hunger, or a combination of both. But I am too invested now to stop and track down food, so I continue reading.

<<ZOYA>>	Sister like your dad is my father.
<<ANNA>>	But that's crazy. Did you tell him that?

<<ZOYA>>   Many times. He's been ignoring me already for months. I've been emailing him all the time, and he doesn't answer. I want a DNK, that's all.

<<ANNA>>   Hold on, let me see what that is.

<<ANNA>>   Oh. A DNA test?

<<ZOYA>>   Yes. Just a DNA test. I will pay for it myself, I don't want money.

<<ANNA>>   But what makes you think he's your father? We left Chernovtsy a long time ago, and he's been married to my mom forever.

<<ZOYA>>   This was before you left. My mother was his accountant. You can ask him about it. Her name was Olga. She died last year and I found some old letters and photos with Pavel Rosenberg written on them.

<<ANNA>>   Sorry to be so blunt, but aren't there hundreds of Pavel Rosenbergs in the world?

Here I stop again and stifle a laugh. It's so typical Anna to come out with that question straight away. It makes me miss her, and hope that she's okay. I also start to wonder what on earth is going on with my dad. It isn't like him to have secrets. Maybe there is more to him than this middle-aged Russian dad who enjoys *Everybody Loves Raymond* and mini golf. Maybe Zoya really is his daughter, from an ex-girlfriend perhaps, and he has known about it all along. Maybe he has another secret family out there. It would definitely explain some of the strange things going on at the moment, especially why he wouldn't explain who Zoya was to me.

<<ZOYA>>   I know he is. Since I was little, my mom told me I had two sisters in America. And then I found his name in the letters, and discovered his profile on Odnoklassniki.

<<ANNA>>   Yeah, okay, but this Pavel Rosenberg? You're sure?

<<ZOYA>>   You can ask him about Olga Oleskin, see what he says. I

	have photos of them together at work.
<<ANNA>>	That doesn't really prove anything, but okay. Let's say it is him...
<<ZOYA>>	It is.
<<ANNA>>	Okay, let's say, for a moment, that it is... If he is ignoring you, it's probably because he doesn't believe you. He probably thinks you want money. We've had people contact us before from Ukraine asking for money, even old friends of his.
<<ZOYA>>	I don't want money! I want a DNA test, that's it
<<ANNA>>	But why? Isn't it a little late for child support?
<<ZOYA>>	It's not for that. I need proof he is my father so I can show I am half Jewish and move to Israel.
<<ANNA>>	Oh.
<<ZOYA>>	I understand that his family is very dear to him. This is why I never reached out to you before. But I must leave Ukraine. This is the only way I know. Please help me.
<<ANNA>>	I'm not so sure I can help you.
<<ZOYA>>	Just talk to him please.
<<ANNA>>	But... Is it even enough to be only half Jewish?

Having lived in Israel for the last five years, I know that it is, so I skip ahead a bit past the explanations. This woman really thinks she is our *sister*? And Papa refused to answer her? It doesn't sound like him at all. And how did this sister come to be? My dad is the farthest away from the cheating type that I had ever met. Was it from an ex-girlfriend? It would certainly help to know her age. I can't help but get frustrated with Anna for not asking how old she is. And also frustrated with Zoya's side of the conversation. I have trouble understanding her, and wonder how much of what she is saying Anna really understood. I wonder, too, what kind of education Zoya has received. But then, of course, I feel bad wondering this. Maybe she is too poor for an education. It's not her fault she hasn't had the privileges I grew up with.

141

I take an ibuprofen with some water from my purse and continue reading.

<<ZOYA>>   ...I'm sorry you had to find out like this. My whole life I've known that you live in America, and I did nothing. But now...

<<ANNA>>   I'm sorry. But I'm still not sure I can help you.

<<ZOYA>>   You can ask Pavel about my mother Olga. Please.

<<ANNA>>   I will try.

The conversation ends abruptly shortly after that and doesn't start up again for another week. I keep going, despite my now-grumbling stomach, because maybe the next conversation will have a clue about her whereabouts.

<<ANNA>>   Hey. What's your birthday?

<<ZOYA>>   May 23, 1987

I pause again. 1987? That would mean she was born after me and before Anna.

<<ANNA>>   Wow. I don't know how it never occurred to me to ask you that. Why didn't you tell me?

<<ZOYA>>   Did you talk to Pavel? About my mom?

<<ANNA>>   Sort of.

<<ZOYA>>   Oh my god. Thank you!

<<ANNA>>   Don't thank me yet. He only admitted to knowing her. He said they worked together. He actually got very mad at me for even asking about you. I really don't think he will take the DNA test.

<<ZOYA>>   He thinks I'm a very bad person. An aferistka.

<<ANNA>>   Aferistka?

<<ZOYA>>   Yes... like a criminal. A bad person.

<<ANNA>> Are you really certain he's the right person you're looking for?

<<ZOYA>> YES.

<<ANNA>> I just don't see it. He's not the cheating type.

<<ZOYA>> I'm sorry. I know it's too late for us to be a family, I am not asking for us to be sisters or for him to pay for anything. I was a happy child. But now, it's different. I need your help.

<<ANNA>> I'm not sure what I can do, Zoya.

<<ZOYA>> I told you already.

<<ANNA>> You really can't stay in Ukraine? Is it because they're still anti-Semitic? My dad says they still hate Jews there.

<<ZOYA>> No. If they do, I haven't seen it. Everyone has always spoken about Jews in a very respectful tone, at least to me.

<<ANNA>> Do you think it's because they knew you were half-Jewish?

<<ZOYA>> There are very few Jews left here. It's harder to be anti-Semitic when you've never even met a Jewish person, I think. It's like hating some animal which has gone extinct.

<<ZOYA>> Come here and see for yourself! I would love to meet you. And didn't you say you wanted to visit?

<<ANNA>> I wish I could, but I don't really have any money.

<<ZOYA>> What about your parents? They can't help?

<<ANNA>> Even if they could, they don't want me anywhere near Ukraine.

<<ZOYA>> Why not?

<<ANNA>> They think it's dangerous. But it's not, is it?

<<ZOYA>> Depends on how you mean.

<<ANNA>> What's it like there? Has it changed a lot? I've always wondered.

<<ZOYA>> It's a very pretty city. Now there are more restaurants and coffee shops, more tourists, sure. For the ones who live here, it's not so different. Most people are worse off than before. The country was better when it was still the USSR.

<<ANNA>> Oh. I'm sorry.

<<ZOYA>>   Anastasia, look. I'm not so good at typing. Can you Skype? I'm supposed to go to a friend's house for dinner soon, but I'd really like to talk to you.

<<ANNA>>   I guess it's okay, but only for a few minutes. I have to get to class.

<<ZOYA>>   To art class? I saw your paintings on MySpace. You're so talented!

<<ANNA>>   No, Algebra. I actually don't really paint anymore.

<<ZOYA>>   Really? Why not? I wish I could paint like that.

<<ANNA>>   You know, people are always telling me that and I have no idea why. It's not, like, a useful skill.

I stop scrolling again. Anna, not painting anymore? Of everything I'd heard today this is possibly the most shocking of all.

<<ZOYA>>   But you're so good!

<<ANNA>>   I guess I don't see the point of it. If I can't make a living from it, why bother putting all of my energy and time into getting better? I might as well find something else to be good at.

<<ZOYA>>   This sounds like Russian parents talking.

<<ANNA>>   Maybe?

<<ZOYA>>   My mama wasn't like that. She always told me to follow my dreams. Problem was I didn't really have any.

<<ANNA>>   What? That can't be true.

<<ZOYA>>   I know we only just met, but you're always welcome to come visit me here. Really and truly.

<<ANNA>>   Yeah? I would love to go… sometime. I've been wanting to go back for basically my whole life.

<<ZOYA>>   That's so funny. I've been wanting to go to America my whole life. Too bad we couldn't switch!

<<ZOYA>>   Here's my Skype name: ZoyaC2007.

Then the conversation ends, and besides a few more innocuous messages that don't amount to anything, it never picks back up. Not on Facebook anyway. But it doesn't matter—because I think I know where Anna went.

OCTOBER/
NOVEMBER 2007

ANNA

CHAPTER NINETEEN

Before Zoya, the closest I came to returning to Ukraine was in high school, during a Baltic cruise, when we spent a day in St. Petersburg. It was a weird trip; even though it was my first time back abroad, I had become anxious the last week, spending so much time locked in a room with my parents, and was looking forward to finally seeing Russia. But being Soviet refugees back in Russia was strange. On more than one occasion we overheard the Russian tour guides joking about how fat and ugly the group from our cruise ship was. They didn't notice we could understand them; that's how American we'd come to look in our bootcut jeans and Adidas sneakers. No one suspected us of being in our homeland. Maybe because it wasn't our homeland anymore. The Jews had gone with the ruble, after all. And like my parents said, we were Jews first and Russians second—at least, this had been the case in the USSR. Our passports listed Jewish under nationality. Who knew, maybe we were Americans first now, or refugees first. I wasn't sure. My identity was such a mess. It was sort of like wearing layers during the time of year that Autumn turns to Winter: when it's freezing out, you appreciate every one. But when that sun comes out, you want to shed half of it to the ground; you feel suffocated. This is what identity could feel like, for me, sometimes. Like wearing too many coats, then not wearing enough.

I didn't know what we were in Russia. Travelers, tourists? In the markets, old ladies asked my parents where they were from; they said we had peculiar accents. My parents were surprised to hear this—how could they have developed accents in their native language?—but they mostly found it funny. They didn't care. It wasn't the same country as the one we abandoned in 1991. This was not a visit home any more than the afternoons we spent in Sweden or Norway. We made our way from site to site like the rest of the Americans, buying souvenirs, old teacups and various sets of Russian nesting dolls, as if we were people who didn't already own these things. We walked around the Hermitage and ate piroshki from street vendors. I wanted to feel the weight and freedom of our past, let it fill me with completeness, but all that happened was that I spent all my money and then got tired from all the walking. I had no connection to St. Petersburg. I'd never been there before. Around seven, we had to go back to the boat.

When we returned to Wisconsin, my parents agreed that one day back in Russia was more than enough for them. On future trips they traveled to China and Australia and London; they had no interest in returning to Russia, or anywhere near it. Had we moved to LA or New York like many of my cousins, perhaps I would not feel whatever deep, deep longing had nestled its way inside me where homesickness once was. But I could not change the past any more easily than I could change myself.

"Hi," I tell Zoya, once her face appears in front of me. Despite our previous internet correspondence, I feel nervous, so I take out another tiny nugget of pot and put it in Sylvia Plath and smoke it. Soon, my emotions dissipate into the air. It is hard to hold onto a thought, let alone a feeling when you are high. I'm not sure I am ready, nor am I sure what exactly you're supposed to do when you see your potential half-sister for the first time, but I no longer feel so nervous about it.

"Hi," a pixelated Zoya tells me from the other side of the world. From my hometown. The place I wanted to go more than anywhere else for years and never could. Even though I can only see her pixelated face and half a wall, I suddenly ache with the need to be there in person.

"Hi," I say again.

Zoya giggles a little. "This is weird," she admits. The lousy resolution resolves itself, and I am able now to study her face, which I do. The first thing I notice is her eyebrows, light brown, plucked too thin for her broad forehead. Then her small blue eyes, which appear a bit sunken behind her full nose. Her upper lip is slim, but her bottom lip is full. Her lips are quite pleasant. As are her shoulders, which are compact and narrow. I expand my vision more outward to try and understand what combination they make, and I conclude quickly that these attributes in no way combine towards something familiar. She is pretty, but she looks nothing like me or my dad. There's nothing in her appearance that would make me think we are remotely related.

This is both a relief and a disappointment.

"So...how's it going? How are you?" I ask, unsure of what to say. If I knew this was, in fact, my sister staring back at me, I would maybe act differently. I'd be dying to know all the details of her life, what her interests are, and what she is like. Even if she were simply a new friend I would want to know these things. Because I don't know, and she is not a random person but someone who believes something that could potentially be very damaging, I am not sure if I should be more cautious or more welcoming.

"Okay," she says, also nervous. I continue to scrutinize her face a bit more: though she looks nothing like us, nor does she seem very Jewish, she most certainly looks Russian. I can quite often spot a Russian person before they even say one word; my whole family can. Though if someone asked me what exactly makes a person look Russian, I don't think I could answer. I just know.

"Alive," she adds, letting out an uncomfortable giggle.

"I've been thinking," I eventually start. "Why don't you move to America instead? It might be easier, at least with the whole Jewish angle."

"America is no longer an easy option. It hasn't been since the nineties," Zoya explains.

"Oh. Really? Why?"

"After the Berlin Wall fell, the prime minister of Israel urged Europe and the States to stop granting refugee status visas to Soviet émigrés, because they were not refugees, they already had a homeland in Israel, and were only moving to America for economic reasons."

"Oh. I didn't know that," I say.

"Yeah. It's okay. Israel is fine too."

"You really want to go there though? With all the crazy religious people and everything?"

"What's your issue with Israel?" asks Zoya, picking up on something I barely register myself. "Israel is great. I went there for three months, and I didn't want to leave."

"Really? Why?"

"The food, the culture, the buildings. It's so...alive. There are people out all the time, eating and drinking and smoking, laughing. They have that here too, but it's mostly tourists. Everyone's poor. In Israel, sure some people are poor, but there's not so much difference between poor and not poor, like here. And at least there's *hope*. There's...life." She turns around and looks behind her at something. "Can you wait a minute?" she asks me, then her head turns into a pixelated blur and disappears off the screen.

This gives me the opportunity to study her living quarters more closely: I see faded flower-print wallpaper, peeling at the edges, spread across much of the room. An old wooden table covered in loose papers. Books stacked on the floor under what appears to be some bus maps. It's not much smaller than my own, but it seems far older, and far more cramped, though this probably comes from a severe lack in organizing skills. There is no visible door, nor any useful furniture besides the foldout couch and table. In combination it resembles the sort of room I've seen in photo albums of old Soviet apartments. This doesn't exactly surprise me. When my grandma Mila last visited Chernovtsy, she said the building next to our old apartment on Ruska St., which had been under construction when we left, was still not done. At that point, ten years had passed.

"Sorry," Zoya says when she returns, now wearing a large purple down coat over her body, re-pixelated. "Our pipes froze again. I tell my neighbors to keep the water running when it's this cold, but they won't do it. They're narcomanee, so what can you do…"

"*Narcomanee?*" I ask, unfamiliar with the word.

Zoya mimes a needle in the arm. "Heroin," she says. "It's a big problem in Ukraine. It's cheaper than cigarettes now."

"Oh," I say. As if I need any more reason to feel for this poor woman. It's amazing she isn't a junkie like her neighbors. I find that I like and respect her all the more given these circumstances, especially seeing that she doesn't seem particularly unhappy, at least any more so than anyone I know in Milwaukee. "I'm sorry."

Zoya shrugs looks into the distance. She definitely knows what she's facing, and is clearly doing everything she can to change her destiny. It makes me feel weak in comparison. I have so many options open to me and yet I still only do what my parents tell me.

"Listen, I have a request to ask of you. But you can say no if you want to," she says. She shifts in her hard, wooden chair and starts pulling at a strand of hair somewhat obsessively. I recognize this tic: the fixation of a smoker wanting a cigarette. There's an ashtray behind her so I'm not sure what stops her. Instead of lighting one up, her face turns serious.

"Go ahead."

"A while ago I found a DNA testing place in America. My friend translated everything for me. The way it works when someone lives out of the country is they ask you to register for a number online, and then you send a cotton swab with your DNA to them in an envelope. The person in America gets a whole kit. They have to send in the kit labeled with the registered number to match up with the cotton swab; then they do the test or whatever," she says. "So I only need your dad's address to send the kit. I'll pay for it obviously."

As the details of this revelation hit me (a tad belatedly, as I have to think about each word for a long time), I snap back to reality. "Oh my

God. No. Don't send it to my dad," I say in English. "That's a terrible idea."

"I was worried you might say that," she says, disappointed.

The thought that she was seconds away from sending my dad a DNA kit! Goodness. Surely she could find his address with a quick search online, at least in real estate records. Does she really lack any foresight? Between the vague message that looked like spam and the idea of sending a kit to my parents' house, I'm starting to wonder if she has a severe impulsiveness issue or a severe lack of intelligence. Or if there is something else altogether I am missing.

"The thing is I already sent in the swab and even got the registered number and everything," Zoya adds.

"Please Zoya. Don't. Let me think of another option, okay?"

Zoya starts to chew on her hair, deep in thought. She doesn't respond.

"What's the big rush anyway?" I ask. "You already waited this long."

Zoya stops chewing her hair and scoots her chair away from the desk. The screen pixelates again before focusing in. She opens her coat to point at something. Right as the connection solidifies again, making the image come into focus, I understand what she's pointing at.

It's a giant pregnant belly.

"Oh," I say.

"I already waited too long as it is," she says.

"How far along are you?"

"Far," she answers. "Six months or so." She looks down at a piece of paper. "98990 w. Oakwood Lane. This is the right address for your papa?"

"Yes, but—" I think about this for no more than two seconds before coming up with a solution. It's two seconds I may come to regret. And yet, I don't see any better options. What if my mom accidentally opened mail addressed to my dad? "Please don't send it to him. Send it here," I say.

"Really?"

"Yeah. Maybe by the time it gets here we'll know more. I can try to convince my dad to do the right thing." *Or I can take the test*, I think. But I don't say it aloud, because I don't want to make any promises so soon.

She looks at me skeptically. "Do you think he will agree with you? That it's the right thing?" she says.

A weird question to ask, if she were to know my dad at all. My dad always does the right thing. He's practically Captain America. He's Captain Russian American. "Of course he will. Once he thinks about it? Definitely."

"Because I'm not so sure he'll agree with you," she adds.

"What do you mean?" Outside, it begins to rain, the drops echoing off the roof. It makes the whole conversation feel ominous somehow. I get up to close the window before responding.

"According to my mom, he knows all about me. She thinks that's why you all left. *Thought*."

"That's impossible," I tell her. *And utterly ridiculous*, I think. We left because we were Jews. Because the Soviet Union was a terrible place. We left because we wanted to.

"*Everything is possible*," Zoya counters, her mood visibly altering. "If you don't know that, then you've lived a very different life than I have."

I frown, annoyed now. "I'll message you my address," I tell Zoya. "Okay? Worst case, I'll take the test myself," I add, even though I probably shouldn't. It seems to me the best option, at least off the top of my head. If Zoya is really my dad's daughter, it will blow up his whole life to take this test. And he must believe there's a chance of it or he wouldn't be so opposed to my talking to Zoya. If he was thinking clearly, he would have already realized that was the best solution from day one, not blocking her and forcing her to contact more family members. I've always thought of my dad as a very intelligent man. How does he not realize that ignoring something doesn't make it go away?

I guess even smart men have blind spots.

Zoya seems to relax now; perhaps it was what she was after all along. "Fine," she mumbles. But it looks like the best option, the more I think about it; I won't have to argue with my dad, and if the test turns out to be zero then no one else has to know about this fiasco. I'm relieved just thinking about it. "Let me know when you get it. And thank you."

"Sure. And write me your address too," I add at the last second. "Just in case I will need it."

"Okay. Thank you, Anastasia. I hope we can keep talking. I would like to get to know you."

"Me, too," I say. I mostly mean it. But the conversation has admittedly irked me. I spend a lot of energy then convincing myself I am doing the right thing. After she logs out, I turn the computer off, and smoke the entire bowl in Margot's pipe myself, until I've entirely annihilated my brain cells into a coma. Then, all day long, I repeat those words in my head: *Do you think he will agree with you?*

For the first time in my life, I don't know the answer to this question.

ANNA

CHAPTER TWENTY

Consequences don't always appear in one fell swoop; sometimes they are jagged, ripping slowly through the course of your everyday life, like dull scissors cutting fabric. One moment, everything is as it always was. And the next? Landslide. I didn't know this, because I had never really done anything before that might produce adverse side effects. I'd never argued with my parents. I got good grades. I paid my rent on time. But there's only so much goodness to go around before the world begins to show you its true colors. Before those colors start to rub off on you like too much paint.

In short: things are about to get sticky.

It starts one day towards the end of November. I'm at the door of Fuel, about to buy myself a Fat Vegan sandwich—I'm not a vegan, but occasionally I try to become one for a few days—when I walk almost directly into Abby. She stops about an inch from my face and backs up.

"Whoa. I did not see you there," she says, in her pleasantly hoarse voice. In her hand is a black coffee thermos, a giant pleather purse with feathers, and a burning cigarette. She leans over and gives me a half-hug. "How is it that I never see you anymore and we live together?"

This is a good question. I'd barely seen her since she tried to burn her clothes in the yard, and my landlord happened to come by and see her. Let's just say he was not happy. Abby had been lying low ever since. The house had been quiet all around, in fact. "Where you going right now?" I ask.

"Foundation. Ed called in sick," she says, exhaling a plume of smoke. "Hey. Have you heard from August lately?"

I shake my head no and steal a drag from her cigarette, if only to get it away from the feathers on her purse. When I give it back, I place it in her other hand.

"He hasn't called me in a while," Abby whines. "Last I heard he was in Atlanta. He went there to introduce a girl to his mom."

"Really? That was fast," I say. "What's her name?"

"Box."

"Box? That's her name?"

"You know train-hoppers," she shrugs. "They're always making up new names for themselves."

"Well, there are names, and then there are inanimate objects."

Abby does not seem perturbed by this. "It's no worse than Twigs the Clown," she tells me. "Remember him?"

A shiver passes through me then, as I remember how I'd made out with him at a bonfire under the bridge. I don't know why, but I'd felt so dirty afterward, like it had rubbed off on me or something. And I was also pretty dirty, I had to shower as soon as I made it home. "True," I manage to agree. "Train-hoppers should really come up with a different word for clown; it's not even in the same genre to juggle swords and spit fire instead of making kids balloon animals."

"I think the city of Portland would disagree with you," Abby laughs.

"About a lot of things, probably."

"Anyway, you know August when he gets a crush." Abby rolls her eyes and puts out her cigarette in an ashtray on the patio table. Then she reaches into her bag for a flask and takes a sip. She offers me some, but it's daytime, so I decline, until she explains that it's kombucha in there and she recently happened to lose all her water bottles. It's actually very good. "Margot is already on the hunt for new roommates."

"She is?" I ask. "But did he say he wasn't coming back?"

"He didn't say it, no. He also didn't mention he *was* coming back. Or send rent money. Which is due soon, in case you forgot." Abby continues to stare at me, confused. "How do you not know about any of this?" she asks. I don't have an answer for her. Perhaps I've been

158

spending too much time in my head, or too much time talking to Zoya online. In either case Abby doesn't seem to want to know the answer to her own question. She checks her watch, a cheap gold knockoff she got with me at the Portland Saturday market last summer, when I went with her to check out PSU. She didn't end up going there, or anywhere. She got to do whatever she wanted, which at the moment involved a late-night radio show for Radio Milwaukee, a ridiculous amount of yoga, and smoking a ton of weed. Her grandparents were really wealthy was what I'd heard; she and her cousins got a monthly stipend of some kind. I didn't really want to know the details so I could avoid being jealous. I mean sure, my dad covered my rent and food, but it was only a few hundred bucks a month, and anything else I needed I'd had to get jobs for.

"Fuck, I have to go. Stop at Foundation later if you're up for it, okay?" Abby says. "You look like you need a drink."

"I always look like I need a drink," I joke back. She's already halfway to Bremen St., her high-heeled boots echoing against the sidewalk. I always *do* need a drink, if I'm honest with myself. Ever since I'd learned about Zoya, I'd been wound up like a toy, waiting for the next shoe to drop. Or anvil, more likely. And yet, I still talked to her several times a week. Not about anything relating to the DNA test, which hadn't arrived. Just in general. I told her about my life, she told me about hers. It's apparently in shambles since her mother died, which I find understandable. I don't know what I'd do if I woke up one day to find myself totally alone. I've never had to face a reality so cruel. It is perhaps my guilt of an easy life that keeps me talking to her. She calls, so I answer. She messages, so I reply. Half the time I don't know what she's saying to me, since my Russian is so bad, but it doesn't matter. She doesn't seem to have many other people to talk to. If I can make her life a little easier, then what harm would it do?

I head inside Fuel to eat lunch. After I drink coffee and study a bit for my Russian Lit exam—we'd just finished Dostoevsky's *The Idiot*, which I thought I would hate due to its unnecessarily large size but totally related to—I take out my phone, which shows a notification that I have three voicemails. Two are from my dad, which surely would kill my mood, so I don't listen to them. One is from my mom, just checking in. I scroll past the number for their house and click on Margot's name. If we really do have to find a new roommate, I don't want Margot choosing on her own, or we'd end up with a house full of her tediously dull friends from school. I'd been the one to convince her to allow Abby and August, who I knew from Riverwest parties, to become our roommates. She'd wanted to rent the extra room to a high school friend with zero conversational skills and teeth so perfect they looked fake. Margot was a magnet for uninteresting people, while I was completely drained by them. I'll take a crazy person over a boring person any day.

"Hey!" Margot chirps, cheerfully, when the phone stops ringing. At least she's not mad at me; the more I think about it the more I realize how little time we've spent together lately. I'm not sure how I didn't notice. But what do I know about friendships? This is the first time since I was in grade school that I've had any. Not like my sister who's had the same two best friends since she was like thirteen. Well. *Had* the same two best friends. It's like the more normal you are the more friends you can have. "What's going on?"

"Are you coming home soon?"

"Uh, no, I wasn't planning on it. Why?"

"I feel like I haven't seen you in a while," I suggest. Before she can argue the point, I ask, "Can we get a drink later? At Foundation maybe? Abby is working the door."

I hear some fuzzy noises on the other end of the line, as if Margot is moving around on a couch. I try not to spend too much time wondering who's couch, if it's not ours. "How does that girl keep her job when she's always letting in her underage friends?" Margot asks.

"I don't know how she keeps any job, honestly."

"It's called tits, Anna," Margot laughs. I hear the clock of a lighter, followed by a deep inhale. "You should know a little about that."

160

"Tits or not, you have to show up for work on time, generally speaking. Or like, at all." Maybe Riverwest didn't get the customer service memo, because half the time I go to Fuel I have to wait forever for the baristas to stop talking to each other so I can order. I lean back into the hard wood of the booth, and cross my legs out in front of me. It's nice to talk to Margot again, even on the phone. "Anyway, do you? Want to get a drink?"

A short pause. "I can't. I'm supposed to go to this party tonight for my friend Julie's birthday."

"Oh."

"Do you want to come?" Margot asks. "It's not that far. It's off of Brady Street. Or maybe Oakland? I can get you the address later."

"Can't you come out here?" I say, disappointed. "It's too cold to bike there at night, and I really wanted to talk to you about something."

"I can't, I promised I'd go, Anna," she says. "I know you hate seeing people on the east side because god forbid you hang out with other college students for one second, but it's not that bad. Just come, we can still hang out and talk there."

"Okay, fine; I guess I'll call BOSS," I tell Margot. The idea fills me with dread but so does staying home, knowing Margot is out there looking for new roommates.

After inhaling another cup of coffee, I hop on August's bike and head back to my house to get more homework done. Around seven, I call BOSS—that's UW-Milwaukee's free taxi service—for a van and take it to the address Margot texted me.

Immediately I realize I've made a mistake, that I probably shouldn't have arrived sober. I never went to them in school, so I am still unsure how to behave at a party. At a Riverwest basement show, I can smoke cigarettes outside with whoever else happens to be as socially anxious as I am, or I can zone out in the basement watching the bands. Not here. Not at a college party that is half potheads in tie-dye beanies and half girls who don't understand it's okay to wear pants in winter. I don't know anyone there besides Margot, and when I find her on

161

an armchair in a back room, legs entwined around a tall, pale soccer player still in uniform, it's too loud to hear what she says. The music cuts through every attempt at conversation we have until I'm left to stand awkwardly beside a large *Big Lebowski* poster, tacked crookedly onto a door, like pretty much every door within a mile radius. Margot looks at me sympathetically and hands me one of her Strongbows, which I chug down in a few large gulps, simply to have something to do until she finally tears her face away from the large-lipped man with wavy brown hair and turns to me.

"This is Jake," she screams over the music, which has only gotten more loud. People start to dance. I'm pretty sure I see a beer pong table in the corner, though I can't be sure since I have never seen one before. A girl in cutoff shorts is definitely throwing a plastic ball at something. I can't help but wonder if this is what all those high school parties I missed were like, and if so, then I'm relieved. Maybe I *was* better off spending my nights at home painting. I kind of wish I could be at home painting now.

Instead, I wave at Jake. "Anna doesn't like crowds," Margot tells him, seeing my face. Jake does not care how I feel about crowds. He starts caressing Margot's arm up and down, a giant smile taking over his face. This is when I finally realize they didn't only meet at this party. They're dating. No wonder I haven't seen her around. Even though she is a self-proclaimed radical feminist, has a Chicks Before Dicks shirt in heavy rotation, when Margot has a new boyfriend, Margot drops off planet earth.

Margot tries to tell me something else, but I can't hear her over the noise, which I'm no longer sure can be called music. It's almost as if someone was making an effort to have every song be worse than the last, then decided on a mishmash of fire alarms instead. But I am the only one to think this, clearly; a group of girls scream with delight at this noise and start dancing against each other drunkenly. One of them falls onto the floor, taking an Obama poster down with her as she goes. Margot doesn't seem to be bothered by any of it, as if she's

162

been here before a hundred times and this is perfectly normal. Which, I suppose might be correct. Despite having art in common, we don't often hang with the same crowds. Margot likes to skateboard and hike in the woods; she enjoys normal things like going out for nice dinners or seeing movies with boys she meets in class, not going to basement shows or drinking endless amounts of coffee in cold cafés.

"Anna!" Margot cries, seeing me getting my sweatshirt and coat back on. She extends a hand towards me, shifting halfway up the armchair. But she doesn't get up, either. I bumpily extract myself from the sweaty, perfumed bodies around us and escape onto the porch.

ANNA

CHAPTER TWENTY-ONE

I stop when I get to the stairs of the porch and take out a cigarette. Outside, thick, white flakes of snow are crashing into the ground in sheets. The lighter I thought I had in my pocket is gone, so I turn to the other person on the porch, a lanky punk rocker-type with bright blue eyes and blue hair. Before I can even ask, he is handing me an ornate BIC with a set of initials on them. TS. His eyes lock on mine, in a way that brings a shiver down my spine. I take another close look at him and notice he is older, likely approaching his thirties, with freckles pooling around his nose and stiff, muscular shoulders. He definitely doesn't fit in with this crowd, but it's college, so who knows how he ended up here. "You can keep it if you want. I have a few."

"Oh no, that's okay," I reply.

"I'm trying to quit," he says. "You'd be doing me a favor."

I light my cigarette then pocket the lighter. It's not worth it to keep arguing. "I should probably quit too, I guess," I say. "But it's not really the best time for me to be making any major life decisions."

The cute guy's eyes are still locked onto mine, deep and penetrating. Instead of turning away in boredom like most would, he asks, "Why not?" While I'm thinking of a non-TMI answer, the door opens and closes behind me, and I turn to see Margot, her thick hair looking more messy than usual, half falling out of her hat.

"Anna, hold on a sec," she says, grabbing hold of my arm and pulling me down the steps, away from the cute guy and into the snow. She takes my cigarette and has a drag before continuing. "I have to talk to you about something."

"Yeah, me too," I add reluctantly. I'm expecting some sort of apology or an explanation about Jake, but what I get has nothing to do with any of that. "You go first."

"Um," she starts. "It's about the house."

"You mean August?"

"Not exactly," she says. "I talked to Bukowski today about replacing August, and turns out he didn't even know there were four of us living there and he's kicking us out. He said it's illegal." Bukowski is our landlord. His name isn't really Bukowski, but that's what we call him because he is an exact ringer for the once famous poet.

"What!"

"He also said he's been getting noise complaints from the neighbors, and that he doesn't want to rent to college kids anymore," Margot says. "It sounds like bullshit to me. Who else would rent that dump if not students? But anyway we have to move out."

"I thought Abby said it was okay. She talked to him when August moved in."

"Well," Margot says, her eyes turning hard. "I told you we couldn't exactly trust her. She's a train wreck, Anna. You have to be blind not to see that." She takes another drag of my cigarette. "I think it was that fire Abby started. It was the final straw."

"What happened between you two?" I ask, finally unable to keep it inside any longer. "One second you're in love and the next you hate each other."

Margot laughs. "In love. Please. We made out a few times, that's it." She steals my cigarette and takes an angry pull. "She could fall in love with a tree branch if it called her beautiful."

I frown. "That's not very nice. What did she do that was so bad?"

Margot shakes her head again. "Forget it. Anna, some people are just not meant to cohabitate."

"What about us?" I ask, visibly hurt.

"I didn't mean us."

165

"Where are we supposed to move in four days? And what about August's stuff? He's supposedly in Georgia. Or headed there, or something, I don't know…"

"That's the other thing." Margot looks away, biting down on her lip. "Don't be mad…"

My stomach drops. Her face shows pity, which is not a good sign. "What."

"Well, with August gone, and the fact that we have to move out, and you know I can't stand Abby anyway…" she says. "Anyway, Jake said I could stay with him during winter break, and then I might move in here, with Alex and Julie until the semester is over. One of her roommates is transferring to Eau Claire."

This hits me harder than anything else I've heard so far. Maybe I really *should* have stayed home tonight. I could cry, if that was something I could ever possibly stomach. I may be many things, but I'm definitely not crying-in-public girl. That is Margot's friend Julie. She is probably crying in there right now somewhere. "What the fuck, Margot."

Margot still doesn't look at me. "Sorry."

"Don't we have a lease?" I ask her. "How can he do that?"

"He can break a lease if there's a violation," Margot explains. "At least, that's what he said. It's not worth it to me to argue about it."

"But we love our house!"

"Sure, I like the house…but I don't like all the Riverwest people coming over as much as you do. Everyone there is so…angry. They're like kids throwing a tantrum or something. Except they're old, so it's not cute."

"I won't let them over anymore," I argue. "And we can ask Abby to move. Done."

"It'll just be for the rest of the semester," Margot explains. "I swear. Next fall, we can get another place anywhere you want."

"Next fall? What am I supposed to do till next fall?"

She thinks about it for a moment. "Live with your parents?"

"There is no way in hell I'm going to do that." The fact that Margot suggested it only shows how distant we have become. It's bad enough I'm already wasting most of my time studying a subject they chose for me, I'm not about to spend the rest of my free time sitting in their horrible house in the suburbs while they ask me where I am going and when I will be back. Plus, I don't have a car. "You just fucking met this guy," I say, waving towards the house. "Now you're going to live with him?"

"For a few weeks, and then..." her voice trails off.

I want to scream. We were supposed to be old ladies together, that was our plan. Now I'm not sure we will make it through the year. I drop the cigarette on the ground and turn toward the street. My fingers are cold and red from the wind and snow, and I shove them in my pockets.

Margot follows me. "Anna, I'm sorry—"

"I'll figure it out. It's fine," I interrupt. I start walking down the sidewalk just for show. But then I realize the snow isn't so bad and I might as well walk the whole way home. Margot attempts to follow me, but I stop and tell her, "Just go back to your boyfriend."

"Are you sure?"

"Yes."

I'm making pretty good time zigzagging northward towards campus, walking past a late-night diner and sports bar on Farwell Avenue, when I finally realize someone has been following me. Not sure how long it's been, but I've definitely heard the same footsteps behind me for a while. Heart pounding, I turn to make sure it's not some deranged killer—though what would I do if it was?—and spot the blue-haired guy from the porch. He runs to catch up with me.

"Hey," he says, his breath forming a cloud into the bitter cold air. "I thought you'd never slow down. Are you some kind of marathon runner?"

"What are you, a stalker?"

"I'm a concerned citizen. You shouldn't be walking around alone like that. It's not safe." He starts to jump around a bit on the soles of his feet like a firecracker, his breath following him in short little bursts.

"I don't even know your name," I tell him. "How is that better than being alone?"

He stops and takes out his hand, and I shake it. "Hi, I'm Tristan," he says. He sweeps his hand out, like the male version of a curtsey. "Nice to meet you." His face melts into a smile, showing off his perfectly straight teeth.

I give him a funny look. "What are you on?"

"Nothing, scouts honor," he says, holding both his hands up. Then he reaches into his pocket and produces a silver coin. "Two months sober today."

"Oh!" I say, surprised. I'm thrown off by such an honest admission. I've never known anyone in NA. Or AA for that matter, although I know plenty of people who could probably benefit from it. I'm not sure how to respond. I also find myself uncomfortable with his gaze; it is focused and excited, like when Abby does too much Adderall and starts cleaning the house fanatically. Except this is a sober gaze, and the intensity makes my body feel a little like it's melting.

"Um. Congrats?" I eventually choke out. Something like electricity passes through us, like a tram as it moves along the cable. To avoid turning into a puddle, or a frozen popsicle more likely, I start walking again.

"Where you headed?" Tristan asks, still following me, his energy at such a high level it almost rubs off on me.

"Oh. Center street. Center and Bremen," I lie.

"Cool. Me too," he says. Now that he is closer, I notice he is not only tall, but he is towering over me by at least a foot. Which would make him close to six foot five.

"Oh really. What a coincidence," I say, sarcastically.

"I am!" he says. His excitement has turned to giddiness now, and he is practically bouncing on his toes. He reminds me of a child in desperate need of recess.

"You can keep following me, but just know I have my hand on my cell and I can type 911 really fast," I threaten. I pick up my pace. It's still freezing out, and getting later by the second. Not exactly the best time to be walking around outside in Milwaukee. Especially with some blue-haired giant.

"Noted," he says. He speeds up his wide-legged pace to match mine. A bus begins driving past us, its windshield wipers working furiously, but I don't try to run to the next stop like I might have if Tristan wasn't walking alongside me. It would also require crossing the entire length of a city block in less than a minute; I'm more likely to slip and fall. I'm no longer in so much of a hurry. I can't remember the last time someone new took any interest in me, and it's not like I have anything else to do now that Margot ditched me for her new boy toy.

"Hey, I didn't catch your name," Tristan says.

"That's because I never told you my name. It's Anastasia," I say. "But people call me Anna because they can't pronounce that."

"Really? And you let them get away with it?"

"What choice do I have?"

"You should correct them. Otherwise they have the wrong idea of you before you even talk."

I watch him, surprised. No one has ever put it like that before, and it's bizarre to hear it from a total stranger with blue hair. "Yeah. I guess that's sort of true."

We turn right on North Avenue, just east of the bridge. The dim yellow bulbs of its streetlamps are barely visible from beneath the swirling white snow, the river below so black it looks like an abyss. "Technically it's not wrong, exactly, being a translation and all. And it's not so bad. My mom's name is Lyubov. You can't imagine the number of wrong ways you can pronounce that."

Tristan asks, "What is that, Russian?"

"Yes. It means 'love' in Russian. Most people call her Luba for short though."

"Are you from Russia?"

"We are Ukrainian, technically speaking. Or Soviet? I never know how to answer that. We speak Russian, and it was the Soviet Union when we left, but now it's Ukraine," I say. "I've never even heard a word of Ukrainian, so it doesn't feel right to me to say I'm Ukrainian. But I'm not from Russia, either. Sorry, that's probably way too much info."

"No, that's dope," he says. He rubs his large hands together for a second then sticks them into his very small pockets. I notice a small tear on the side of his black jean jacket, next to an assortment of patches with band names on them. Punk bands, if I had to guess. I remember seeing similar logos in Masha's old room that is now an office.

"I think it's confusing," I shrug. We keep walking down Farwell, watching the cars swim through layers of slush and snow and dirt, my toes getting soaked and the frigid wind burning the thighs of my legs into numbness. But I ignore my frozen limbs. I am actually starting to cheer up a little. Something about the combination of physical effort and discomfort clears my mind, like meditation. I almost forget I'm not alone, until I catch a blue smear in my periphery vision and remember.

"What about you? Are you from here?" I ask.

"Nah, I'm from Virginia originally. Then Austin, and New Orleans for a while. I've been traveling around a lot."

Passing the Oriental Theater, then a crowd of smokers outside Landmark Lanes, we hit a red light and stop moving. For a second, we stand there, silently. Tristan is close enough to me now that I can smell the patchouli on his clothes. I dissect his river of blue dreads, his bright blue eyes, his nearly invisible eyelashes. He, too, seems to be scanning me. I try not to wonder too much what he sees; my face is likely bright red from the cold, my hair, falling halfway out of my hat, is wet and slowly turning into icicles. I am completely sober and aware enough to count off all my physical defects; my short stature, my sensitive skin, my slightly crooked teeth. That said I also know I'm not ugly. Tristan seems to be making the same or a similar assessment. Because out of nowhere we start kissing.

When we're done, the light turns green and we continue our

conversation like nothing has happened. Except it has. My stomach is giddy with butterflies. I try to ignore it, and circle back to what we were talking about before.

"I wish I could travel more," I say. "I wish I could move, really."

"Yeah? Why don't you then?"

"My family, I guess. They would be really upset. I don't have the balls to leave."

Tristan purses his lips, lets out a little whistle. "I wish my dad gave two shits what I did."

"He doesn't?" I ask.

"He has this whole new family now. Doesn't even remember to call on my birthday." He creases his brows into what appears to be a grimace, before letting it melt away into impassiveness. "Whatever."

"Sorry. That sucks."

Tristan shrugs. "He's Cuban. We didn't really get along when I was little. I think he called me a fag more often then he used my name." He doesn't seem sad expressing this information, which makes it even sadder. We stop again at another light, and kiss again.

The kiss lasts a long time, considering the circumstances. It's a very good kiss. But it's impossible to stay focused on it, with the blizzard still swirling around us, and people walking by. Cars, too, continue to drive through the flooded street. We also happen to be a block away from my grandparents' house. Visibility right now is nil—and yet, all I can do is worry they might see us. What would my eighty-year-old grandparents be doing walking around a blizzard at night? Who knows. But I can't get it off my mind.

Tristan stops suddenly and looks around. "Hey, this road doesn't go to Riverwest."

"Yeah, I am actually not going that way. I just said that to throw you off."

"Where *are* you going?"

Should I really tell a stranger where I live? I wonder. Then I tell myself to stop thinking. What has thinking ever done for me? Nothing good. However, neither has catching pneumonia. I point north towards Prospect Ave. "That way. Sorry."

He looks at me again like I'm a textbook he's studying. "If it makes you feel better, I'm leaving town tomorrow. I'd like to keep hanging out with you, but no pressure."

"Oh," I say, unsure how to feel about this. "Okay."

"You wanna check out this shitty college bar a couple blocks from here? I'll let you beat me at pool."

I'm freezing, and could definitely use a real drink, so I agree to this without much thought. The door guy is so busy texting someone on one of those new smartphones that he barely looks up when he sees us, and even though Masha's old ID is expired, he doesn't seem to notice and waves us through. Inside, the place is dark and dank and reeks of sticky beer. But it's so much better than that party I could puke. I'm surprised to find Tristan with a decent-sized wad of cash in his wallet, and I allow him to buy me several drinks in a row before we actually get around to a pool game. He doesn't let me win, however, like he promised. In fact, he seems to actively be sabotaging the game. The more we drink the more hyper he gets. He starts poking me with the pool cue, and finding ways to wrap himself around me to show me what I'm doing wrong. When he isn't doing that, he is juggling the pool balls. Eventually I stop trying, and he wins. By then, I've figured out that pool is only an excuse to touch me, and I'm drunk, so we go back outside into the cold to share a cigarette.

Tristan is in great spirits now. He starts massaging my shoulders while simultaneously smoking without use of his hands, a feat I have never been able to accomplish. While we stand there, this skinny old bearded man we in Riverwest call Rabbi walks by with a grocery cart of old flowers and asks us if we want any. I say no, because I always say no to Rabbi, but to my surprise Tristan reaches into his pocket and hands him a five, and before I know it, I have an individually wrapped daisy in my pocket.

"I can't believe you did that," I say. "That's so nice of you. I see that guy every day and never think to get anything."

"You know he gets those flowers out of dumpsters and sells them for crack money, right?" he asks me.

"*No*," I say.

"He's not even a rabbi."

"What?!" I frown. "You really just ruined this guy for me. I always thought he was a cute little old man."

"Look at his eyes. And his teeth."

"I don't look at his eyes or his teeth. I look at his pants. They're like halfway up his stomach. It reminds me of my grandpa."

"That's kind of sweet." Tristan smiles and puts his cigarette out so he can kiss me. When he's done, I ask, "Can we go? I'm freezing."

After that, we start walking again, practically running all the way back to my block despite a red light. Tristan, a gentleman, places an arm on my back, steering me away from puddles that have formed from melting snow. Then, when we are only a block from my house, out of breath, we slow down again. The snow has finally stopped, and the streetlights here seem brighter than the rest of the neighborhood. For the first time I notice Tristan's clothes are not only black and a little ratty, but that he's wearing Carharrts and a bandana. I somehow hadn't realized he is not so much a punk as a train-hopper. Suddenly I find myself wondering how we managed to cross paths.

"That party doesn't really seem like your scene," I say, out of breath.

"It's not," he says.

"What were you doing there?"

Tristan looks around in both directions, then reaches into his back pocket to show me a pair of wallets. "I was working."

I stop and look at the wallets. One is leather, and filled with cash. The other is a silver purse with a fake diamond clasp. "You're a thief?"

"Well, I prefer the term pickpocket," he says, then laughs. "Just kidding. I don't give a shit."

"Cool," I can't help but whisper. Then I remember we're not in a movie, that he stole things from people, from Margot's friends. I don't like Margot's friends, but still. "Why would you tell me that? We just met."

He licks his lips, then puts the wallets back. "Because I have a feeling you'd be good at it." he says, rubbing his hands together for warmth. "It's better with a partner."

I cross my arms over my chest. For a moment I forget the cold. "I don't think so. I would feel bad." I scratch my head, itchy under my hat. Then I start walking again; either for warmth, or to give myself space from Tristan, who is not exactly what I expected. Maybe it's my fault. The blue hair should have been a clue. But having spent so much time in Riverwest, I'd stopped noticing those things.

"Why? You don't need money?" he asks, pointing at my torn shoes.

"I could get a job, like a normal person."

"Is that what you are? A normal person?" he asks, smiling. "Come on, Anastasia! Why should rich people have all the fun? The system is rigged against us from the day we're born. I'm just evening the scales a little."

"So you're Robin Hood?" I ask.

He grabs me by the hand and turns me towards him, both a question and an answer in his gaze. It's so intense my entire body turns into a flutter of nerves. I feel like he can see into my soul or something. "Want to be my Maid Marion?" he asks.

I look at him skeptically. "What?"

"That's Robin Hood's girl."

"I didn't know he had a girl."

"Oh, there's always a girl," Tristan says with a wink.

Then we start kissing again. If I had been thinking of anything else before, it was all gone in a flash. It doesn't matter how many times a man touches me; it always feels like I'm about to jump off a gigantic cliff. And despite the warning bells going off in my mind, I have to admit I find the pickpocket thing sort of intriguing. Sexy, even. I don't want to contribute, of course, but I would like to hear about it. There's something about him that makes me feel like we've known each other for years, not less than a few hours.

We reach my house and stop right outside the door. I watch as Tristan paces back and forth against the sidewalk. "Maybe I'll stay a couple more days," he suggests. "How would you feel about that?"

"I think I would like that very much," I say, and I let him into the house.

ANNA

CHAPTER TWENTY-TWO

In that elusive slice of morning between getting another drink and getting breakfast, hard metallic pings and the smell of alcohol wake me up out of a deep, deep sleep. Is it raining whiskey? Am I in a sauna? Confused, I open my eyes and look around the small, dark space. No, I'm in my room. Snow is melting and dripping from the rooftop, the radiator is working overtime and an empty liquor bottle has spilled a little onto the floor. My confusion is replaced with an inexplicable feeling of doom and a dire need to drink water. The doom I cannot explain away, but I can hydrate, so I roll out of bed and crawl over Tristan to get to the door. I tiptoe to the kitchen in my underwear, trying not to wake anyone up. I make a stop at the bathroom too, since I am already out. By the time I get back I'm wide awake, and my body is buzzing with the need for a cigarette. Tristan is sleeping through all of this, even the cat-like screams the computer makes while warming up. He is passed out face down, mounds of long blue hair spread out across the pillow like a river, his arms covered entirely in tattoos. He looks sexy, and I should probably go back to sleep. And I would, if it wasn't for this feeling I can't shake, like the reoccurring dream I have where I am driving my parents' old car down a hill and the breaks don't work. So instead I head to MySpace to see if anyone is online. Truthfully, I just want to talk to Zoya more. And I'm in luck, as she happens to be online. It's daytime where she is.

<<ANNA>> Hey. How are you doing?

<<ZOYA>> Hi! I'm good. I'm getting ready to go to work. What are you doing up so late?

<<ANNA>> Can't sleep.

<<ZOYA>> Why? What's wrong?

<<ANNA>> Nothing. Never mind.

<<ZOYA>> Tell me!

<<ANNA>> It's not a big deal… but I have to move in a few days, which I'm sad about.

<<ZOYA>> Oh, I'm sorry.

<<ANNA>> That's okay, don't worry about me, I'm sure you have enough problems.

<<ZOYA>> That doesn't mean you can't have your own. Can you stay with your parents?

<<ANNA>> Frankly I would rather live with my grandparents than my parents. They're way nicer to me. No, they're not an option.

<<ZOYA>> I don't get it. You all seem so happy in your photos.

<<ANNA>> Everyone seems happy in photos. If they looked sad, they'd throw the photos away not post them online.

<<ZOYA>> Not here. Haven't you seen any photos from the USSR?

<<ANNA>> Oh yeah, that's true. I remember my dad telling me how strange it was to come here and have everyone smile at him. For years he thought Americans were all crazy.

<<ZOYA>> What is Pavel like, anyway?

<<ANNA>> He… Works a lot. Loves my mom. Really into the whole "family" concept.

<<ZOYA>> Why is family in quotes?

<<ANNA>> A real family accepts each other's differences. Or they pretend to, at least. Not my dad. Everything has to be his way. You either become a sad sack doormat or you have to blow up everything, like my sister did.

<<ZOYA>> Your sister that's in Israel? I tried messaging her too, but I never heard back.

<<ANNA>>   She's religious, so she doesn't really go online much … I'm not sure she even knows what MySpace is.

<<ZOYA>>   How did she end up there and you're here?

<<ANNA>>   She never got along with my parents. They fought constantly. Then she had some problems in college that she didn't deal with very well. I think she would have gone anywhere as long as it wasn't here, but she happened to go on birthright on her winter break.

<<ZOYA>>   Are you two close? I've always wanted sisters.

<<ANNA>>   Not really. When we were kids, maybe.

<<ZOYA>>   Why not? She isn't nice?

<<ANNA>>   It's not that… She isn't mean to me. She's just not… present. I don't know what it is. We're too different maybe.

<<ZOYA>>   Well, like I said before, you are welcome to come to Chernovtsy anytime you want. I will show you a good time.

<<ANNA>>   Really? You aren't just saying that to be polite?

<<ZOYA>>   Of course. That's what family does, isn't it?

<<ANNA>>   I may take you up on that. One day, when I have some money. I need to get a job or something.

<<ZOYA>>   You've never had a job?

<<ANNA>>   Oh I have. I've worked on and off since I was fourteen. But my parents insisted I focus on school so they are paying for my rent right now. Does that make you hate me?

<<ZOYA>>   No, I don't hate you. I only wish I could have that kind of support.

<<ANNA>>   Your mom wasn't supportive?

<<ZOYA>>   We were best friends. But no, not financially.

<<ANNA>>   You probably won't understand, but you are probably better off. Money is just paper.

<<ZOYA>>   That sounds like something only someone with money would say.

<<ANNA:>>   We were never rich, Zoya. My most expensive pair of pants were like twenty dollars.

<<ZOYA>>   Sorry. Forget I said that. Shouldn't you go back to bed?

178

<<ANNA>>   I should… But there's another reason I'm awake right now.

<<ZOYA>>   Does it have to do with a boy?

<<ANNA>>   Yes, haha. A cute one.

<<ZOYA>>   Well, just be careful. You don't want to end up like me, haha.

<<ANNA>>   I've been meaning to ask you… are you speaking to the father of your baby?

<<ZOYA>>   At the moment, no.

<<ANNA>>   Does he know about your condition?

<<ZOYA>>   He knows. He told me to get rid of it. Like mother like daughter, I guess.

<<ANNA>>   Wait. What? My dad told your mom to get an abortion?

<<ZOYA>>   That's what she says.

<<ANNA>>   No way.

<<ZOYA>>   Yes, she did.

<<ANNA>>   I don't believe it.

<<ZOYA>>   Only two people know what really happened. One of them is dead.

<<ANNA>>   You don't understand. My dad loves kids. He's a REPUBLICAN.

<<ZOYA>>   Maybe now he does. In Ukraine, there are no republicans. There are only communists and traitors.

<<ZOYA>>   I'm sorry Anastasia. I shouldn't have said that. Forgive me. I don't mean to make things hard for you.

<<ANNA>>   You're wrong about him. He's not the monster you are making him out to be.

<<ZOYA>>   You're right. You know him, I don't. We've never had the pleasure of meeting. I'd like to remedy this, but he doesn't. Did you get the DNA kit, by the way?

<<ANNA>>   No, not yet. Did they tell you how long it would take?

<<ZOYA>>   Anywhere from a few weeks to six months, I believe. It would be easier if we lived in the same place.

<<ANNA>>   I wish I could come visit you. I'd just take it myself and we would know right away.

<<ZOYA>>   Can't you, though? Maybe your parents can loan you the money. You said you've always wanted to visit here, maybe now is the best time.

<<ANNA>>   I already tried that route. My parents were furious. They don't want me anywhere near Ukraine.

<<ZOYA>>   Maybe if you explain how much it means to you…

<<ANNA>>   I did, trust me. It was the biggest fight we ever had. I don't intend to repeat it.

<<ZOYA>>   Oh okay. It was only a suggestion.

<<ANNA>>   Don't worry. We'll get this sorted out. We just have to wait a little bit longer.

<<ZOYA>>   I don't know how much longer I have, Anastasia.

<<ANNA>>   Why? Are you in trouble?

<<ANNA>>   Are you?

<<ZOYA>>   I have to get to work. Bye for now.

YOU'VE BEEN SMOOCHED!

ZOYA HAS LEFT THE CONVERSATION.

ANNA

CHAPTER TWENTY-THREE

Tristan is gone in the morning. I'm not surprised, but I do spend ten minutes making sure he didn't steal anything before I go to the kitchen to have breakfast. As far as I can tell, everything is in place. Still, I text him to see what his plans are for the day. I remember him saying something about extending his trip to Milwaukee a few more days for me, and I'm curious if that was alcohol talking or if he really meant it. I grab my backpack and am leaving the house for my least-favorite class of all time, Astronomy 101—who knew it wouldn't be about horoscopes?—when I see my dad's car parked in the driveway, sitting in a cloud of fumes. Still high from my unexpected romantic encounter and so tired from a lack of sleep that my brain is fuzzy, I don't assume it's terrible right away. But when he gets out, slamming the door furiously and dressed up like he's come straight from work, or right before work, I guess, my heart plummets.

My dad heads straight for me with an envelope in his hand. He doesn't stop till his head is practically touching mine. I can smell his cologne, the nicotine gum in his mouth. "What did you do?" he asks.

I back up, onto the sidewalk. "What are you talking about?"

"I'm talking about this!" Here, he dumps out the contents of the thick manila envelope in my face. Inside, there appears to be some kind of scientific kit. And a letter, printed out in Russian.

A lump forms in my throat. This must be the anvil I've been waiting for. "What is that?"

My dad hands it over and I read—well, skim, it's a lot of tiny text—

what's written on the page. It seems to be a list of directions. Directions how to take a DNA test properly and where to mail it when it's ready. On the sides there are some images accompanying the directions, in case you're like me and zone out anytime you see a list of anything.

"Oh. Wow," I tell him, my heart racing. I hand it back over. "Is that what I think it is?"

"Why are you so surprised?"

"What do you mean?"

"Where did she get my address, if not from you? Aren't you the one talking to her?"

"I didn't give her your address! I told her not to send it to you, in fact. She just…" I don't finish the rest of the sentence, which is that she asked me about his address, and I confirmed it was correct. Because, oops? Maybe I shouldn't have done that. But then why had she kept asking me if the kit had arrived? Wouldn't that imply it was en route to *my* house, not my dad's? Or did she mean my dad's house all along? If she sent a DNA test to my dad, who ignored all her emails, why would she expect him not to ignore that too?

"I knew you were still talking to her," he says. My dad, who is now bright red in the face, begins pacing back and forth like a lunatic. I quickly glance around to make sure no one is watching us; what if Tristan chooses this moment to return? Or, worse: what if he doesn't return? But there is no one outside so early in the morning. Only mountains and mountains of snow surround us, and cars trapped underneath them. A few people far in the distance are out there with shovels, but most, because it's the east side and full of college students, are still asleep. It is mornings like this I am relieved not to own any vehicle besides a bicycle.

"This is insane, Anastasia. What am I supposed to do?" My dad is still pacing, his pants getting wet around the ankles due to the fact that my landlord hasn't been by to shovel yet. The pacing is making my own anxiety spike. I sit down on the cold concrete steps by our door, to allow more space between us. The smell of cigarettes is so strong

I worry he is smelling it on me. It certainly couldn't be coming from him. He'd quit years ago, when my mother had gone through a little health scare. "Can you imagine what would have happened if your mom got home before me and saw this?"

"I only talked to her like one more time," I explain to my dad as patiently as I can. Or three more times. Maybe five? "I *definitely* didn't tell her to send you a DNA test."

My dad stops and leans against his car. He looks to the sky, as if he will find an answer in the gray clouds. "You must really hate me," he spits out finally, in Russian.

"I don't hate you," I mumble

"Then why would you believe a stranger over your own father?"

"Who said I believe her?" I look him straight in the eye. "Do *you* believe her?"

My dad turns away. "I told you," he says with an annoyed sigh. "She's blackmailer. Apple fall far from tree." He lowers his head back down and starts shaking it in frustration. I start to feel like he is really overreacting. How is any of this my fault? She found him. She found his address. I did nothing but try to help them and fail. "Do you have any idea what you've done by talking to her?"

"I'm sorry," I say. I am sorry, but I also feel defensive. "But why would she target *you*? And why would she ask for a DNA test, not money?" I ask. Mulling it over, I guess I really didn't believe her. And yet, now, I am questioning the entire idea. If she was a stranger to him, then why would he be panicking so much?

No answer from my dad.

"You really didn't date her mom?" I probe.

He gives me a piercing look, as if to tell me, *See? I knew you talked to her*. "I fired her. She was mad. She started trying to blackmail me."

"Blackmail you for what?"

"You know this, Anastasia, we did all sorts of crazy things in the USSR. I had to bribe everyone from the brick layer to the manufacturer just to get anything done. She wasn't the only one to try to get us all in trouble."

"Why would she blackmail you though? What did she want in return?"

My dad shakes his head. He returns to English now, having calmed down a little. "It was crazy place," he repeats. "People did stupid things. Forget it."

"And you really didn't date her? Not even a little?" I pry. "Mom told me once you used to be quite the ladies' man when she met you."

A long pause ensues, at the end of which my dad seems to deflate. "I did not date her. But…" He pauses again, his expression now less defiant and tense.

"But what?"

"I did not date her," he continues, deflating more; looking relieved even. "We had…relations, after a work party. There was a lot of vodka involved."

I want to laugh when he says this. I've never been in shock before, but maybe that is what shock feels like—an unbearable urge to say that's so ludicrous it's funny. Preposterous. For a moment I can't catch my breath. I realize then that I never really believed Zoya. My faith in my dad's honesty trumped anything she could ever say to me. Now I have no idea what to think.

"Oh my god!" I say finally. My dad looks back towards the house anxiously. This has all been a story to me, an investigation; play acting, almost. I haven't considered him at all, not really, not what this would mean for him if Zoya is correct and she is, in fact, his daughter unknown to him for most of her life.

He might actually have another daughter.

I might have another sister.

My grandparents might have another grandchild! And what about my mom? What would she now have?

"I told you to stay out of it, Anastasia. But you never listen. This all your fault."

My heart starts pounding all the way into my ears. I feel myself start to get angry. All I ever do is listen. "Dad—" I stop, lowering my voice. "All I did was answer a message."

"No. You gave this woman hope."

"But if she's really not yours, as you claim, then why are you so worried? Just take the test!"

My dad dumps the contents of the envelope, which he's been gripping tight this entire time, onto the ground. "I know it's my fault you have lived a very sheltered life, but please, don't be so naïve."

My legs begin to feel rubbery, and I am suddenly glad to be sitting down. "What do you mean?"

"You understand that if I do this, she'll never stop coming after me? First, it's a test. Then it's $500. Then it's $5,000, then it's everything I have." He puts his hands on his hips. "This is how it works in Soviet Union."

"It's not the Soviet Union, anymore, Dad," I protest, meekly.

"You think because it's called something else now it's a brand-new place?" he says.

"No, but…"

"You can't wash dirty dishes with dirty water, Anastasia," he says in Russian. "That level of corruption doesn't go away because rubles are now hryvna."

"I don't know about all that…. But if you would've just taken the test, this could all have blown over by now," I start. "If you're really her father, a test is nothing! Even if she asks for money later, don't you owe it to her, if you're really her father?"

My dad looks at me like I'm the biggest idiot in the world. And maybe I am. But that doesn't mean she's not his. Does it? "Anastasia, trust me. I'm not."

"But you don't *know*," I say. This conversation has made me feel physically ill. At the very least he cheated on my mom. At the worst, he is an absentee father and a liar. How can he stand there judging *me*? How can he ever judge me again? "She's pregnant, did you know that?"

My dad rolls his eyes. "Sure." He crosses his arms over his chest. I start shaking, either from the cold traveling up through my torn jeans, or something else. "Oldest trick in the book. Her mother used the same one on me."

"But maybe they're both telling the truth!"

"This is not a mail from truth teller, Anastasia," he continues. "I've been around block few times. Once you live a little longer, you might know some things too."

Despite this admonition, I cannot help but stand up for Zoya. She may have gone about fixing it the wrong way, but if she's right, it was her life he'd messed up by leaving. "She's not the criminal you think she is. She's nice. She wants to do what's best for her baby. Don't you even care that she might be your daughter?" I ask, teeth chattering. "I mean...don't you want to meet her, if she is?"

"The last thing I need is another daughter," my dad says, his jaw clenched. He stares at me with an expression I've never seen before. Like he's looking at a stranger. A stranger he doesn't like very much.

I don't even try to come up with a response to this. He never wanted a daughter to begin with. How he was hoping for a son is practically all I ever hear about when he tells the story of my birth. How he'd asked the doctor over the phone to check again and make sure. He means it as a funny anecdote, but to me, it's always felt like I was born a disappointment. Where do you even go from there but down? Add to that upending his whole life for his kids, and I may never escape from his swamp of expectations and guilt.

At the same time, could it really get any worse than it is already? Maybe now is the time to make some changes.

"This agreement we have, paying for school, and your rent...it ends today," my dad says, getting back into the car.

"What?"

"You heard me. You think I can afford it now? If she starts trying to claim I'm her father in court—she could sue me for everything I have!"

"She won't! How could she?"

"Who knows how much this is all going to cost. Maybe you'll finally learn what it means to have consequences," he says.

"Fine!" I say. "I didn't even want to go to college. You made me go."

"Great. Then everyone wins."

Without another word or glance, he gets in his Toyota and drives away. Only once he's gone do I take the contents of the envelope from the ground and shove them into my pockets. I'm mad at Zoya for sending it to him, but it's better to keep it in case I need it later. Now that I know she might really be his, anything could happen.

ANNA

CHAPTER TWENTY-FOUR

Needless to say, I miss my astronomy class.

I'm sitting on the porch feeling pretty sorry for myself and smoking what has to be the fourth cigarette in a row when I see August and his new girlfriend walk up, covered in dirt and carrying giant army-green bags on their backs, guitar cases in hand. For a second I'm so happy I forget how mad my dad is at me, how I may have totally messed up his life. And mine, too.

"Hey!" August says, waving at me. He looks pretty chipper for having spent weeks on a moving train. He's also filthy; even his dimples are covered in dirt. And didn't someone tell me August was far, far away from here?

"I thought you were in Georgia!" I say, standing up, and stretching out my arms.

He comes in for a hug.

"Jesus." It's hard to describe the smell of a train-hopper the moment they've gotten off a train, but you can often recognize it from across the room; up close it's nearly unbearable. It's not quite homeless person, but it's far past patchouli-wearing Riverwest hippies. It's somewhere in between scented oils and lack of bathing, with a tint of bonfire. Not entirely unpleasant, just powerful. No that's not true. It's pretty unpleasant.

"I know. I'm heading straight for the shower," he laughs. He steps back, grinning, and introduces the girl next to him. "This is Box." I turn to look at her. She's pretty, despite being dressed in tattered clothing; black jeans, torn beige shirt, multiple facial piercings. A giant mole covers the bottom of her chin, surrounded by smears of black ash. Her eyes are soft and kind, a tint of green in them. They don't seem to belong with their surroundings. Like a pretty flower that's been plucked from a garden and planted in a sea of weeds.

"Hi," she practically whispers.

"Hi."

August has dropped one of his bags on the ground and is taking two hard ciders out of it. "You want one?" he asks. "We stopped at the Whole Foods dumpster on our way. Got all sorts of goodies."

I usually avoid drinking when the sun is still out, but today is not one of those days. Today, I chug down half the cider in one instant. "What's going on?" I ask, momentarily hopeful. "How was your trip? Are you staying?"

"I'm still on it. I'm only here to get my stuff," he says, smiling at Box, who beams back.

"Well, damn. Margot was right." I finish the rest of the cider and crumple up the can, leaving it in a pile of snow. "Where are you going?"

"New York, for now. Box's sister lives there," August says. He puts his bag back on and starts digging around in his pockets.

"Oh. Awesome. I love New York." I take out my keys, as they're always attached to my jeans with a carabiner, and unlock the door for them. "What's your real name, Box?"

"Oh, we don't talk about that," August says. An awkward smile passes over his face. He looks down at the crumpled Strongbow can, then back at me. "Anna? Everything okay?"

"Yeah, sure. Just having a weird day." I turn back towards the door, opening it.

We walk inside the house. "How are you moving your stuff?" I ask.

August and Box drop their things on the floor of the kitchen with clear relief. "My friend is coming by with his truck. How about you? Where are you going to go?"

This is, indeed, a good question. Without an apartment, or money coming in from my dad, I have no idea where I am going to go. I try to think back to how much I have saved in my checking account. A few hundred dollars maybe? How long could I live off a few hundred dollars? What could I sell? But of course, I have nothing of value at all. Some portraits that no one will ever buy, because people only buy paintings of themselves or their kids, and who could blame them? The most success I'd had, besides commission work, was with tiny paintings of dogs I'd sold at a show titled Mini Art, where all work had to be under a hundred dollars, and you could take it home right off the wall. But I don't have even one painting to sell this year, because all I've been doing is homework for classes I couldn't care less about. And drinking. I can't remember the last time I painted. Although, if I can finish my former guidance counselor's commission in the next four days and also get him to drive down here to pay me for it, that's another five hundred dollars. That could hold me over for a little while, if I'm not paying rent.

Or I could work with Tristan, I think for a moment, before shaking this thought away. No. I can't steal from people. That would be wrong. Plus who knows if I'll ever see him again.

What's the point of any of it, if my dad really won't pay for next semester? Would I be going to college at all, let alone living in Milwaukee, if he isn't? I had never considered any other options, because my parents were so insistent on my going to college nearby that I had no space to wonder what I would want to do if it were up to me. The only place I would have wanted to go, had I had the time to consider it, was the Art Institute of Chicago, where a few people I'd been in shows with ended up, every day posting pictures of new elaborate projects while I burned away my time clicking. So my dad wants to cut me off. So what, then? No more college? Is it so horrible that I won't be forced to spend all my time using Adobe InDesign anymore?

No. No it would not be so horrible. Actually it would be kind of great. Right then and there, standing in my kitchen like some kind of deranged lunatic, I feel a spark of hope for the first time in a while. I think of the photos I've seen of skyscrapers of New York, the cozy patios of Austin, Portland's bridges and coffee shops. I imagine showing up to each place with nothing but a backpack of clothing and art supplies. Getting a job waitressing in some small desert town, like Liz Parker. Living, without the heavy weight of expectations, whatever combination of survivor's guilt and tremendous fear of the unknown my parents have insistently forced me to carry. Just being and painting, all the time, like I've always wanted but couldn't admit to myself. Or hell. Maybe I'll just go straight to Chernovtsy.

I don't even notice how long I stand there staring blankly until August comes by and waves a hand in front of my face.

"Hey. Hello? Talk to me," August says. Part of me forgot he was in the room, but no, there he is in front of me, lighting a rolled cigarette and then handing it to me. I suddenly feel dizzy, and like I need to sit down. "You okay? What boy drama did I miss while I was gone?"

"No boy drama," I say. I take the cigarette, but I'm not quite ready to speak more. My brain won't stop turning. Should I even bother finishing the semester?

"What's going on?" he asks me.

"I'm fine," I tell August. I take in a deep breath and turn. "Sorry, I just have to do something quick." I walk past him and into my room, which is uncharacteristically messy, so I hope August doesn't follow. The bed isn't made, my blue and green striped comforter drooping to the floor haphazardly, next to a pile of laundry. The ashtray is full and surrounded by old coffee mugs. I ignore it all and press the power button on my computer, and while I wait for it to load, I change my mind and carry a few of these mugs out to the kitchen sink. It's extra slow today, so I have time to dump out the ashtray and make my bed all before the computer is awake and logged in. I open my MySpace account, and click on the messenger function.

"Hello? Anna?" August is asking, trailing behind me. It occurs to me that he has been talking this whole time and I didn't hear him. "Are you listening?"

"Sorry. What did you say?"

"Come with us to New York," August suggests.

"You mean... train-hop with you?" I ask, surprised.

"Yeah," August says. "I think you'll like it."

I think about this for a second. Should I go? I'd been asked plenty of times before—before August left he'd asked, in fact—but I never really considered it till now. I try to remember all the times I had secretly fantasized about going on such an adventure, how I'd never let myself get very far in this illusion because I knew I could not go, not with my parents around, checking up on me regularly, pulling the purse strings. It does seem fun. Whoever has real adventures anymore? Everything is on Google. Everybody is on MySpace, telling you where they are and with whom. All the crevices of the world have been explored and excavated and monetized, even your deepest insecurities. August and his friends are the only people I know who don't play into it. They go where the train takes them, sometimes without any destination. They don't have plans and to-do lists and transcripts of vaguely useless skills. They don't check a map four times before stepping foot outside. They just go.

My eyes finally focusing again, I look at August, in his all-black clothes and greasy hair, dirt-streaked cheeks. This lifestyle really suits him; he looks great. He comes off more weathered, more mature. Happier, too. I let out a breath so long it's like I've been holding it all morning. "When are you leaving?" I ask.

"So you'll come?" he asks, excited.

"I don't know. I'll think about it," I say.

"What about your dad?" August is asking. He begins stretching his arms over his head, then bends over to touch his toes. "He won't freak out?"

"He's not going to be a problem for a while."

I turn to the computer and start writing out a message to Zoya: *Hey! Why on earth did you send my father the DNA test instead of me?*

"Why not?" he asks, curious. "Did you finally stand up to him?" August raises his hand for a high five but I don't meet it. I'm not exactly happy about our current state of affairs.

"No," I say, blushing. I click refresh on my internet browser. Zoya is online, which means she might answer me soon. August is now sitting on the floor and stretching his arms over each leg, one at a time. "How long till you leave again?"

August pops up straight to answer me. "A day or two. You can meet us there if you're not ready by then."

I shake my head, the fantasy bursting like a bubble. I feel silly for even considering it. I can't even imagine getting on a train all alone. How would I do it? Why? And is now really the best time to go somewhere? "I don't know, August. I don't think I have the uniform for it," I joke, half-seriously, half about to cry.

He stands and puts a hand on my shoulder. "I don't think you have the uniform for this either," he says, waving a hand in the direction of the room, the house, Milwaukee.

"Why do you say that?" I ask.

"I don't know. Doesn't it feel like you're always one floor removed from everybody else?" he asks.

"No. It's more like we're all on the same floor, but I'm in a different building," I explain.

August laughs. "I'd say a bit of both." I turn back to the screen, to see if Zoya has responded, but she hasn't. August returns to the floor to stretch. He is mid-bridge pose when the door opens, and Box walks in nervously, looking years younger now that she's clean, a towel wrapped around her wet hair. She can't even be eighteen, I realize.

"Thank you so much for letting me use your shower," Box says. She bends over and ruffles August's hair, and before I know it, August has jumped out of the bridge pose and is on his feet again. He gives Box a tight squeeze.

"Hey, kid. You need help packing?" Box asks him. The two of them are cute together. They look happy, or at least more content than

193

anyone else I know. It makes me wonder if maybe they understand something about life that I don't; something like you can't be satisfied with everything until you can live with nothing.

Maybe this endless want of distraction is what the absence of beauty in your surroundings replaces. My parents should have been happy enough with getting us here, but no; then it became a series of newly desired accomplishments. European cruises and expensive clothes, new floors, healthy savings accounts. Honor roll and college degrees and clean-cut Jewish life partners for their children; money, money, money. It would never end. It would never be enough. Like when you've missed eating all day and then try to eat, but no matter how much you consume, it's too late, you don't ever feel full.

"That shower was *perfection*, darling," Box says, taking the towel off her head and hanging it on my doorknob to dry. "I feel so *fancy*." She runs her fingers through her short hair and doesn't ask for a comb. I notice that she's still in the same ratty clothes she came here in, a band t-shirt worn so thin I can't make out the band name, and black jeans at least one an inch too large, torn in the knees. I feel suddenly very much like giving all my things away so I can be free too. It'll be less stuff to move, at least.

"Anna might come with us," August says, grinning at Box. Her eyes go wide with surprise.

"Really?" she asks. "Have you gone before? That's exciting."

"It sounds fun, but I'm not so sure I can actually hop a train," I tell them. "Isn't it dangerous?"

"Nah," she shrugs. "It's fun."

Maybe they're not entirely crazy, these train hoppers, to remove the shackles of daily existence in order to be free. Who wouldn't benefit from a little freedom? We live in buildings we can't see the bottom of and use machines we don't know the first thing about recreating. It's progress, and so much of it is necessary, but it separates you from your natural state. It's like there is no natural state anymore.

I start looking through my drawers for clothes I've been meaning to

194

take to Goodwill that I can instead donate to Box when August grabs me by the shoulder.

"Hey—who's that guy downstairs?" August asks. "He's huge!"

I look out the window, at where he's pointing, to see a young man is standing there, blue hair streaming out of a thick gray hat. In his hands, he has two large Fuel coffee cups. He rings the doorbell.

I smile, without meaning to. My stomach fills with butterflies again. "Oh, that's Tristan," I say. Part of me had thought I'd never see him again. But the other part... No, I knew all along he'd be back, that something had started between us last night, because maybe I was wrong to trust Zoya, but I've yet to be wrong about a guy being attracted to me. Some things you can't hide. Or maybe I just know how to look. Certainly if I met Zoya in person, I would have a better idea what her intentions are. But online? It's impossible to gauge tone from some text.

Right as I'm about to go over there and open the door, my computer makes a noise: an incoming message from Zoya on MySpace. I slump back into my seat.

I'm sorry, it says. *Can we talk?*

When the doorbell rings again, I turn to Box and August, who are now making out by the window. "Can you let him in?" I ask August. "Please? I just need a second here."

"Wow, look at you, juggling more than one dude!" August says, slapping me on the back, assuming I'm flirting with someone on here not demanding answers from a girl who thinks she's my sister. He and Box exit the room and head down the hall as I write, "My dad was so pissed he threw the test on the ground," I explain.

"*Anastasia, it was a mistake*," she writes. "*I didn't know till you messaged me.*"

"*That wasn't cool. We had a plan*," I write.

"*Let me explain. The truth is, when we first started talking, I had already sent the DNA kit to Pavel. I didn't think I would ever hear back from you*," she writes. "*So when you told me to send it to your address, I contacted the post office and begged them to change the delivery address. I called so many times, Anastasia. I even called the United States."*

"How am I supposed to believe you now?"

"I swear. They told me on the phone the address was changed to yours. I don't know what happened. Maybe they only said it to get me to stop calling," Zoya explains. *"I'm really sorry."*

A knock at my door jolts me out of this conversation: it's Tristan. "Hey," he says, smiling. "I got coffee."

"Hi! And here I thought you'd disappeared on me," I say, turning my head. I try to swallow my rage, if only for a moment, but my entire body feels like it might burst into a million pieces. It's just all too much to take.

"No, I just remember you said you like Fuel coffee," he says. He hands it over, followed by a cigarette.

"That's really sweet," I say, taking them both. When I look back, Zoya is writing me again:

"What about the test?" she is saying.

I drink some coffee and light the cigarette, hoping to feel more relaxed but only feeling less so. Like I'm at the edge of a cliff. *"I think it might still be okay, but I need to look at it more."*

"Do you think you can convince your dad to take it?"

"What's that about?" Tristan asks, hovering now behind me. "Is that Russian?"

"No, I don't," I write.

"Anastasia. I understand if you don't want to get involved. But can you please take the test instead? I am begging you."

My heartbeat starts to race. Should I really get involved more than I already have? I feel transported into an entirely different story than the one I've been telling myself. In this one, I'm not so sure I'm the hero. And I'm certainly not capable of making any important decisions. Not before I figure some other things out first. And definitely not before I drink my first cup of coffee.

"I will think about it," I write. I log off the computer, as if that will

make what she said disappear too, and turn to face Tristan. And then, feeling the overwhelming need to get it off my chest, I tell him everything.

FEBRUARY 2008

FEBRUARY 2005

MASHA

_____

CHAPTER TWENTY-FIVE

I scroll to the end of Anna's and Zoya's conversation, then back up to where I left off, pre-Skype call, and reread the initial conversations. I wish I knew what they spoke about on that call, because everything that follows is so out of context. First Anna sends her address; then Zoya is checking in about something almost daily; then Zoya sends her address in Ukraine for a second time. After that, they never speak again. Not on Facebook anyway. When I check the Skype history, it shows seven calls, two of them missed, and three of them less than two minutes' long. Two calls, however, were nearly an hour each. They could have talked about anything in that amount of time. They could have become friends, or enemies, or both.

I sit back and think about things for a long time. I have so many questions. Why had Anna engaged with this woman for as long as she did? Did she have information that I don't? Why didn't she reach out to me about it? And is Zoya involved in her disappearance? Anna was so excited when Zoya said she could come visit her in Chernovtsy. Combined with the fact that I can't find her, it makes me wonder if she hadn't up and gone to Ukraine to meet Zoya and take the DNA test herself. Why else had she sent her address so many times? Maybe that's why Anna needed money so badly she decided to steal it from people. If I didn't know from years of unanswered entreaties how much Anna had always needed to see Chernovtsy again, this could be considered a huge leap. But she'd wanted to go back there since the day she learned that it was the place from which we'd come, like a moon forever orbiting a planet that could never really be hers. I tried to tell her to forget about it; I'd been there, I'd lived it, and it wasn't worth the bother. Why waste so much energy wanting something that never wanted you? But I should have known better; the more you tell someone not to feel a certain way, the more they are going to feel it. The older she became, the more Anna's nostalgia grew on her like a tumor. There's a word in German that explains it perfectly: Fernwah, which means homesick for a place you've never been. Despite what I imagined when I'd left—that she had replaced her desire for Ukraine with a desire to make art—maybe I was wrong. Maybe I only thought that because it was easier than asking her about it.

What if she'd actually gotten on a plane, without telling any of us, and gone there? If she had the means now, I doubt anything would stop her. We don't know anything about this Zoya woman. I definitely don't trust her to take care of my sister.

If she did go to Ukraine, there has to be a way for my dad to find out. Ticket receipts, bank account statements, something. He'd know better than I would. Even though I am still slightly furious with him I immediately search the house to track him down. I find him drinking espresso in the kitchen while attempting to make a frozen burrito on the stovetop. The sight of it temporarily distracts me from the entire ordeal I'd read about and my new hypothesis.

"Papa, no. Just… oh my god." I take the burrito and pop it into the microwave. My dad watches me take the frozen sack away from him, and he doesn't fight. "You have to defrost it. Then it goes in the oven. Unless you want to eat a frozen bean icicle?"

"Your mom did all the cooking," is his only response. The peach-colored walls—also my mother's doing, I imagine—make his face appear even paler than it was before. I notice, for the first time, that he has dark bags under his eyes too. Papa has had insomnia on and off his whole life, and it is suddenly clear to me that he has not slept much, if at all, over the last few weeks.

My previous anger at him begins to shift into pity. "Well it *is* 2008," I say, softly. "You could learn to cook too. It would probably take you the same amount of time to make a burrito from scratch." The microwave beeps and I place the burrito in the toaster oven on high, with a timer on so he can't screw it up. "It's beans and rice, Papa."

"Sure," my dad shrugs, blankly.

This despondent look makes me remember why I'm there in the first place. I should probably tell him where I think Anna disappeared to, but surprisingly, what comes out of my mouth is this: "Why did Anna stop painting?"

Papa narrows his eyebrows at me, confused. "I didn't know she had. Why?" He leans against the shiny granite countertop, his hands looking for space to rest, but not finding any, because it's so cluttered with kitchenware and old, dirty glasses. How long had my mom been gone, anyway?

"Well, did you see anything new at her apartment? Were her arms ever covered in paint?" I pry.

"I do not notice these things, Masha, you know this. I busy man."

"But she's not majoring in art, correct?"

"I not throw my money in toilet."

My blood starts boiling again, replacing pity with frustration. The same frustration I've always had when it comes to my parents, but twofold, because I'm supposed to be the one protecting my sister and I've clearly done a terrible job. "Anna *needs* painting, Papa," I explain. "She needs it like we need..." I wave towards the toaster oven. "Like we need to eat food. She's not herself without it."

My dad doesn't roll his eyes at me, but I still have the impression of him doing so. Perhaps he is thinking so intensely in his mind how ridiculous I am that I can feel it. Or maybe I am imagining it because I know him too well. We'd had some similar arguments when I'd decided to make Aliyah, but in the end, he couldn't really say no. When you're a Jewish refugee, there's a special place in your heart for Israel, knowing that you can always go there if you ever have to flee. Plus, I was twenty years old and Israel paid for my ticket. It didn't matter, in the end, what he thought. Maybe that's what Anna is learning too. "It just hobby, Maria. So what, she doesn't paint a few months? School more important."

I shake my head. "Not for Anastasia. You weren't around when she was in middle school. She was so unhappy. She used to eat lunch in the bathroom, do you know that?"

My dad looks stricken. "This is gross." He crosses his arms over his chest, as if he can protect himself from this information; or maybe he is trying to look tougher than he is. It doesn't work, either way; his outfit, a loose white tank top with America written across it and plaid pajama pants, keeps the impression of toughness far at bay.

"People are cruel to kids who are smart and sensitive. You didn't grow up here, so you don't know what it's like." Here he frowns again, and I know he's about to say something like *It's all the same everywhere with kids*, but I don't let him speak. Because it's not. Not exactly. And even if it was, my dad was always popular in school. He wouldn't get it. "Without painting, she's just that girl eating lunch alone again. She'll attach herself to any distraction not to be that girl again."

I expect my dad to wave this off, but he surprises me by taking it in, absorbing it. "I did not know this," he says, almost sadly. I find him staring at a framed childhood photo of us hanging on the wall near a light switch; in it, we are both wearing bright red snowsuits and are standing outside our old apartment building in Chernovtsy. It's one of only a few pictures of my childhood that are in color, which probably makes it that more difficult to look at for him. Like he is remembering exactly how it used to be back then, at that house, in those difficult but rewarding years. Or maybe he is thinking about how much easier it was, even in the Soviet Union, to raise little kids, as opposed to grown women. With him, it could go either way.

"It's not something you really tell your parents," I explain. "Especially when they're working two jobs just to feed you."

"I did not move from Soviet Union so kids could eat lunch in bathroom," he says, a little bit irate now.

204

"Yes, I know. You also didn't move from Soviet Union so that we could wear ripped jeans or work in grocery stores," I say, giving him a knowing look.

"Okay, okay, now I am joke," he says.

"No, Papa. Not everything we do is a reflection on you. Only what *you* do is a reflection on you."

"What you saying?"

I can't believe I have to explain to him what is so clearly obvious. The man may understand math, but he does not have a clue about how people work. It's too late for our relationship to be like it once was, but maybe it's not too late for him and Anna.

"If she wants to be an artist, can't you let her try? Even if she fails at least she'll know she tried. She won't resent you for the rest of her life." Papa has such a blank look on his face I wonder again if I am accidentally speaking Hebrew. But I know I'm not. This is a different sort of mistranslation, one that has nothing to do with language. After all this time he still doesn't know how to be supportive of anyone pursuing a path that might differ from his. Clearly, he learned nothing from all of our altercations and my subsequent absence.

"If you do, I'll tell you where I think she went," I say, crossing my arms over my chest.

His eyes go wide. Now I have his attention. "You found her?"

"I found her computer." I pause, waiting to see what he says. "She left it here, didn't you notice?"

He thinks about this and shakes his head. "I never go in her room."

"No wonder you've had zero luck finding her. Have you even *tried?*" I ask. The toaster oven timer goes off and we both stare it, before I move forward and remove my dad's gross-looking frozen burrito and hand it to him. His arms drop to his sides.

"So, get to it!" he says, not taking it from me, as if he forgot what he was doing in the kitchen in the first place.

I put the burrito down on a plate, and without turning around to face him, I say, "You're not going to like this."

"I don't like any of this, so?"

"Well, I found an old conversation between her and this woman called Zoya. The one you asked me if I knew about?" I rotate to face him, and see his eyes widen in horror. "Anyway it looks like Anna might have gone to Ukraine. To, uh, Chernovtsy."

He leans his hands against the counter, letting his shoulders sag a little, like he's a balloon deflating. This is clearly not the answer he expected. What did he expect exactly? That Anna was hiding in Riverwest, still? That she'd taken a train to Chicago and we could just drive to pick her up? He probably assumed she was with her boyfriend somewhere because it was easier. And maybe she is—but I am no longer so sure.

"You're telling me Anna is in Chernovtsy?" he asks.

"Well, this was a month ago. And I'm not sure, it just kind of seemed like it...I was reading between the lines a little." I take out a cup from the cupboard next to him, and fill it with water. "Maybe you can look into it? Don't you have access to some of her accounts?"

"I do not need. I know she cannot afford."

"Can you please look anyway?" I decide not to tell him my theory on *that*. "Or you could talk to this Zoya woman. Do you know her? I would have messaged her from Anna's profile but she deleted her account so I can't write back. MySpace too. Didn't she write you too?"

"She did, but there's no way..." He starts shaking his head emphatically no. "I'm not writing her."

"What? Why? Don't you want to find Anna?" I say. "She probably went to Chernovtsy to meet her. She could be there with her right now!"

"Even if I wanted to. Which I do not. I blocked her."

My pity turns back to anger. "Papa..." I start. I think of the German word verschlimmbessern: to make something worse when trying to improve it. Though I'm not even sure where to apply it: Anastasia, or my dad? "No offense, but it seems like I'm the only one here actually trying to find Anna. This woman claimed to be your

206

daughter, and Anna may have believed her. So maybe figure out how to un-block her?"

My dad looks up at me for second, then turns back toward the counter without acknowledging that I know about his little secret now. For a man who has always advised 100% transparency, he sure doesn't practice what he preaches.

I shake my head. "No wonder Mama flew off to New Jersey," I say. "Is she...? I mean, does she...have proof?"

"She's lying, Masha."

"Papa, Anna must have a reason that she believes this girl over you."

"What can I say? She angry with me."

"You don't know Zoya's mom or anything? Wasn't she your accountant?"

"Where did you hear that?"

"I told you, I read their messages."

No explanation from my dad arrives, but I know without him telling me: he had an affair with this woman. If he hadn't, there would be no reason for Anna or my mother to listen to a stranger in Ukraine. He doesn't want to know if Zoya is his. It'll be easier to deny it that way. Or maybe he does know and isn't telling me.

"You never dated her mother?" I try again.

Papa sighs, but he doesn't say no. He looks tired, not defiant.

"But you slept with her?" I ask. He still doesn't answer, but he can't look me in the eye. I guess I don't blame him. This is the most uncomfortable conversation I've ever had, and it might be his too. Or, one of three, anyway. "Papa?"

When he still refuses to answer, everything I understand about the situation in Milwaukee changes in an instant. In all the time that I was reading their online correspondence, I didn't once consider that Zoya might *actually* be his daughter. But she could. He basically admitted it with his silence. This girl, whether or not she approached it well, could be our *family*. By Jewish law, we have to help those in need. When it's family, there's no question about it. It's a fundamental principle of Judaism, and it's the obvious moral thing to do. Even the worst Jews on earth would be able to see that. I'm telling my dad all this, but he shakes his head at me.

"Bunch of crap. This nothing to do with being Jew."

"Shtuyot b'mitz," I say.

"What?"

"That's Hebrew for 'nonsense in juice,'" I explain. "It means exactly what it sounds like."

I look at my dad, the too-bright lights above us making his face even more pale and tired-looking, to the point where for the first time in my life I realize he's an old man. In my mind, during all these years away, he was always so strong and intimidating; bigger than life. Now, I'm not so sure what he is. At best, he's a cheater. At worst, an absentee father to a poor orphaned girl. I know that despite his mistakes he is still all the other things—the doting husband, the reliable protector— but right now I'm so livid I can no longer stand being in the same room.

I turn to leave, then change my mind. I may be mad, but I still need to follow through on my search. "Actually, can I borrow your car?" I glance at the clock. I have about thirty minutes until Shabbat, so if I leave now, I can get to Milwaukee right on time.

Papa looks lost in thought and waves me off. He doesn't ask me what I need the car for, but he is clearly relieved to be done talking about Zoya, so he points to some keys hanging by the door. "Fine. Take your mom's."

208

MASHA

CHAPTER TWENTY-SIX

I arrive back in Riverwest right as the sun is setting, and park the car by Rose's house for the night. I turn the corner and head into Riverwest's very-popular tiki bar, Foundation, which is also on Bremen Street. Then I order a drink. Sure, I told myself I'd come out to look for Anna's roommates. But the truth is, I'm not sure I have any right to look for her, nor do I feel at all equipped to find her. I'm not saying I give up, but maybe I am giving up for the night. And don't I deserve a break? It's not like any of this is my fault, and my dad is barely trying to find Anna. I feel totally overwhelmed doing so much heavy lifting. And what I used to do when I felt overwhelmed was drink.

I guess I haven't changed that much after all.

I chose Foundation because Liam suggested it, but also because it's my favorite bar on the planet. I used to go to here every other day. The bartender has an actual barbell mustache, waxed on both ends. There isn't a single TV, and the tables all have little candles on them. It's like another planet. No, it's like it exists outside of time. In Foundation, it could be 1985 or 2020. As soon as I get swallowed up by the smoke and the blowfish lamps and Jim Croce singing about New York, I even start to feel a little better.

Sipping on a Mai Tai with a fun straw, I study every face that walks in the door. But no one looks familiar. I don't recognize even one person; not anyone I used to associate with, or the tattooed hipsters Anna was living with. Maybe it's harder to get a fake ID now than when I was her age. Whatever the case may be, it's a bust. I am sitting between a girl with pink hair reading a book and a middle-aged man with a motorcycle helmet, waiting to close my tab, when I see what the girl is reading: *Skinny Legs and All* by Tom Robbins. This is so Milwaukee that I can't help but comment.

"'The new American Dream is to achieve wealth and recognition without having the burden of intelligence, talent, sacrifice, or the human values that are universal,'" I tell her. "Doesn't that just totally explain reality shows?"

She looks up, confused. "Huh?"

I point at the book. "It's a line from the book you're reading," I explain.

A nervous smile replaces the confusion on her face. "Oh, sorry!" she says. "I don't think I got to that part yet."

I try again. "'The purpose of art is to provide what life does not,'" I say.

"Ah! I love that one," she says. "I think I highlighted it."

"I did too. It sounds deep, but now that I'm thinking about it, I'm not sure that it's true," I say. "Shouldn't art provide exactly what life provides, but in a different way? Like that book for example. That's life too, but presented in an orderly fashion, a story within a story, pages bound by paper and glue." I explain the word Maya, Sanskrit for the mistaken belief that a symbol is the same as the reality it represents.

The girl's eyes go wide with either surprise or discomfort, it's hard to tell. Maybe I'm talking nonsense; I don't know, I have had some powerful drinks. Then she merely shrugs, and sips her beer—something dark and frothy—and puts it back down. "I don't know. Like, I think art—or at least books—do provide something life doesn't. Like, I don't know, closure, or something?" She smiles without looking in my direction. "There's a beginning, and there's an end, and you know when both of them happen. In life, you don't remember the beginning, and you usually don't know when the end is coming. And you definitely don't get closure, about pretty much anything," she says.

Then, she turns to face me, and I see her cheeks are pink.

I nod, surprised. "I guess you have a point."

Blushing more, she adds, "Also, I love how he makes the inanimate objects characters who talk. It's so cute." She smiles again, then turns back to the book. I leave her alone this time, because who am I to bother someone who is so deep in a book they can read it at a bar? I'm just glad people still read at all. On her birthday, I used to buy Anna copies of my favorite books—*History of Love, The Unbearable Lightness of Being, One Hundred Years of Solitude*—but I couldn't get her to read a single one after she read Harry Potter in sixth grade so eventually I gave up and sent her art books instead.

I pay my tab with the cash my dad threw in my bag, and walk to Bremen to give it another shot. There isn't a show happening, so it's fairly quiet compared to my previous visit. I sit at the bar and ask the bartender for a drink. It looks like the guy who was working with Rose previously, but I can't be sure. There are so many bespectacled boys in tight pants around here they are starting to blend into each other. It must be though, because he tilts his head in recognition, as if wondering where he knows me from.

"Are you Anna's sister?" he asks.

I nearly choke on my vodka soda. "How did you know that?"

He crosses his arms over his chest and smiles proudly. "I'm good with faces." He reaches across the bar and offers me his hand. "Jared."

"Masha," I say back.

Jared shakes his head in amusement, still smiling. "You two look so alike," he marvels. "But also...not at all alike."

Broad statement as it is, I understand what he means. At first the two of us look like we could be twins, until you start to look at our faces more closely. By the end of which you're not sure if we are related at all. "How did you know my sister?"

"She used to come here every day and use the computer," he says, pointing to the aging desktop in the corner by a side entrance. "I'm not nosy or anything, but I think she was looking for art fellowships or

211

something like that."

"Really?" I ask.

Jared seems excited to have my attention. He perks up a little. "Yeah. I definitely saw her filling out forms with university names on top. I don't remember which, but it looked fancy."

"Did she ever come in with a tall guy named Tristan?"

He shrugs. "Not sure his name was Tristan, but he was definitely tall." He stops to think it over. "I couldn't tell if they were together or if he got friend-zoned. You'd think I'd be an expert."

He is certainly right about that. He seems like he's been friend-zoned a lot in his life. I can hardly believe my luck, after so much resistance for information, and I decide to take advantage of his chattiness. "Have you seen much of her lately?" I ask.

Jared shakes his head. "No. It's been a few weeks now. She got some bad news or something on the computer, then she left and never came back."

"Really?"

"Yeah, I mean, I felt kinda bad for her. She looked really sad, and she doesn't seem like the overdramatic type. I tried to give her a hug but she just kinda ran out of here." His expression changes instantly from jovial to concerned. "Wait. Is she okay?" he asks.

I swallow the rest of my drink in one gulp and place it down on the bar with a shaky hand. "I don't know." Placing a five-dollar bill on the table, I stand to leave. "I'm guessing you don't have her number?"

"I don't think she had a phone. I let her use our phone a couple times," Jared shrugs. Then, mulling it over, he adds, "Let's just say if she did, I would have asked for her digits. Your sister is a hottie, sorry."

I try not to cringe. I know my sister is pretty, but it is unnerving to hear it phrased like that and I can see why Anna didn't give him her number; he does not have the best understanding of social cues. He is also clean-shaven, nervous, and dewy-eyed, like a newborn deer. Not her type at all. "What about her roommates? Did you ever see them?"

"Only remember the tall guy. Sorry. I hope you find her."

212

As I walk to the door, I feel dizzy. Now that the last drink has settled in my stomach, I realize I'm more drunk than I thought. I sit back down on a patio chair and have the strongest sensation of falling. Something about Milwaukee turns me into my worst self. Or maybe, sometimes, you have to walk your way through a bad thing to get to a good thing. I don't know. I'm no longer thinking straight. I have a cigarette and a water from my bag and try to sober up a little, but I am not very successful. I stumble my way back to Rose's house and let myself in, heading straight for the couch.

MASHA

CHAPTER TWENTY-SEVEN

A few hours later, I am nursing a massive headache when I hear a doorbell followed by a loud banging on Rose's door. I assume it's my dad again, that he has grown impatient and didn't want to wait for me to call him. So when I go down there, I am very surprised to find Liam. In an actual coat and pants this time.

"What's up with your phone?" he asks me.

I think about this. Does he need the real explanation? I choose not to give him one. "It's dead," I say. This is not a lie, unless you count it as one by omission. Although, it is a slippery slope. This is possibly why I never came back to Milwaukee, to avoid the temptation to be bad. I am terrible at avoiding temptation, if the last day and a half is any indication. "What are you doing here?"

"Rose told me you were staying with her."

"I mean why are you banging on the door and calling my name?"

His face breaks into a grin. "You better thank me with a kiss," he says. Then, when he sees my horrified expression, he puts his hands up. "I was just kidding, Jesus. Relax. I came because I know where your sister is."

"What? For real?"

"Tao's friends are at the trainyards. They're leaving tonight."

"So she's there? She's there for sure?"

"Tristan is there. Tao saw him somewhere and they got into a huge fight about the shit he stole, which Tao lost from what it sounded like,

214

but I guess they made up because they're going together."

"Shit. What time is the train?" I ask, suddenly full of adrenaline. The blanket I had around my shoulders falls to the floor. A gust of bitter cold air rushes in and makes me shiver. Behind Liam, I notice his old white conversion van sitting impatiently in its fumes.

"I don't know, man, do I look like a crusty to you?"

"Sort of." I let my glance fall over his ripped black jeans and boots and stretched-out black t-shirt of a metal band he once drummed in.

To my surprise, Liam laughs. "Do you know how many times I tried to tell people how funny you are? No one believed me."

"Would it be online?" I ask. "The schedule?"

"No, it would not be online," he says, still laughing. "These guys guard their train manuals like gold. You better just go now and hope for the best."

My brain works quickly, despite the mix of emotions I'm now feeling; excitement, relief, anxiety, exhaustion. I remember from old friends of mine that the yard to catch a freight train is about three miles south, somewhere near Second St., past downtown. I have no idea how I am going to get there at night. I am busy trying to mentally coordinate bus schedules and cost of fares nowadays when I hear Liam clear his throat. "Fine, fine, I'll drive. Just don't ever say I never did anything for you."

Relief blooms in my chest. Maybe I hadn't been entirely crazy to like this guy. "Thanks, Liam. I mean it." I turn to grab my stuff and put on my shoes. I take my phone just in case, and a charger too. It may be dead, but it's better to have it on me. Worst case I can always find a nearby store or restaurant with an outlet to charge it. Or maybe I'm scared to be without one, like everyone else. The new adult-version of a security blanket. It's crazy how quickly you can get used to things. Not that long ago the idea of a phone you could carry in your pocket would have sounded like a trinket out of the Jetsons.

Once I'm in the hallway, and the door is locked, Liam puts an arm around me, and squeezes. I let him. "You're lucky Melanie is still

215

gone," he says. And I'm so relieved he found Anna I don't even ask him what I've slowly started to suspect: that Melanie isn't just on a weekend getaway.

That she is, perhaps, gone for good.

MASHA

CHAPTER TWENTY-EIGHT

It's after ten-thirty when we make it to the trainyards. By then my nerves are totally frayed, my heart beating into my chest so rapidly I'm unsure how Liam doesn't hear it. I'm not exactly a fan of dark, abandoned fields, or approaching groups of strangers in general, and here I am about to do both. I wish I could tell my dad the lengths to which I'm trying to help him—help Anna, really—but I know already I can never relay any of this to him. One heart attack was enough.

"You need to relax," Liam says, laughing. "They're like dogs; they can smell fear."

"Hilarious."

"Not a joke, actually."

The moon is full now and slightly ominous, the wind cold and making the van sound haunted with its wails. I continue, unsuccessfully, trying to force down my panic. "How about you come with me then?" I ask Liam, finally.

He shakes his head, grabs a cigarette out of his coat pocket. I catch a glimpse of something long and shiny tucked under his shirt—a knife maybe? Part of me wishes I'd thought to bring something like that; David would have insisted, had he been around. "This way is funnier." Then he lights the cigarette and turns off the car. "If you're not back in fifteen, I'm leaving you here."

"What a gentleman," I say, and get out of the car. I'm officially on my own.

As I walk through the field, I tell myself they're just kids wearing strange uniforms, filled with strange ideas about the world; lost, maybe, but nothing to be scared of. They're no different than those who had come before them, people I'd known and talked to. There's no reason to be so nervous! And yet, when I look down, my hands are shaking.

I slide my hands into my coat and focus on the task at hand: making it through the field without falling on my face. I don't have a flashlight, so I meander bumpily through the field to a wall of trees, beyond which, I understood from Liam, is where I would find everyone. I'm lucky there's a full moon. I can't see any train tracks nearby, but I imagine they must be close since I can hear the low rumble of cars moving slightly back and forth, as if being adjusted into place on a rail. Eventually I get far enough to hear some hushed voices. Some are laughing, others deep into conversation. I walk over more loose branches and wet leaves until finally, a group of figures emerges into my view, along with a very strong smell of something flowery mixed with smoke.

"Is that a bull?" someone asks right away, starting to get up. I almost laugh at this, that they imagine I am some hired security guard meant to find them. My night vision is so bad I can only see the shapes of things, not what they are. Or maybe that's been my problem with everything since I returned. Otherwise, shouldn't I have found my sister by now?

"It's just some girl," a man's voice answers, letting out a long cloud of smoke. From my brief experiences with drugs, it looks like they're smoking opium. I see a lighter meet the edge of a butter knife, underneath a hollowed-out milk carton. Someone moves over and puts their lips over the spout and inhales. Another person stands up and heads my way. A girl in black overalls and dreadlocks tied up in a beige bandanna. Not my sister.

"Are you lost?" the stranger asks.

Frozen in my tracks, I look around, hoping that my eyes can focus enough to find my sister's face. Or not. It will certainly be better if I don't find Anna here. Would I even recognize her in this condition? With a mess of unwashed hair instead of curls, an assortment of torn black clothes instead of purple bows and purple shoes? I'd watched her grow from adolescence into adulthood online. I knew it when I left. There is always a cost of leaving—my parents had sacrificed home and community, my grandparents had lost everything they'd ever owned and known over and over again—and being distant from my entire family, including my sister, was the cost I'd agreed, silently, to pay. It was the cost I'd *wanted* to pay. I was never going to stay in Milwaukee. If only I had stayed in touch with her more, though. Maybe I could have convinced her to join me in Israel. Standing there in the dark, surrounded by half-empty beer cans and aggressively angsty homeless youth who liked to imagine themselves vagabonds or perhaps superheroes on the right side of history, I can't help but wonder if leaving had been worth it. I'd had friends who rode trains when I lived in Riverwest, sure, but it was more of an amusing anecdote, not a decision, not throwing your life away. And none of them had ever been *junkies*.

But no, there's no point in wondering. After what happened to June, nothing on earth would have kept me in Milwaukee. For so long, until David really, who had experienced far more death than me and spent years telling me it wasn't my fault until I finally believed it, I blamed myself. It was easy to do, since everyone else had. Would I blame myself now, too? For the condition I might find Anna in?

Suddenly I hear a familiar voice call out to me, and relief blooms in my chest for a brief moment. Then it turns back into dread. Because when I turn and look towards who has called my name, my eyes fall on Tristan.

Just Tristan, no Anna.

He stands up, wiping his dirty palms on his dirty jeans, and heads my way. I find myself at a loss for words. I was so certain she would be here. There are 7,000 languages on earth (almost 1,000 of those are in Papua New Guinea alone) and yet, it's hard to find the right ones when you need them the most. There's a language in Botswana that consists almost entirely of five clicking sounds. So many options and yet we humans are constantly failing at communicating properly.

Tristan, now close enough that I can smell several weeks of non-showering on him, motions for me to meet him farther away from the group, near a cluster of trees. I follow him. He may not be my sister, but he is the closest I am getting to her at the moment.

I get straight to the point. "Where's Anna?"

"Anastasia? She's long gone," Tristan shrugs. At least this time he isn't pretending not to know who I'm talking about. This is a step in the right direction.

"Gone where?" I ask.

Tristan shrugs again, but he must know more than he's letting on. The fact that he's calling her by her Russian name clues me in that their relationship is more serious than I previously thought.

"We, uh…" he pauses, looking a little bit ashamed. "Didn't end things on a great note. Whatever. It happens."

"So you haven't spoken to her? Then why were you at my friend's house yesterday?"

He shrugs. "It's still a good idea. Your sister is hella smart," he says.

I find myself scowling at him, then fix my face. It won't help matters to show my disgust. "Yeah. Just imagine if she put that brain of hers to good use."

Tristan's eyes narrow at me. "How do you know she isn't?" he says. Then abruptly his glance falls on something behind me. I turn, and Liam is there.

I frown. "What are *you* doing?" I ask Liam, before turning back to Tristan.

"She's fine," Tristan tells me, starting to back away. "Stop looking for her. She can take care of herself."

"I can't do that," I say. "She's my sister."

He softens a little. "It's really cool how much you care about her. I wish I had someone out there looking for me," he mumbles. Then he shrugs again, backing away some more until he is almost too far to hear. "But if she doesn't want to be found, you have to respect that."

He has a point, but not one I particularly want to admit to right now. Tristan seems, despite his ragged appearance, to be a nice and loyal person. So maybe Anna isn't so confused after all. Of everything going on in Milwaukee right now, her actions appear less and less terrible the more I learn of them. Except for the stealing anyway. But everything else? My dad's appalling behavior could explain a lot of it.

Abruptly, I hear the sound of sticks breaking, and then Liam is propelling himself beyond me. He stands between us, a nervous laugh tumbling out of his mouth. "I have to give you some props," he says to Tristan. "I'm tough to surprise."

"Can you give us a second?" I ask him, annoyed that he followed me out there, after I specifically asked him, and he declined. Why did he change his mind? And right when I was getting somewhere. "Go back to the car."

"Fuck no," he says. He takes out the knife I'd seen moments earlier and points it in our direction. Tristan doesn't even blink. He must have already noticed it. He raises his hands in the air innocently.

"Is there a problem here?" He lets out an arrow of smoke and then drops the half-finished cigarette on the ground. My heart rate begins to speed up. I have to keep reminding myself this is my life, that I'm not watching a movie play out in front of my eyes. This is me in the woods at night with two angry guys who look ready for a fight. This is me using nothing but moonlight and the smallest remainder of nerves to keep standing upright.

"Yes, we have a fucking problem. I want my goddamn money back, you fucking junkies," Liam says, pointing the knife at Tristan's face in a manner that makes it pretty clear he'd never aimed a weapon at anyone before. I know from Krav Maga and watching way too many detective movies with David that someone could make one move on Liam's wrist and grab it in less than a second. More, I don't buy it. He isn't a violent person. For a moment it makes me less scared, remembering

221

this. I am level-headed enough to ask him what's going on.

Tristan sighs again. "Dude, you're really not as interesting as you think you are," he says. "Just because you were the cool guy in high school—"

"Can you put that thing down?" I ask Liam. "You don't really intend to stab this guy for twenty bucks, do you?"

Liam snorts. "More like eight hundred bucks. She took it out of the drumhead in my closet when I was sleeping." The ends of his mouth curled. "Like a *whore*."

"*She?*" I ask.

"The fuck did you call—" Tristan starts.

"Yeah, I called your little girlfriend a whore, because that's what she is," Liam says.

"What? Are you talking about Anna?"

"Her name is Anastasia," Tristan says. "She doesn't like the name Anna."

"Since when?"

"Since always."

I move on to the more important questions: "Why would you keep that much money in a drumhead?" Then, confirming my growing suspicions, I ask, "Why was she there when you were sleeping?"

Liam shakes his head at me like I'm a moron, which, maybe I am. "Why do you *think*?"

As all the information begins to settle on me, I become more and more confused. Even knowing she was stealing, I hadn't really considered *how* she was stealing. With the Craigslist scam, I assumed she would only come to people's houses and report back to Tristan if it was worth breaking into. But now it looks like she took money from people herself. It sounds like something a stranger might do, not my happy-go-lucky kid sister Anna. I'd never once imagined her being able to use people like that. Or being involved with someone like Liam, who is his own type of addict, someone she would never have a future with. He was never letting go of his open relationship doctrine, it was obvious. Not to mention Tristan and his blue hair and his train-hopping. At least Liam had a house.

More importantly, if she really is dating either guy, and they are both *here*, then where is Anna?

"You need to take your petty grievances with you and leave," Tristan tells Liam. But Liam has no intention of fleeing. While we are standing there staring at each other, out of the corner of my eye, I see Liam shift, the glean of the knife reflected by the moon; then, even faster, Tristan moves past him, until the two of them are suddenly wrestling on the ground. A second later, Tristan is sitting on top of Liam and has taken the knife out of his hand.

"Not cool, bro," Tristan says, standing up, sliding the knife into a pocket of his pants. He gazes up at me with a look I can only describe as tiredness. Tired is the last thing I am feeling. My heart is beating so fast and so loud it's like a drum. This would never happen in Israel, I think, yet again. When you fall, there are too many people there to catch you. Here, when you fall, there are only people to pull you farther down; if there's anyone at all. The nuclear family ideal has consequences.

I kneel down on the grass beside Liam, and take my bag off my shoulders. "Here," I say, reaching into my bag. "You said he owes you 800 dollars? I'll pay you back, okay? I have some money from my dad, and I can get more. It's not a problem."

Tristan looks at me, then at Liam, then at me again.

My heart is racing now. What if he decides to wrestle me to the ground too? But Tristan merely stands, flicking the dirt from his jeans onto the ground and wiping his brow of sweat.

"Tell Anna, if you find her…" he licks his lips, and stares at the ground. For a moment, I see the real version of him. The one underneath all the layers of bravado and indifference. "Tell her I'm sorry. And…tell her the money went where it was supposed to go, and she shouldn't worry."

"What money?" I ask. Did he mean the money they made stealing?

The money I thought was used to get the hell out of dodge, possibly to Ukraine? I stand up, and extend a hand for Liam.

"She'll know," Tristan says.

I help Liam up, and buy the time I turn around again, Tristan is already out of sight. The fire is nothing but smoke. I am left there with nothing but the moon and a Liam trying to catch his breath. Well. Not only did I fail at finding my sister, Liam got beat up in the process. It's really a good thing I'm not in law enforcement. I offer my old friend a pat on the back, even though part of me thinks he deserves it, pulling a knife on someone like he is in an action movie, when he is quite certainly high and has never taken one self-defense class.

"Did you really think that would work?" I ask him.

"I forgot the fucking guy was into Judo or Jiu Jitsu or whatever," he says, standing up, rubbing his chest. "Fuck. He kneed me right in the chest."

The whole thing probably took five minutes, but I know I'll be unraveling it for weeks to come. I've definitely failed at retrieving Anna, but after talking to Tristan, a small part of me *does* understand why she would go, and why she might not want anyone to know where.

If we knew, we might stop her. Now I'm not so sure I *want* to stop her.

I remember how it feels to leave with nothing but a backpack strapped to your shoulders. We aren't the type to sit in an office and click away on a keyboard for eight hours a day, like our parents, like that entire generation of Russian Jews who'd come here for a better life, always striving and striving and never being able to say *this is enough*. In Israel, nineteen-year-olds don't have the luxury to disappear, because everyone has to join the army. In Ukraine, they are generally too hungry to do anything but find jobs. But Anna and I are lucky. In America, you can do pretty much anything. Wrong or right, we are able to choose our own paths, to make them up from scratch.

I hear the flick of a lighter behind me; Liam has a cigarette in his mouth, his eyes unmistakably dark. I stare at him, taken aback by his sadness. "You really liked her, didn't you?" I ask. I finally realize it's not his girlfriend Melanie he's been mooning over since I saw him yesterday. It's Anna. No wonder he looked so surprised when I mentioned her name.

Not that he will admit it. Instead he frowns at me and starts walking back towards where he parked. "I like everyone, Masha," he says.

JANUARY 2008

JANUARY 2008

ANNA

CHAPTER TWENTY-NINE

Turns out it doesn't take all that much for me to consider stealing, once I run out of money and get used to the idea. It probably helped that I'd stolen before; if I thought I could get away with it, I'd walk right past a gas station register with a water bottle I'd already opened, or peanuts or a magazine from a booth at the airport. No one is ever paying attention at an airport. Because I am always broke, I like free stuff. But those were rare instances, small inexpensive things, small thrills. What Tristan does is different and takes more getting used to. Luckily for him, I get used to things quickly.

The first party he takes me to is in Shorewood, a cozy suburb just north of Milwaukee's east side. It's only a ten-minute bike ride from Riverwest, but it's practically another state. Every house we pass is a different level of ostentatious, and there's so much space between the houses you could fit another two or three buildings if you want to. I choose to marvel over this later, as it's barely twenty degrees and we are chilled to the bone. Parking the bikes near the garage behind some bushes, we rush inside to warm ourselves with barely a glance at the exterior. Only once we're inside do I notice how gigantic it is. It's a three-level brick mansion with nearly a dozen windows, a portico, and a view of the lake. No one I know would live in a house like this, and I am dumbfounded how there's a party with so many people my age until I notice the family photos hanging in the foyer. One of them shows a blonde, athletic-looking guy wearing a UWM shirt, flanked on

229

both sides by a very well-dressed middle-aged couple. A minute or two later, I hear someone shout: "Dude, your parents should go to Greece more often!" Then I understand.

Now that I can feel my toes again, I grab Tristan's hand and pull him into the living room, where I'm a little shell shocked by the vast amount of people and alcohol and bongs I've found myself facing. I don't move when the door opens behind us, letting in a group of giggling girls drenched in various perfumes. Tristan pulls me to the side so that they can pass us.

"Did I mention I hate parties?" I ask Tristan, my eyes wide with horror.

"Only a hundred times," Tristan laughs, giving my hand a squeeze. It calms me down, but only for a second. The place is full of people I might have gone to high school with—khaki pants with actual pockets in the sides, clean-shaven faces and hair with blonde highlights—and we stand out like sore thumbs. I try to swallow the dread that has been growing in my belly all day and meander through the crowd to get to the kitchen. A place like this has to have vast amounts of alcohol in the fridge. I'll take any kind at this point, but my fingers are crossed for vodka or rum. Instead, I only find beer. In the far back, on the bottom shelf, behind the beer, Tristan grabs me a full bottle of wine with a twist-off cap. I open it and fill a plastic cup to the brim. Then I drink it all, and refill it again.

"You look like you're gonna throw up," Tristan tells me, his eyes narrowing in concern, but his mouth twisting into a smile, like he finds it a little bit amusing. I keep drinking and shake my head.

"I never throw up."

"Really?"

"Really."

"Okay, then you look like you're gonna pass out," he adjusts. I refill my cup.

"I'll be okay," I tell him, finishing that cup too.

"How about you just watch me first. Will that make you feel better?"

I nod. I don't feel like explaining that my issue is more related to social anxiety than concern over stealing a wallet. I can't shake the feeling that I'm once again in a high school cafeteria, surrounded by people who don't notice I am there. I need time for the alcohol to work its magic, so I tell him, "Yes, actually."

Tristan gets straight to business. Not that watching does me any good. He's so fast at grabbing the wallets out of men's back pockets that I can only tell when he's stolen something because his coat is wider. By the third or fourth wallet, I've finished more than half the bottle of wine and have learned absolutely zilch. My anxiety is spiking, having to stand in the kitchen alone, so I disappear out back to smoke a cigarette with a few others. In our puffy winter jackets it's almost difficult to tell that we've come from such different worlds. It's dark, and therefore hard to notice the holes in my clothes, which I suddenly feel self-conscious about. I sit on a patio bench and finish the cigarette far too quickly, then go back inside, where I realize I've also now lost Tristan. The place is crowded, wall to wall, with belligerent students. A beer pong table has been set up on the other side of the room, and a group of the drunkest students are playing against each other. Several people are making out, not even bothering to go into a room.

Suddenly, someone is touching me, and I nearly jump out of my skin. I turn to find Tristan.

"There you are," I say, breathing a sigh of relief. I feel his arms wrapping around me from behind. I feel him slide the wallets from his hand into my bag. To the left of us, I watch a group of men yelling "Chug! Chug! Chug," while a girl swallows beer from a plastic funnel.

"They won't even feel it, losing fifty bucks. For us, that's food. To them, it's a manicure."

My heart flutters with nerves. Now that the time has come to emulate him, I no longer feel so lighthearted about it. "I don't think I can do this," I whisper in his ear.

Tristan kisses me again. "You can do anything," he says. No one has ever said this to me before and it makes me a little bit giddy. It makes me want to prove him right. That, combined with the stream of alcohol I'd just imbibed, sends a brief surge of temporary calm into my system. Maybe I really can do it. Tristan is right. These people will barely notice the absence of twenty, thirty dollars, and for me, that's lunch for a week.

I finish the rest of my wine in one gulp. "Do you think they will know it was me?" I ask.

"Nah. You look like a college student. You look like one of them," he says.

"Not to them I don't."

Tristan slaps my butt. "See? Use that anger. It'll make you less nervous."

"Who said I was angry?"

"Aren't these the same fuckers who made you sit in a bathroom for lunch?"

"I really wish I hadn't told you that."

"I don't. I want to know you."

I almost smile, hearing him say that. He is really quite sweet for a criminal. Considering his upbringing, it demonstrates a lot about his nature. As an attempt to procrastinate, and pretend we are here as nothing but partygoers, I ask him, "Where did you eat lunch at school?"

"I didn't." Tristan leans against the granite countertop of the kitchen island and crosses his arms over his chest. "If I went to school, I was usually shooting up by lunch somewhere. In my car, likely."

"Oh," I say, sadly. "I keep forgetting you were so...into drugs."

"You don't have to worry," he says, licking his lips. "Those days are behind me."

"I know." I expand my focus to the rest of the party again, and my glance lands on a bright yellow purse that's been left on the floor. It's sitting next to a six-pack and a stack of winter coats worth more than a year's worth of rent. For a moment I try to imagine myself walking by and taking it, as casually as if it was my own. But this image is replaced by another one—being chased down the road by an angry mob of perfectly tousled blonde hair. I start to second-guess my ability to pull this off.

"I'll be right here," he says, and that's all I need. Where is everyone else who promised the same? Nowhere to be found. Tristan means what he says, and he cares about me. Whenever I'm around him I feel like I can be myself, and I've never had that feeling before in my life. It feels like freedom. And sure, it comes with certain costs. But I like trying new things. Generally, going out of my comfort zone is more exciting than scary.

Plus, the people here are so drunk; it's the perfect setting to make a first attempt at theft. If I get caught, I can claim it was an accident, that I mistook the purse for my own. I take a long breath. I let go of Tristan, then stride across the room. My heart is beating into my chest like I've just run a mile. When I reach the purse, I swallow the knee-jerk inclination I have to look around and make sure no one is watching. Instead, I try to be cool. I bend over like I'm tying the laces of my all-black converse shoes. Then, rather than take the entire purse, I reach into the bag and feel around for a wallet. Soon my fingers land on a smooth pleather pouch filled with coins, cash, and cards. I snap the pouch closed, slide it into my right coat pocket, and stand up. I'm not as fast as I would like, but I'm fast enough. No one seems to notice anything; I don't feel anyone watching me or hear anyone screaming for me to stop. Immediately I cross the threshold back into the foyer and, seeing some stairs, practically run to the top of them.

Tristan is only a few seconds behind me. He pins me against the wall of the hallway, and starts kissing me.

"That was dope," he says, smiling.

My heart is pounding so hard I feel it in my ears. But I'm also totally energized. Is this how Tristan feels when he's doing drugs? I wonder. "Did anyone see me?" I ask him.

"No. You did great," he says. He kisses me again. My body is full of adrenaline now, but also something else. Not guilt. Relief. Excitement.

233

I'd actually gotten away with it. And possibly solved my money problems at the same time. At least, temporarily. I drag Tristan by the arm into a closed bedroom on the second floor and try to catch my breath. As happy as I am to have my freedom, I would like to continue to have it. All I want to do now is hide.

"Did we get enough stuff?" I ask. "Can we go?"

"We can go whenever you want," Tristan explains, lying down on the bed. "Fuck this is comfortable. How much do you think this bed costs?"

"I'm really bad at that game."

"More than a grand, I can tell you that much for sure."

"Who pays more than a *grand* for a bed?" I ask, but of course, I know the answer to this question. Rich people. They spend money on expensive items just so other people can see they were able to afford it. Why else do all my aunts and uncles need three-bedroom homes in the suburbs when none of them have any children left in the house?

Out in the hall, I hear a duo of drunk girls trying to find the bathroom. One of them opens the door to see us standing there, mouths an O of surprise, then closes it with a giggle. I get up to lock the door and return to sit by Tristan, who is taking his shoes off and making himself comfortable.

"See? I told you it would be easy," Tristan says triumphantly, running a finger up and down my arm. "No one would ever suspect you."

"It's only because they're wasted." I look down at my outfit; ripped black jeans, black t-shirt, thick black down coat. Even my hair is so dark it's almost black. The girls who not two seconds ago saw us in there were half glitter and one hundred percent fake tan. "I don't exactly blend in."

"Have you ever gotten a compliment before in your entire life? Jesus, girl," Tristan laughs. "You did a good job."

He starts to pull off my coat, the inside nearly stuck to my arms from sweat from the heat of the house. It doesn't seem like he is in any hurry to leave. Since no one is out there chasing us down, I figure it's okay. I'm also weirdly turned on by the whole endeavor, my adrenaline still spiking and causing my entire body to buzz. I roll on top of him and we start to make out. Having spent the last few nights on an acquaintance's couch, Tristan and I haven't exactly had any alone time together. I'm hoping this little escapade will give us enough money to get a hotel, or a temporary sublease for a room. Or a ticket out of Milwaukee. Anything.

"Do you think we got enough? Should we find a checkbook or something?" I ask Tristan, between kisses.

"We're good." He flips me around so that I'm under him in one seamless move. "You're sexy when you talk like that."

I let out a nervous giggle. "What was I before? Hideous?"

"No," he says, taking off my pants. "I've been wanting to do that all day."

It doesn't take long for us to be fully undressed.

Afterward, we make a quick exit down the stairs. Sobering up from both the wine and the adrenaline, I can't help but steal a glance at the purse I'd stolen from, and am relieved to find it hasn't moved. That's good. Whoever left it there, she won't know yet that anything is gone. She probably won't notice until morning, if she's as drunk as everyone here looks. Because I'm feeling confident, I even grab one of the North Face coats on the table as I walk past so I won't freeze on the way home. Now I focus on leaving. The kitchen is so packed with bodies the windows and glass patio doors are starting to steam. A boombox is playing a rap song I've never heard before. A large group of frat guys keep themselves busy tapping a keg in the middle of the room.

Tristan nods his head toward one of the guys near the keg, which I take to mean he's going to swipe his wallet too, so I stop at the fridge and search inside for the rest of the wine bottle I'd started. I've only ever had boxed wine, so my standards may be low, but it's the most amazing wine possibly ever made and I wouldn't mind some more.

Quickly, I grab the bottle and close the door. I'm in such a hurry I slam it too hard, and cause a note to fall from the fridge to the floor. I pick it up and try to put it back in place with a magnet. Then I notice the entire door is covered in sticky notes. In the middle of them all, there's a big calendar of the month of December, with every Tuesday and Friday circled in red. The note beneath it says, "Don't forget to feed Frida." Below that, there's a photo of a cat. And the numbers 1416.

Right as I get the note back in its place, Tristan pulls on my arm. "Time to go," he says. He drags me forward and pushes me toward the door. Not the front door, where we first came in, but a side door that leads to a laundry room and then opens into the garage. From behind us, I am pretty sure I hear a woman shout: "Oh my godddddddd! Where's my wallet!" Another voice shouts, "I bet it was that shady-looking elf!"

When I hear this, my knees become so weak I think I might fall over. But I don't have time to fall over, because Tristan is pressing the garage door button and breaking into a run, still holding my hand. I follow him blindly, skirting the edge of the house back toward the bushes where we'd left our bikes. Just as we're mounting the seats, three or four girls begin pouring out the front door, pointing in our direction. But they are drunk, and we are fast. We are already pedaling. Their shouts disintegrate into the cold winter air. We don't slow down till we've biked several miles down Lake Drive, back into Milwaukee, where we belong.

ANNA

CHAPTER THIRTY

It's my idea to break into the mansion in Shorewood. Between the calendar and the notes I discovered on the fridge, I am pretty sure that the place is unoccupied, except for the two days a week that the only child of whoever owns the place arrives to feed the cat. Tristan thinks it's too risky, but he says he is open to convincing. It takes me a few tries, but eventually, I persuade him to bike up to Shorewood with me and watch the place around midday so I can show him it's okay. We park our bikes across the street, in the thick enclave of dead trees that line the other side of the road.

"What are we looking at?" he asks me.

"You'll see," I tell him. I lean my bike against a dead tree and sit down on a dry patch of leaves. "Sit down. It might be a while."

"Okay, lady. You're the boss." Tristan sits and we both light cigarettes, watching the smoke blend into the clouds of air coming out of our mouths. It's not as cold as the night we came for the party, but it's not far above twenty degrees. "What's going on with that half-sister of yours?" he asks. He puts sister in air quotes. "Have you heard from her?"

"Yeah. She keeps asking me to take that DNA test."

"Are you going to?"

"I don't see how it would help her or my dad," I shrug. "It's not enough to get her to Israel."

"Hm."

I poke him in the side. "What?"

"Nothing."

"What, Tristan? Tell me."

"I just…I can't see her letting it go," he says.

"Maybe not," I admit. I take another long inhale. "It's getting kind of annoying actually. Now that I don't have a computer, I can only check my accounts at the desktop at Bremen, and it's not like I have all the time in the world to go there."

"So you're ignoring her," he says. He starts shaking his head. "I told you not to do that."

"I have more pressing issues. Like where are we going to live?" A white van slows down in front of the house next to the mansion. I perk up. "There! Watch this!"

"I know you don't believe me, but this girl is conning you," Tristan says, keeping his gaze on the road.

I roll my eyes. "You think everyone is conning everyone." I point ahead. "Are you seeing this?"

"Everyone *is* conning everyone. In some way or another," Tristan says. But he follows my gaze across the street. Right as I'd suspected, the mail van skips the mansion and continues to the next building, another multi-level brick home with a balcony, and a matching large white fence wrapping around its lawn.

"What does that prove?" he asks me. We both watch as the postman sticks his hand out of his window and deposits a stack of papers into the box at the end of the driveway—I'm reminded again that we are no longer in the city, where the mailboxes are by the front door and require post office employees to walk through every kind of weather Wisconsin has to throw at them.

"They have a mail hold," I explain. "It was the same thing yesterday."

"Maybe they didn't have mail yesterday," he says. He takes off his hat and itches his thick head of hair, then begins to make a series of little jumps into the air. Now that we've been off the bikes for a while, the sweat we accumulated biking is making it feel even colder. I pedal my feet up and down, trying to get the feeling back in my toes, but I'm wearing a pair of ripped converse shoes, so it does no good. I may as well be wearing nothing at all.

"I checked the nearby mailboxes; everyone got the same coupons from Sendik's yesterday. Plus, like I said: I heard someone at the party say they were in Greece."

Tristan stops staring at the mail truck and turns to give me a look I still have to get used to seeing: one of awe. "Your brain is sexy," he says, lifting his eyebrows. Will I ever get tired of hearing this phrase? My whole life it has felt like my brain has been a nuisance. My peers either get jealous or don't fully understand my meaning or intentions, my parents use it as an anchor to force me into an education I don't want. It definitely didn't please my teachers to have their assignments questioned and analyzed.

Tristan blows into his hands then crosses his arms across his chest. "But what if the kid comes over unexpectedly?"

"Then we climb out the window," I say, pointing at the row of windows on the first floor. In addition to the bottom windows, there are more the next flight up. "Or jump," I add, pointing at one of the patio couches, a teal and brown one with clear plastic over it.

"All right," Tristan shrugs. I thought it would take more convincing, but Tristan has a bad back. Sleeping on an actual bed appeals to him more than the danger of it scares him. Once I found myself asking him how he's been managing on-and-off homelessness all these years with a bad back and turned to find him miming a needle to the arm. That put an end to the questions for a while. I didn't like that he had the same answer to every one. His past filled me with awe but it also scared me.

"Let's head out," Tristan says. "I want to come back tomorrow to make sure the mailman skips the house again."

The following day, he gets his confirmation, and around sunset, we park our bikes in a small cluster of trees behind the house and get to

239

work finding a way into the back door. Normally, in Milwaukee, I'd be wary of neighbors, but a house in a suburb is—for once—an ideal location. The houses are spread out, and since people in the suburbs love to pretend they're in nature, a burst of trees and wild vines or flowers extend between almost every yard. Standing next to the back door, we survey the landscape to the left and right of the raised deck, and are relieved to find you really can't see anything but trees. Plus, it's now dark, and there are no streetlights anywhere close by. All we have to guide us is the half-moon in the sky and a pocket flashlight attached to Tristan's keys. There is the problem of actually getting into the house, though. Tristan starts looking under pots and rocks near the patio door.

"Most people hide a spare key somewhere," he explains. I had assumed we would go through a window, but this is a better idea, I have to admit. Except that there are a lot of places to look. The patio is adorned with an array of knickknacks and potted plants, trees, flowers. "Try the front door. Under the mat."

I stumble over the paved pathway in total darkness, grazing the brick of the house with my hand for balance, until I reach the front of the house. I expect a long exploration to commence but I find the key almost right away, under a turtle statue next to the welcome mat. I find my way back to the patio, where Tristan is still bent over, looking, and hand him the key. He grins at me.

"Nice job, Nancy Drew," he says, opening the back door. I am half expecting someone to catch us as we enter the house, but the place is empty, as I had thought. I reach for the light switch and the giant chandelier in the foyer flickers on, illuminating the perfect wood floors, oriental rugs, and grand staircase. Someone must have come to clean it after the party, too, because the place is spotless; not an empty beer can to be found.

The second we put our bags down, an alarm begins beeping.

"Shit," Tristan says, picking up his bag again. "I told you this is a bad idea."

I hold up a finger. Without a word, I turn to look at the walls on either side of the door. I locate the alarm system pad next to the front door and type in the numbers I saw written down on the fridge: 1416. The alarm shuts off. Tristan looks at me with awe.

"Soon you'll be better at this than I am," he says.

"No," I say, shaking my head. "I just notice things."

"What do you think makes a good criminal?" he jokes. He puts his bag down on the floor, and lifts mine off my back and places that on the floor too. Then he carries me into a bedroom, a different one than the one we'd discovered at the party, and drops me on the bed like we're newlyweds. This one is a huge king size with a tufted royal blue headboard and sheets so soft they feel like silk. They probably are silk, I later realize. It's nicer than a hotel room. The bed is made military style, not a crease or unfolded edge. Tristan pulls off the comforter in one grand sweep and places me inside.

"Did I mention how sexy your brain is?"

"Only every day." He kisses me again, and for a while, I forget about everything.

Afterward we both take showers at the same time—there are four showers on the first floor alone—and luxuriate on one of the couches watching bad TV for the rest of the day. I find a stash of wine in the basement and by the second night we've made quite a dent. We don't dare venture outside, other than to smoke in the closed garage, enjoying the warmth and luxury of furniture that probably costs more than my parents' entire home. We drink and watch TV and take tons of showers and sleep, as if we are on vacation. The following day is Friday, however—which means we will need to be out before dawn, since there is no way of knowing when the student will come by to feed the cat. I spend several hours beforehand cleaning, a sad attempt to make it look like no one has been there since the party. I don't think I do a very good job. I've always been good about organizing and keeping things neat, but I almost never mop or wipe counters and keep imagining I am missing something that must be right out of sight.

Margot was always getting mad at me that my room was spotless but I never remembered to wash my dishes, and didn't know where the broom was. But Tristan tells me it looks great, so I choose to believe him.

After helping myself to coffee from the automatic espresso machine in the kitchen, I find Tristan in one of the bedrooms, counting cash. "How much money do we have?" I ask.

He doesn't look up. "Almost five hundred dollars. Those frat boys really love to carry cash on them. I bet they were planning to score some coke or E for that party."

I let out a little whistle. Despite spending half my life living in a middle-class home, I've never seen that much money at once. Between the house and Tristan and the cash, I'm feeling pretty good right now. I'm feeling better than before my life got derailed, somehow. It makes me wonder: What's the point of following all the rules, when people still find ways to make you feel bad? Better to just do what you want and not listen to anyone. There is a freedom to making all of your own decisions, whether or not they are good or bad, that cannot be explained without real life experience. Had I known all of that, I might have made some changes far sooner. "Nice. Should we spring for a hotel?"

Tristan still doesn't look up, just deposits the envelope into his bag.

"Not with this," he says. He stands up, shoving the envelope into his back pocket. "You ready to go?"

I nod. "You go first, so I can set the alarm again. So as not to arouse any suspicion." I bite my lip, looking at his back pocket, the envelope still in there. "Where are you sending that money?"

He shakes his head. "Don't worry about it."

"But…" I pause, feeling nervous suddenly. "I thought that was both of ours."

"You'll get your half. I promise," he says. He reaches into the envelope and takes out two twenties, handing them to me. "Here, that'll hold you over for now." Then he grabs our bags and heads out the back door without further explanation.

We don't talk for the entire bike ride, and when we arrive back in Riverwest, Tristan says he has an errand to run and leaves me by the door of Bremen Café, alone. "I'll be back in a couple hours," he says, then disappears down Bremen, towards Humboldt Avenue.

I lock up my bike and head inside, using the cash Tristan gave me to buy a breakfast bagel with eggs and cheese, a pack of cigarettes, and another coffee. Then, since I have nothing better to do, I sit down at the desktop computer near the side entrance to use the Internet. Bremen has two desktop computers with internet that any customer can use. Most people own laptops, and this will likely become redundant enough to remove within a year or two, but for now it's a lifesaver, since I left all my things at my parents' house and haven't returned since.

I begin by looking for an apartment sublease; but there is nothing in my price range of almost no money, not even one with the five hundred dollars Tristan disappeared with, so next I begin searching jobs on Craigslist. Sure, I had stolen one wallet, and broken into someone's home. But I'm not intending to *continue* going to parties and stealing wallets. Surely I could find a job, at least a temporary one till I figure out what my next move is. It wouldn't even have to be in Milwaukee necessarily. It could be in Chicago. The Greyhound to Chicago is only ten dollars. I could swing that. The problem is that after an hour of searching, I don't find anything I am qualified for that doesn't pay minimum wage or sound horribly soul-killing. The closest thing to real money would be cleaning apartments, and even that is only $12 an hour to start. I even check if anyone needs Russian or English tutoring, but there's not much demand for foreign language skills in Milwaukee. Only a couple of ads requesting Chinese lessons.

I take a break from this depressing endeavor and head to MySpace.

Ignoring the several apologetic and concerned messages I've received from Margot, I open a second browser window and login to my Facebook. I want to check in with Zoya. But Zoya's accounts on both Facebook and MySpace have been deactivated. Strangely this doesn't sound any alarm bells in my head. I figure there must be some kind of technical issue on her end. But then I log in to my university email.

In between some notices from UWM about my lack of securing payment for the next semester resulting in my temporary suspension from school, there are a few new emails from Zoya. The first one is dated yesterday.

"*Hey, sistreechka,*" it says. "*I don't appreciate the 'cold shoulder,' as they say in America. We are running out of time.*"

The following email is less nice. I will spare you the colorful language. The basic summary of it is that if my dad doesn't take the DNA test and acknowledge her as a daughter for her Israeli immigration application, Zoya would sue him for eighteen years of child support. I don't know if that's legal—or an option—here in the US, but my first reaction is only that it doesn't sound like her to write something like this. I should have expected it, but I'm still in total shock. This isn't what we agreed to. Even if she didn't have a chance of winning, it would destroy his marriage, and possibly his whole life. I scroll down the end of the page, my heart in my throat.

"*We can avoid all this if you just have him sign the attached letter acknowledging he's my father. Of course, if he sends me $5,000 for moving expenses, I can be convinced to let it go. Or you can send it; I really don't care. But I will not be ignored any more. If I don't get either the signed letter or the money within one month of this email, I will tell everybody what your family has done to me. Including your mother. And a lawyer. Then we can let the court decide how much money I am owed.*"

This message, so different in tone than her previous correspondence to me, sends a shiver through my spine. Tristan was right. Zoya had been conning me. Was that whole mix-up with the DNA test a lie? Our friendship? Was that too a lie? I reach into my new pack of cigarettes and light one, hoping it will soothe my spirits, which had been so high before, in the cloud of seclusion I'd created. That's all gone now. Where had Tristan gone with our money? What does Zoya intend to do? I can't let her destroy my parents' lives. Not when the whole thing is my fault. I'd been duped, not my dad. I would need to get her the money somehow, I realize. And that much money in so little time? I couldn't exactly go the legal route. I would need to use my overactive brain to get us out of this mess without any more people being hurt. I sit there and smoke and think for what feels like a very long time. I consider all the ads I saw on Craigslist, and everything Tristan has told me about his past, and an idea starts to form in my mind. With a sigh, I click on the email and open a new message to reply.

"*Zoya. Leave my parents alone. I will get you the money.*"

ANNA

CHAPTER THIRTY-ONE

I know from the calendar in the Shorewood mansion that whoever lives there will return in a matter of days, and I have no other leads of places to sleep, so after the first home I "clean," a nice condo in Bayside, I tell Tristan we need to find a better solution. This is when I discover Tristan already has an apartment. Turns out the place he told me about when we first met, where he was staying with friends, was really only one friend, a bartender named Chris who was leaving town for the entire month of January. Tristan said we could have been staying there the entire time, but that it was more fun to see what I came up with. I found this revelation bothersome, but chose to ignore it, because I was so relieved.

I expect some dank, dirty studio loft without a real kitchen and am happily surprised to find it otherwise. In reality, it's a two-bedroom apartment at the outskirts of Riverwest, just past a new park that was an abandoned concrete slab of graffiti only months earlier. The apartment is astonishingly modern for Riverwest; it has brand-new hardwood floors, two large, open living rooms, and a kitchen with recently installed granite countertops and new wooden drawers and cabinets. Chris the bartender is apparently also Chris the carpenter. He'd refinished the entire place after it became an abandoned warehouse. There are even built-in bookshelves and bike hooks where we can hang our bikes; a far cry from the hobbled-together assortment of furniture at my former apartment, where every couch and armchair were a different color and material, and we had more art supplies than dishes. This place is actually nice.

For a while it is easy to imagine we are a normal couple living together. We get into a good rhythm. I meet with my potential "clients," clean their homes, and report back to Tristan if I see anything worth taking. If there is, I set up a time to meet for our lessons at the Alterra in Bayshore Mall, because the parking lot is such a nightmare there it gives Tristan and me a good cushion of time to prepare an exit strategy. Having the actual stealing happen out of sight is a nice perk, and leaving the homes spotless alleviates some of my guilt, though I don't really feel as bad as I thought I would. Because Tristan is right: rich people have insurance. It's really the insurance companies we are hurting. These billion-dollar industries can afford a few hundred dollars' loss.

The one thing I don't know and don't care to know is how and where Tristan sells most of the valuables he finds. It's easy to remain ignorant; all you have to do is not ask. It takes us only a few weeks to amass four thousand dollars, which is good, because Zoya hasn't stopped checking in and I know can't hold her off for much longer. I also understand this scheme can't go on forever—Milwaukee is small, and people talk. I try to change my hairdo and clothing style every time I go clean, but there's no changing my face. Sometimes I wear huge earrings or a bandanna, other times I go in khakis and polo shirts I buy from Goodwill. Only once, when I didn't have time to change, did I go wearing my own clothes. This was probably a mistake.

Another problem is Tristan's ego. Correction: his restlessness. Once he's enjoyed a couple of weeks of freedom to read and drink as much as possible, he begins to get so antsy that I become antsy too, even when there's no reason for it. His energy is just that encompassing. Now it's not enough for him to break and enter; he wants to do more, go bigger.

"What's bigger than stealing from rich people?" I ask him, rolling over in bed one morning after he's brought it up yet again. The sun is bursting inside through the slats of the window blinds, illuminating the mess that has taken the room hostage. I may attempt to be a neat person, but Tristan does not; because we have no furniture for the bedroom, besides the mattress, I suppose I can't really blame him for leaving clothes and empty food bags on the floor, but it's still unpleasant to look at. At first, I tried to maintain some order, but it soon became apparent that cleaning the place would be a full-time job. Now I really try to avoid the apartment as much as I can when I'm not asleep. Tristan is the opposite; after so many years of traveling and couch-surfing he is elated to spend most of his time in bed smoking cigarettes and reading Joseph Campbell or taking naps. Well, he was. Now he spends all his time inventing new schemes for us.

Tristan reaches for his pack of cigarettes and lights one. "There's this guy I know," he says, blowing out smoke.

"You want to steal from a guy you know?"

Tristan circles his hand in the air. "Well, *knowing* is relative, right?" he says. He takes another long, intense drag of his American Spirit. "He's not a friend. He sells shit."

"Sells what?"

Tristan makes a point of looking out the window, which is framed by an inch of snow and sleet. Down below, a couple with a stroller is walking south down Meinecke screaming incoherently at each other. "Uh, you know. Coke, acid, shrooms. Whatever."

I sit up abruptly. "What?"

"It's whatever. He's so out of it he keeps his cash at home. He's basically asking for someone to take it."

"You want to rob a *drug dealer*? You are not allowed to say 'whatever' again during this conversation." I get out of bed, looking for my pants. "Is that where you went the other day?" I ask, thinking of his recent disappearance. "Did you buy drugs?"

"I know where he stashes his money," Tristan says, ignoring me. "How many more necklaces do you think I can sell? These suburban fucks keep all the real money in safes and banks. This guy, he doesn't trust technology. He's one of those, uh what are they called? Doomsday preppers. He has so much cash he doesn't know what to do with it. He wouldn't even notice if we took some."

"I'm not going to steal from a drug dealer, Tristan." I say. "That's insanely stupid."

"Why? It's not like he can call the cops."

"There are worse things he could do if he catches us." I finish getting dressed, and grab my bag so I can leave. I don't want to entertain this idea any longer. "You can go without me if you want, but, uh, no."

Tristan gets out of bed, following me towards the door in nothing but his tattoos and a thin pair of old boxers. He grabs a hold of my arms and looks me in the eye. "I promise you won't have to do anything. You'll just act like you want to buy something. I'll go pretend to use the bathroom, but I'll really be in the closet getting the money."

"Why do you need me for that? You can take anyone."

"You have a trustworthy face."

He is right; I do have a trustworthy face. At least I did before I started hanging around with Tristan. I break eye contact and turn to look for my coat, which I find a moment later underneath a stack of boxes.

"Trust me, we do this one thing right and we'll be set for the rest of the year," he says, practically jumping up and down on his toes now. There's a spark in his eyes I haven't seen since we first started our craigslist scheme, and I know it's careless, but I can't help but want to say yes. I've never been good at saying no to people. He takes me in his arms and squeezes me tight, like precious goods.

"After this, we'll be done. You can pay Zoya, and we can get an apartment, if you want…or you know what? We can take the money get the fuck out of here. I'm getting sick of this town. What are we waiting for?"

I have to admit I like the sound of that. I've been getting sick of Milwaukee, too. The weather alone is enough to send anyone packing this far into winter, and now I have no friends to go out with, no classes to attend. Really, the only thing keeping me around anymore, besides getting Zoya's money, is my grandparents. And even though I'm not speaking with my parents at the moment, the thought of leaving them too has been an anchor wrapped around my leg. But I can't stay here forever because of it, I know that. "I really just have to stand there and pretend to buy something?"

Tristan's mouth spreads into a wide grin. He kisses me. Then he says, "You'll need to actually buy something."

"Oh. Like weed? I guess I can do that."

"This guy doesn't sell weed."

I give him a knowing look. "Are you sure it's a good idea to go to a house full of drugs?"

Tristan waves his hand in the air like its nothing. "I'll be fine," he says, kissing me on the cheek. He goes back to the mattress and lies down, adjusting the two pillows I grabbed from my parents' house behind his neck and starting his cigarette again.

"I don't know, Tristan," I say again. It's one thing to steal from an empty house, but quite another to risk being caught, let alone by a drug dealer. "I don't think it's a good idea. I have a bad feeling."

He grabs his book from next to the bed and opens it. Then he looks up again, annoyed. "Didn't we already agree on this? What else is there to talk about?"

I look at him, sitting half naked in the bed like he doesn't have a care in the world, and I can't help but wonder if this is the man I fell for, or if he has been hiding behind a gentler version of himself this entire time. When we'd met, he seemed so stable. He had quit everything; not just drugs but alcohol and cigarettes too. Eventually the cigarettes came back, followed by the alcohol. Had he returned to drugs, too, without my noticing? It's not like we spend every second together. I'm not the jealous type, so I don't generally monitor his whereabouts.

Maybe I should.

I close the door without arguing more, and head out to linger around Riverwest with my sketch pad like I normally do nowadays.

But all day long the feeling of dread grows in my stomach. Not the nervous kind, like when we went to the party and stole wallets, but the kind that tells you not to do something, if you only care to listen. Tristan doesn't believe in premonitions, or fate, so it's no use sharing the information with him.

When I get back from Gordon Park, where I'd been sketching a dog playing fetch in the grass, Tristan is already dressed and outside, like he'd been watching for me out the window. He hands me a roll of bills and slaps my butt till I get on my bike and follow him. We bike all the way down Center Street, passing a show at Valhalla and several groups of smokers at Mad Planet. We keep biking past Holton for several blocks, then turn left on Martin Luther King Drive and head south. I've never gone this far into the "hood," and the further out of Riverwest and into Harambee we go, the more my pulse drums in my ears.

The feeling of dread intensifies when we get to the house on MLK drive. The duplex, a green and brown Polish flat like much of Riverwest, looks at first like any other house around. Until you get closer and notice the windows are boarded up, the front porch is caving in, and there are three German Shepherds barking at us from the backyard. The only thing separating us from them is a thin dilapidated fence. Outside on the steps several Latino teenagers in baggy clothes are smoking cigarettes and drinking forties. One of them nods to Tristan in greeting.

"Tristan," I say, gripping my bike handles tight. There is no part of me that wants to get off my bike and go into that house. "I don't like this. It's a bad plan. A *really* bad plan."

"Anastasia, don't be racist," he says. He hops off his bike and motions for me to do the same. I stare at him and don't move, other than to take off my hat. He ruffles my hair. "I'm just kidding. You gotta relax."

"Oh, yes, please tell me how I need to relax. That totally always works."

251

Tristan places his arms on both my shoulders and blinks. "No matter what happens, I'm going to protect you," he says, serious for the first time since he came up with this horrible idea. "You don't need to worry about that. Just take a breath."

I take a breath. Then I take two more. Then I force my legs to move and release the bike. We lock them to a nearby pole with a "no parking" sign attached to the top, which is a little loose in the cement and could likely be taken out if someone has the energy or wherewithal to do it. I can only hope no one does have the energy, because I will need to get out of here way faster than my nervous legs would be able to take me. And we are now at least a mile from Riverwest, if not more.

"It'll be over in no time," Tristan says into my ear. He even kisses my neck softly, right where he knows I like it. "Just do what we said."

I nod, but my breath comes in short and choppy, and my body is filled with panic in a way it hasn't ever been before this night. I squeeze his hand tight, like he's a life jacket and I'm lost in the ocean. The dogs start barking more incessantly the closer we get to the door, and one of them is tall enough to reach its snout over the fence and snarl at me.

I push my body into Tristan's, even though trying to hide is useless. Soon there is someone at the door. A thin, tattooed man with half his head shaved and the other half black and down to his ear. He is wearing a leather coat and baggy black jeans, and I can't make out if he's a punk or in a gang or both. "Hey," he tells Tristan, then opens the door wide to let us in, but not wide enough that I don't have to squeeze past him and smell his peculiar mix of sweat, cigarettes, and cologne.

There are more dogs inside, a boxer and a lab, sitting on one of the couches. They don't look up when they see us. I have to bite my lip to hold in my shock. I've seen punk houses plenty of times, but I've never seen a drug house, and they may as well be different planets of disarray. From where I stand, I can count three or four dirty mattresses without any sheets scattered about the bedrooms, and even more couches and armchairs that look like they've been snatched out of the junkyard then repeatedly beaten with sticks. There are empty pizza cartons filled with cigarettes and circular pieces of cardboard with old cheese stuck on, an array of empty soda bottles and cans that would make a recycling aficionado burn with delight, except that they are also filled with old cigarette butts. It probably goes without saying that the smell is enough to knock me out.

"This your girlfriend?" asks an olive-skinned, very tattooed pot-bellied man who Tristan introduces as Santiago. He coughs, clearing his voice of its phlegm, without covering his mouth, and doesn't get up from where he sits between the dogs. "Shitttt. Nice job," he tells Tristan with an approving nod to my chest, his voice thick with an accent and possibly a massive amount of marijuana or pain killers. His eyes are red and half-closed like he could fall asleep at any moment.

"Uh, yeah, thanks," Tristan responds, trying to brush it off.

Santiago stands up and reaches for my hand, then kisses it. "How may I be of service, miss lady?"

I swallow the lump in my throat and try not to scream, which is what I feel like doing when his skin touches mine. Instead I reach into my pocket and hand over a rolled-up wad of bills that I know amounts to a hundred dollars. So that he doesn't notice my hand is shaking I shove it quickly into his grasp and clear my throat. "Two eight balls and a quarter of mushrooms," I say. "Thank you," I add afterward.

"Polite lady, I like it." The man nods approvingly, pocketing the cash and nodding at a third man, a tall and skinny one in plaid who is sitting on a different couch with yet another dog. He gets up and heads into a back room.

"She's Russian," Tristan says, out of nowhere. I look at him, surprised, then back at Santiago, whose eyebrows are raised, then down at the floor. I just want this to be over. But Santiago asks me to sit down on the fraying corduroy couch next to him and I have no choice but to go.

"Russian, eh?" he asks me, reaching across the couch to cut up some lines of a white powder already lying on a silver platter among the old soda cans and bongs. "Any wise guys in your blood? Those fuckers are brutal."

I lick my lips, take another big breath. "Not that I know of," I say. "I do have an uncle who looks like Al Capone. People are always giving him better seats at places."

"Ha!" Santiago says, almost smiling. He slaps his knee. "Fucking A. Other day I see a program about those spies back in the day, what you call them?"

"The KGB?"

He points at me and smiles. "Yeah, those fucking guys." Then he shakes his head and repeats what he said before. "Brutal." For a moment I think the guy isn't half bad. But then he snorts a line of the powder up his nose with a rolled-up bill, and when he's done, points at Tristan. "On the house, dude."

"Oh, no, I'm good," Tristan says.

"Come on," Santiago says. "It ain't fun to party alone. Get the fuck over here."

"Nah," Tristan repeats.

Santiago now eyes us both suspiciously, and Tristan starts doing the thing where he gets anxious and hops a little on his feet, until I give him a look to stop it.

"You must have a magic pussy to turn this guy straight," Santiago says, with a mean laugh. He gives me the rolled-up dollar bill and implies that I take the line instead. I look at Tristan again. He's standing perfectly still, not five feet away, but it may as well be an ocean.

I've had coke before, but I didn't like it. It's also hard to tell what this powder is. It could be heroin for all I know. If I believed in God, I would have prayed to him right then and there: not only that the coke wasn't laced with something, but that if He let me out of this mess alive I'd never do drugs again. I would mean it, too. In my previous life I would refuse to put anything up my nose unless I knew where it came from and had seen others do it first. But there's Tristan's sobriety to uphold, so I take the bill and snort the next line like I have often done with Adderall. But this isn't Adderall. Immediately, my entire body feels like I've injected coffee and happy pills straight into my brain.

"Pretty good stash, huh?" Santiago asks me. Then he waves Tristan over again. "Get the fuck over here, man, you're making me nervous. Let's have a good time already."

Tristan ignores my pleading eyes and sits down on the floor. He snorts a line of the powder, then reaches over and drags a finger across some loose powder and rubs it on his gums.

"That's a good boy," the guy laughs, patting him on the back. "None of this sobriety shit in my house."

Tristan stands up, shaking his head like he just swallowed something spicy. Still avoiding my eyes, he asks, "Dude, can I use your shitter?"

The guy turns to him with an appalled expression. "What do I look like, a preschool teacher?" he asks, shaking his head. "You gonna raise your hand to talk, amigo?"

Tristan lets out a small, tight laugh, then disappears into the hallway without looking at me. I try not to think about where he is going or what he is doing. If I do, I might pass out from worry. Plus, now that Tristan is gone, I have bigger concerns. Santiago moves closer to me on the couch, and keeps shoving the dollar bill in my hands. "I won't bite," he promises.

I have no choice but to take another sniff. Tristan is gone, and I can't let this guy go looking for him because then we would be in even worse trouble than my being a little high. Even my skin is buzzing. In my mind, I am praying to a God I do not believe in to get us out in one piece. But my mind and body have separated.

I grab the bill. The powder burns my nose as it goes up, and the chemical aftertaste pools in my mouth a moment later. My heart rate, which was already faster than I've ever felt it, is now working overtime. My teeth feel numb and alive at the same time.

"How did you meet my amigo?" the guy asks then. He relaxes into the couch with his arms raised and wide. I'm so relieved he isn't forcing me to do more drugs that I tell him the truth.

"At a horrible party," I say. "He was there taking wallets."

He seems amused by the story. "And what were you doing?" he asks, with a smirk.

"Looking for a friend of mine," I explain. In any normal circumstance I would have shut up then, but the coke is making every thought in my brain flow out of my mouth. "My best friend. Margot. She kind of ditched me for this guy, and I hadn't seen her in a while, and I wanted to talk to her about that and some other stuff, you know, but then I got there and she couldn't even get off his lap for a second." My mouth dry, I swallow my spit and catch my breath. "So I leave and she follows me out, but not to apologize or anything, to tell me she's moving and we all have to find new apartments." I start shaking my head now. I know I'm in a room of men who couldn't care less about me and Margot's problems, but for some reason it's sort of a relief to get it off my chest. I hadn't really thought about it since it happened. I'd relegated it to the back of my mind, along with everything else in my previous life, before my dad cut me off and Tristan swooped me up into his world. "And that was all after I found out my dad cheated on my mom and might have had another kid with her. She's been messaging me from Ukraine."

"Damn," Santiago says, the smirk moving from the corners of his mouth to his eyes. "That's a lot."

The other man still sitting on the couch with the other dogs shakes his head. "Women," is all he contributes to this conversation. I sort of forgot he was in the room. I turn and scan my surroundings and suddenly notice that I am a woman alone in a room of men I don't know. I find myself craning my neck, looking for Tristan to return.

"Don't stress, chica," the guy says. "I got a daughter your age. How old are you anyway?"

I swallow, my throat even dryer than before. "Nineteen."

"Nineteen," he says. "You're practically a baby." A look passes between Santiago and the other man.

"How old is your daughter?" I ask.

"I got four, can you believe it? The oldest just turned eighteen." He taps his chest a couple of times, and gazes into the space ahead of him with genuine awe. It was a good call to ask about his children, I realize in the moment with a flutter of hope. "She's an angel. Gonna rule the world one day."

Everything stands perfectly still for a moment, and I start to think the danger has passed. I even forget what it is we are doing there. But then his thin friend with the half-shaved head returns with my drugs, and breaks the spell. He has two little baggies, which he places in my hand, making sure to touch my hand a little longer than necessary. I stifle the urge to cringe. I stuff the drugs into the front pocket of my backpack and put it back on my shoulders right away. Now I am starting to actually get annoyed at Tristan. He better hurry or I'll have to get the hell out of here without him. If I am allowed to do that.

"What's her name?" I ask, as an attempt to return to our previous casualness. "Your oldest daughter."

"Isabella," he says with a grin. "Real smart, like you. Not like her Papa. Don't know where she gets it. It sure ain't from that bitch of a mother, god rest her soul." Here, he crosses himself. I want to ask what happened to this mother, but I'm not sure I want to know the answer. Then I regret not asking more about her, because Santiago chooses that moment to look behind him. A crease of uneasiness crosses his face. "What did this fucker eat before you got here?" he asks, forcing a small laugh. "Damn."

"McDonalds," I lie, because I know when he has eaten it in the past he also spent a lot of time in the bathroom. "He didn't feel well after." This must not be an uncommon reaction because the guy nods and doesn't push it. He reaches over to the table and takes out a cigarette, and offers me one. It's almost like he offered me a lifeboat, I'm so happy to take it. But maybe my McDonalds lie wasn't as good as I thought, because I catch a look pass between the men, and soon the other one is up again. Presumably to check on Tristan. My mood towards him shifts from annoyed to furious. He put me in a terrible position. He claimed to know where the money was. If he does, then what is taking him so long? Not to mention he broke his sobriety over this dumb plan. I stand up under the premise of going to the pet one of the dogs on the couch opposite ours, the black boxer-lab. I need to put some space between me and Santiago. "Is she friendly?" I ask, walking over more spilled trash and another bong and what looks like a broken guitar being used as a table.

"As a housecat," he laughs. I pet the other dog instead. The coke recycles my emotions in waves, like a Ferris wheel, for moments terrifying me, and then filling me with a confident joy that is totally out of whack with the present situation. It throws my intuition completely off, and I don't even feel that there's a man hovering behind me, until his hand has grazed my backside.

I can't help but jump a little. Then I correct myself and move to sit next to the dog. I try to tell the dog to save me with my brain. But Santiago seems to merely be having fun with me. He lets out a brief chuckle and picks up an ashtray that is sitting on the table next to us. Then he returns to his previous seat on the couch and pretends like I'm not even there.

Petting that dog like it's my only lifeline, my anger returns with a vengeance. I keep the cigarette in my hand and smoke it slowly in case I will need to use it as a weapon. It's gone quiet and still in the living room, and this isn't a good sign. Any moment they are going to start looking for Tristan, and any moment they will find him somewhere he shouldn't be. And in the midst of all these contradicting emotions and worries I somehow find a moment of clarity: that my life has gone *completely* off the rails. That I need to get away from everything that is keeping it off the rails; Milwaukee, Riverwest, and most of all: Tristan. Of course, this is the moment Tristan chooses to make his reappearance. He materializes, as if out of nowhere, and sits beside me on the couch. He puts an arm around my shoulder and squeezes. I have no idea if he found the money and if so, where he is hiding it.

"Sorry, man," he says. "Something wasn't sitting right."

"We've heard," Santiago says pointedly.

So quickly I wonder if I imagined it, I feel Tristan's arm move down from my shoulder and deposit something into my backpack. Then he stands up like a bottle rocket, and pulls me up by the arm too. "Well, thanks for the hospitality, man. Appreciate it."

"Anytime, amigo," Santiago says. "I was just getting to know your girl. One more before you hit the road?"

"Sure, man," Tristan says without hesitation. To my total surprise, Tristan and the man do another long line of coke. As if we are only here as party guests. This one, unlike the first, seems completely unmotivated by pressure. He *wants* to snort more coke. He isn't being forced. My anger turns to outrage. Has he been coming here and doing drugs for the last few weeks, and I just didn't know about it? How else are these two so friendly he knows where the money might be? I decide I've had enough. I came as a decoy. There is no way I am sticking around here and watching him get high.

"I'm going to go unlock the bikes," I tell Tristan as he remains hovered over the table. "Okay?"

"See you in a sec," he says without looking up. I'm pretty sure he does a second line of coke but I don't stay long enough to find out. I walk straight for the front door and open it.

I am half expecting someone to follow me and chase me out the door, but when I turn around, no one is looking my way at all. Someone has even started a joint. Could he really be getting away with such an abysmal endeavor? Is he going to stay and smoke with them? I know in that moment that Tristan was right: Drug addiction is a prison with no room for visitors. There's no space for others. And that includes me.

Whatever. At least I made it out of that house in one piece. I practically run across the street, past the barking dogs and the caved-in porch and whoever is left out there smoking, if there's anyone at all. The cold winter air has never felt so good on my skin, after what I experienced inside. That level of illegality is a step way too far for me to take. Skirting the rules a little is one thing; but now we are flirting with actual felonies and prison time. Even if I didn't do the drug dealing or the stealing, I could easily be considered an accessory. What if the guy took my picture when I wasn't looking? What if there are cameras? Had Tristan even considered that? How did I let myself get so sucked into this bubble? I need to be as far away from this place as possible. Even if it means leaving Tristan in there alone, and abandoning his bike without a lock. If a stolen bike is the worst thing that happens to him today, he should count himself lucky.

My hands are shaking so hard it takes me four tries to get the bike lock off, and Tristan is still not out. I get on August's bike anyway; I decide I will wait one more minute. The dogs are going nuts, and even though the men are off the front porch, I know they're still close by. It's quiet outside, but that doesn't fool me. It's a tense sort of quiet, not one of calm. The coke has nearly left my system already, and I am pure adrenaline now. I need to get on this bike and *move*. Right as I'm about to start pedaling, Tristan starts running toward me at full speed, followed by an angry dog nipping at his heels and then the thin man, who is holding a gun. The gun goes off before I have time to even think to duck. A bullet whizzes past both of us and hits the tree across the street. Lights start to go on around the house in windows that were previously dark. I know I should start moving but now I'm totally frozen with fear. I just stare at Tristan and don't move. It takes Tristan pushing my backpack to get me to notice. I still don't move, and he keeps pressing me. Finally I start pedaling, to put a stop to the pushing, but almost fall off the bike because my legs are so wobbly. They feel filled with water instead of muscle.

"Anastasia," he whispers. "You'll have time to be scared later. Right now, we gotta get the fuck out of here."

The man shoots at us again, the bullet landing in a different tree. "Don't you fucking show your face in this town again or I'll really kill you!"

"I didn't do anything, man!" cries Tristan.

"José saw you, man," the guy says. "Fucking dumbass junkie."

I look at Tristan, a question in my eyes. "He didn't see shit, don't worry. Just that I went into the room."

The guy is still out there, and is getting angrier by the second. But he's also barefoot and coatless and doesn't want to walk through the piles of snow that now separates us. He points the gun at his dog, and says, "Get him, Michael Jordan!"

The dog reaches us in a second and starts growling and barking in circles by our feet. Tristan kicks it, but this only makes the dog angrier. I see the dog's mouth latch onto his ankle.

"Anastasia, go!" Tristan says, trying to shake off the dog. Something about the dog breaks the spell I'm under, and I am no longer frozen in place. I start pedaling again, with more success this time. I don't look back even once, I just bike. I bike faster than I've ever biked before and probably ever will again. I don't notice the cold gushing against my ears because I've somehow misplaced my hat in all this mess. I don't notice my frozen toes, which are soaked from the snow and slush. I don't notice that Tristan isn't behind me. I barely notice the tears rolling down my face. I don't stop to notice anything, not until I reach Riverwest. Then I slow down. Then I look around. Then I stop. I drop my bike on the corner of Center and Pierce, and sit down on the freezing earth, so out of breath I start hyperventilating. I lie down on the wet ground, trying to catch my breath. I am totally spent, but I am also so relieved I could laugh. I even do start laughing, but because I am lacking in oxygen it only turns into a cough. It is in this state, lying prostrate on the ground in someone's front yard, when I notice a man standing over me like an angel. His dark hair is surrounded by the yellow glow of a streetlamp, and he smells like sweat. He smells familiar, actually. It isn't till he pulls me up by the arm that I realize who it is. Not Tristan, coming after me. Not his drug dealing friends.

Liam.

ANNA

CHAPTER THIRTY-TWO

"Anna?" Liam asks, a Camel Light hanging out of his mouth and a forty in his hand. Once I am standing again, he looks at me curiously. "What the hell happened?"

When I don't immediately respond, he walks me and my bike half a block over to the back of his house where there is currently a show going on. He sets the bike down in the yard, and by then my heart has slowed down enough to realize what nearly just happened to me. "Holy shit, girl," he says. He reaches around me for a hug. "You're shaking like a leaf."

I'm still too in shock to speak. I'm about to take my backpack off my shoulders to look for cigarettes, when I realize I don't have my backpack. Either I dropped it in the scuffle, or... or Tristan took it from me as I biked away. I guess I can add that to the things I am furious at him about. Whatever, I say to myself. I'm done with him and this entire thing. He can have it. As soon as I regain the feeling in my legs and lungs and heart, I'm getting out of here and never looking back. First, I swallow some air and try to find my voice. Liam takes out two cigarettes from his pocket, one for each of us, and even lights mine. Without asking, I take a sip of his beer. When he doesn't protest, I drink the entire thing. It's more out of intense dehydration than anything. I generally detest beer. But my water is in the backpack that's no longer on my back, like so many other things.

"Are you okay?" Liam asks again, looking at me with genuine

concern. I nod at him. He takes a seat on the elevated deck and motions for me to follow so I do. For a moment we sit there in silence and watch while in the yard, someone has started a small bonfire, and people begin gathering around plastic lawn chairs, getting louder by the minute. A typical Wednesday in Riverwest. Well, for everyone other than me.

"So...um..." I start, wondering how I can explain this. And I realize the truth would actually work. "I got robbed, I guess?"

"No shit? Are you okay?" he asks. In his glasses, the reflection of the fire twists and curls, then disappears. My heart soars so high and so low in one moment it turns into some kind of numbness. I take another last sip of his can.

"I will be," I say. I mean it, too. It's the worst night of my life, but in some ways it's the best, because I've learned exactly where my line is. And that I don't have to go down this road just to prove something to someone who isn't even watching.

"Here," Liam says, reaching into his coat pocket for a flask and handing it over. I take a long, long sip, feeling it burn all the way down my throat. The whiskey is a better repellent of the coke that is still in my system. It succeeds in taking my heart rate down a notch, but barely. The coke is really potent. I'm so afraid of my own body I never want to do another drug again. Also, now that I've seen where it can lead, I am *extra* done with drugs. If I find a way to do what I want with my life and get meaning from that, I won't need it. This is all very clear to me in a way that wasn't before.

"You want to tell me what happened?"

I shake my head. "It's a long story."

Liam lets out a little grunt, then continues to smoke his cigarette. He pats me on the leg in a friendly, not sexual, way. "All right."

"Sorry, thanks."

We sit there in silence for a while, at least the length of two or three songs, before Liam speaks again. "Where the hell have you been, lately?" he asks. The way he asks is almost shy. He seems uncertain, which is unlike him. "I feel like I haven't seen you in months."

I shrug. "Around."

Liam narrows his eyes. "You didn't answer my calls."

"When did you call?" I ask, dumbfounded.

He shrugs. "A bunch of times. I wanted to know what you've been up to."

I nod in understanding. "Melanie left you again."

"Now why would you assume that?" he asks.

I let out a sigh. I do not have the energy for that conversation. It's enough that I had to compete with her once already. A month ago it was all I could think about, but now? A relationship with Liam is the furthest thing from my mind. Instead of answering, I watch as a bunch of metal heads in studded leather coats stream into the backyard, drinking cans of beer and smoking something that's not a cigarette over the bonfire. Liam takes a long sip from his flask, then licks his lips. Two of the punks by the fire look in our direction like they might know us and come over. But I've never seen either of them before.

"Friends of yours?" I ask Liam, after they've checked us out a second time. I look closer, and they don't look familiar to me at all.

"No, I think they're looking at *you*. That's why I've been calling," Liam says. He reaches into his back pocket and produces a piece of paper from his duck taped wallet. On the paper is a drawing of a face. My face.

"Doesn't this look just like you?" he asks. I look at the drawing again, and have to admit it really does have a strong resemblance to me. Almost as if they got me to draw the thing myself. I read the text at the bottom. It says: "The Milwaukee Police Department is searching for a person of interest in several local robberies. If you have seen this woman, please call the number below."

My breath escapes in a sudden gasp, my hands letting go of the flyer. The paper falls to the ground, and Liam picks it up. "So it *is* you," he says. "I thought you just had a doppelganger out there robbing people."

I stand up, wobbly legs be damned, and take a very long breath. I don't have time to relax at a party. I need to make myself scarce. "I really gotta go Liam. Thanks for the booze. And the cigarette."

"Wait," he says, standing up too, and grabbing a hold of me. "Why don't you stay? Just for the night."

"I'm really not in the mood for a party."

"We can go hang out in my room if you want," he says. "Come on, it's getting late. And you seem really fucked up. Let me be there for you."

I look at him, weighing my options carefully. I've never been more certain of anything in my life than what I know in that moment: I need to get the hell out of Milwaukee. And in order to do that, I would need to make some sacrifices. Starting with Zoya's money, which I no longer have access to. I don't have a clue where Tristan has been keeping it, and my backpack is gone. And who knows if he was even able to make it out of there in one piece, with that dog on his leg. When he does, I doubt the first thing on his mind would be to find me. He'll need to find a doctor. It gives me the perfect window to go without having to also break up with him. But it also leaves me broke. "Do you have a computer?" I ask Liam.

"What am I, Amish?" Liam asks, laughing. "Of course I fucking have a computer."

"Okay. I just need to stop at home for second to grab a few things."

ANNA

CHAPTER THIRTY-THREE

Tristan isn't back at the apartment, which doesn't surprise me. As much as I don't want to see him, I'm sure he doesn't want to see me. First, he had put me in real danger. Then he threw his sobriety out the window like it was nothing. And to top it off, he stole my bag. I have a lot of things I need in that bag. My sketch pad, an extra set of clothes and underwear, an iPod with headphones, the expensive winter coat I took from the party, and my beloved (if not very in need of repair) Converse. Now I'd be stuck in my shitty winter boots for who knows how long.

Admittedly, I have bigger problems than a few missing items. I keep my wallet in my coat, so I still have ID and about fifty dollars cash, but without Tristan, that would be all the money I have to my name. Plus, my face is all over the walls of the Milwaukee Police Department. If that isn't a sign to get the hell out of Dodge, I don't know what would be. I don't even bother to look for our money because I know there's none in the apartment. I simply grab an empty garbage bag from the kitchen and start filling it up with everything I need. I would not be coming back ever again.

It doesn't take long; I left most of my things at my parents' house. Not ten minutes later, I'm back on my bicycle heading west to Valhalla. I go straight to Liam's room to find him totally passed out in his bed. I'm half annoyed and half relieved. I think about leaving, but then I see his computer is on and I sit down for a minute to write Zoya.

I don't even open the two new emails I received from her, because I already know what they're going to say and I've had enough of people threatening me and trying to use my good nature as a weapon. It's time I start taking care of myself.

Dear Zoya,

Go ahead, tell the whole world what my dad did. I am no longer taking responsibility for his actions. It's time I start making my own decisions, poor or otherwise.

P.S. My dad would probably rather deplete his entire life savings on lawyers than pay you a dime, so really, good luck in court.

Anastasia

I breathe a sigh of relief, knowing that is no longer on my plate. I tell myself I won't give it another thought. Now, I really have no one stopping me from doing anything I want. And, unlike before, I know exactly what that is. It's definitely not going to Ukraine; I've flirted quite enough with danger, I don't need to risk more. And it's not going back to school. It's something else altogether. I pick up Liam's cell phone from the floor and call a number I have used so many times that I have it memorized.

"Hey," I say into the speaker. "Where are you right now?"

FEBRUARY 2008

MASHA

CHAPTER THIRTY-FOUR

The following morning, I wake up yet again to a very loud banging on the door.

"Masha!"

I sit up, hitting my head on a hanging plant. "Ow," I say aloud as I walk to the door, rubbing my head with a palm. Who would be knocking like that so early in the morning? Who even knows I'm here? It certainly doesn't sound like Rose. She has a spare key hidden somewhere, and, as always, she doesn't seem to enjoy being home. Spending so much time in her apartment without her there reminds me why I moved out so quickly after she'd replaced June; Rose was practically never there. And Emily, she'd disappeared almost entirely, too, after June had died. I couldn't blame her now, though I did, then. We should have both moved out right away, instead of trying to live there like nothing had ever happened. Because everywhere we looked, we saw June's dead body; I saw it every time I passed the door of her old room, I remembered it when I used her dishes, I dreamt of it, so cold and blue, my sleep. She may not literally have been haunting us, but in a way, her presence did plague us. And because I never addressed it, it only grew from there. Soon she began haunting Center Street, and Riverwest, and the entire city of Milwaukee, until I had to get as far away as I could.

I'm not sure why I no longer feel her here—maybe time really does heal—but now, I am starting to remember what I used to like about

Riverwest, not only the bad stuff. How every other block, you run into people you know, or at least look familiar. How cyclists speed by you no matter what the weather; it could be blizzarding out and a guy in all black would still ride past you through the snow, covered in winter gear. Most importantly, it's so small; you could walk from any bar or cafe in Riverwest all the way home in less than fifteen minutes. And this, the fact that people will show up at your door with no warning and knock on it. It's like we're living in the eighties.

"Who is it?" I ask. I turn to check the clock on the microwave and am surprised to learn it's eight in the morning. I'm so tired I thought it could still be the middle of the night. Or, maybe I'm hungover. Yes, that's it. I'm hungover for the first time in years.

"It's your dad," the voice answers. Either I am still half asleep or unusually bewildered, but I can't figure out why my dad would be here. So I open the door partway, trying to blink the sleep away from my eyes.

"You're not answering your phone," Papa says in Russian. "I've been worried."

I open the door further to let him inside. The blanket I am wearing around my body falls to the floor, and a shiver passes through me momentarily before I can get it back on. "Papa, I told you I wouldn't be able to call you or drive back. It's Shabbat. No phones, no cars."

He lets out a breath of air, as if he's been holding it since we last saw each other. "I didn't know that. Sorry."

"I told you that like three times!" I complain. Is fifty-five is too young to have Alzheimer's? Or is it just the constant lack of sleep eating away at his memory skills?

Papa doesn't move from the doorway. "Maybe you did. I can't remember."

If he didn't look so worried, I might be annoyed at him, possibly angry, too. But he's too pathetic-looking to be angry with. This stuff with Anna is clearly getting to him. I'm sure it doesn't help that Mama is gone. My dad was never good at being alone; he went straight from his parents' house to living with my mom and her parents. Then we came along, and it had been a full house ever since. The quiet, vast emptiness is likely starting to get to him.

"Come inside," I tell him now, gesturing towards the very messy living room.

"This is okay. I came to take you to your grandparents," he says. "They calling me nonstop."

"Oh," I say, grabbing my coat and bag. "Okay."

"How did you even know where I was?" I ask Papa, sitting down across from him in the car.

"I remember house," he explains.

"Did you talk to Zoya?"

"No," he says. "I didn't."

"Papa! I'm doing everything I can out here and—"

"I tried. I couldn't get. Odnoklassniki where we talked. The account is deleted. Emails got returned."

"Sorry, I shouldn't have snapped at you," I say, looking out the window as we zoom past Gordon Park and over the Locust Street bridge. "I'm tired."

"What about you?" he asks. He moves away from me, a funny look on his face. "Other than getting drunk, did you find something?"

"Maria?" my dad asks again.

"Sorry. I did make some progress. I got some phone numbers from a friend of mine," I say. "Got" is probably a nice way of putting it; I had forced Liam to write down the numbers for me before I would get out of his shitty van. "For her old roommates."

"Da?" Papa looks pleased. He reaches into his cigarette carton and takes one out to light. "That could help."

"Problem is…."

"Shabbat." He smiles a little. "See, I do listen." He looks out the window in thought, then opens it to let out the smoke. The sound of birds twittering enters the room, and for a moment, I feel relaxed. It's easier now when my dad is relatively calm. When he is nervous, or

273

anxious—which happens often—it's like there's so much of it inside him it spills over onto me and I can't feel anything else. It's probably why I am so much more relaxed in Israel. "Okay. Well, I can call them after grandparents."

He turns down Oakland Ave, and becomes quiet for a moment. Then he gazes at me with a strange expression. It's part wistful, but disappointed or angry too. "Did you know your sister smokes?" he asks.

"What? No."

"She thought she could hide it from me…" he starts, then shakes his head. "I'm not as stupid as I look."

"I can't imagine anyone calling you stupid," I grimace.

Papa inhales deeply. "No matter what I try to do for you two, you just do the opposite."

I swallow. "She's nineteen. I'm sure it's a phase."

My dad looks me right in the eye. "Was it a phase for you?"

I turn away. I don't think he's talking about smoking anymore. "Give her a break," I say. "It's not like it was when you were her age. People don't have time to ask questions when they're starving."

"And this better?" Papa says, gesturing to the ceiling of the car, meaning the entire world of 2008.

"In some ways it's better. In other ways, it's worse," I shrug. "But that happens with every generation, don't you think?"

Papa sighs, then pulls into a parking spot on Farwell Avenue. He puts his coat back on and opens the door, all in one swift motion. I follow him outside as we walk into the apartment building more familiar to me than any of our previous homes because my grandparents hadn't lived anywhere else in nearly twenty years.

"Did you look at Anna's bank accounts at all? Did you find anything?"

He shakes his head. "Nothing." Then he goes into his pocket and reaches for his wallet. "That reminds me." He shoves a bunch of cash in my face.

274

"What is this for?" I ask. He's so close to me now I can smell his generic Dove soap. I back up a little.

"It's not from me," he explains. "It's from your grandpa."

"Oh. Nazi money?" I ask, taking the pile. It's probably my portion of all the quarterly reparation money he gets from Germany. There's like over a thousand dollars in there. I figured once I left he would give my half to Anna, but it doesn't appear that way now at all. Or maybe he did give money to Anna. Maybe that's the money she used to leave town. "Wow. That's a lot of German guilt right there."

Papa slides his hands into his coat pockets and starts walking up the stairs. "I guess maybe we know where Anna got the money to leave," he says.

MASHA

CHAPTER THIRTY-FIVE

"Mashinka!" Dedushka cries out with joy. "Finally! You're here!" He wraps me in a suffocating hug, before allowing my grandmother to do the same. By the end of which I have to sit down on their itchy couch to catch my breath. This is hard, when it's probably eighty degrees inside. I wave a hand over my face, hoping they will get the hint. They do not.

"What took you so long?" Dedushka asks me instead.

I turn to my dad in confusion.

"They calling me nonstop since you landed," he repeats in English. "But you had…enough to deal with." The way he says it makes me understand: they have no idea that Anna is gone. Maybe they don't even know my *mom* is gone.

"Excuse me," I tell my grandpa, the closest phrasing to 'I'm sorry' that Russian has. "I was really busy."

"Too busy for your grandparents?" Babushka chimes in from the rug-covered couch. It disturbs me slightly that she hasn't bothered to put on real clothes for our visit. She's in a long, cotton dressing gown with several large stains on it, and holds a thick blanket over her lap that smells like it didn't dry well enough before she took it out of the dryer. "Who practically raised you? Oy, such ungrateful girls you have Pavel."

My dad explains: "Mama. She only arrived yesterday."

"I'm here now," I say, trying to relax them. "Isn't that good

276

enough?" As I begin to peel off my coat, which is now stuck to me with a layer of sweat, I take the moment to look around the apartment. Was I expecting it to be different? If so, I would have been disappointed; it is exactly the same. I don't think even one old framed photo from the long array of our school yearbook pictures has been moved. Like a time capsule from the nineties. No, like a time capsule from the Soviet Union. Because they still have all their old flower-patterned dishes and hand-painted tea sets and beautiful glassware sitting behind a glass case, as if in a museum collection, practically untouched. They never made friends here, not really, and I doubt people come to visit them other than my dad. And sure, most people in the building are old and Russian, some of them even related to them. But they probably have nice china of their own. What reason would my grandparents ever have to take it out? Even on their birthdays, we always went out to eat, or for the major ones, had parties in Russian restaurants.

"You're getting old. Why don't you give me any grandchildren?" my grandma starts. "You know I don't have much time left." I don't bother responding to this age-old request. I'm too hot. I fold my coat over my arm and stand up. Then I turn into the kitchen, which is only a foot away from the living room, hoping the air will be cooler here, but it's not. In the sink, I notice, there are a few nice glasses and plates standing in water. Dirty.

"Babushka, you have grandchildren," I say. I sit down at the small dining table, which is littered with photos and mail. "I think what you mean is great-grandchildren."

"Masha, stop being such an elitist. You know what I mean," my grandma says, nearly making me choke with laughter. She has a point, perhaps.

"Anastasia's nineteen, and I'm not married or ready for kids in any way," I explain. I gaze quickly at the clock, a Hebrew one they got on their last visit to Israel with an image of a praying rabbi in the background, says it's a little past noon. My grandma went nuts buying things with Hebrew writing on them—besides the clock, there is also a mezuzah, several oversized T-shirts and caps, and at least ten different candle holders—all so she could practice reading them upon her return. In another life, she could have been a linguist. In another life I could have, too. "Sorry. You may need to wait a little longer for great-grandkids."

I start rifling through their mail so I don't have to look at them and come off as annoyed. This topic of conversation is always draining for me. I can't think of a good excuse to leave already, although I would prefer to come back tomorrow or when I have less on my mind. I still have so much to do; I'm not any closer to finding Anna. She could be in danger. She could be in Ukraine! She could be in danger in Ukraine. I'm about to say I have lunch plans, but then I remember my dad knows I ate because we ate together, at Beans and Barley, about ten minutes before we arrived.

"I don't have time to wait," Babushka complains. "I'm practically dead already. What about this boyfriend of yours? Is he Jewish?"

"Mama, please," my dad says.

"Of course he's Jewish. I live in Israel."

"You live in Israel? Bozhe moy. How could you do such a thing to your parents?" Babushka asks. Then she stops as if remembering something. "Well at least he's Jewish. Tell him to marry you already so I can see your children before I die."

"Babushka, you've been telling me you're dying for about twenty years," I explain. "I think it's safe to say you're not actually dying yet."

"Nothing safe about being alive, young lady," she merely replies. "Especially not at eighty."

"You're eighty-three," my dad corrects. He is standing next to the table with his arms crossed, looking more impatient than I am. I look back to the scattered piles of mail. Most of it is junk, but then I notice a handwritten letter sticking out of an open envelope. Who would be writing my grandparents handwritten letters?

"Once you reach a certain age, who cares?" Babushka shrugs. This is true, but my grandparents have never really known their exact ages. My grandma's mom forgot hers, and my grandpa lied about his to avoid getting conscripted into the Russian army for an extra year or two after the war ended, so he no longer remembers his actual birthday, either. We celebrate it on Yom Kippur. Which, as it turns out, was the day my dad called me to return. In the chaos, I had completely forgotten to wish him a happy birthday.

"Dedushka, Happy Birthday!" I say, standing up again to give him a hug. "I feel so bad now that I didn't call you."

"Oh, thank you," he says, surprised, but smiling again. As I hug him, my coat falls from my hands onto the floor. I bend over to pick it up. The slight draft knocks over the letter I had noticed onto the floor and flips it over, so that I see the return address. I remain on the floor an extra moment to look at it to make sure I'm not imagining things.

Nope, I'm not. It's a letter. From Anna. With her current address. I shove the envelope into my pocket and put the letter back on the table as I stand up. Relief blooms in my chest, and I am calm for the first time since my dad dropped me off in Riverwest.

Somehow, I manage to get through ten more minutes of small talk with my grandparents before my dad is satisfied we've stayed long enough.

"Come back soon," Dedushka says. He glances over at my grandma, who is chewing on what looks like a cold leg of chicken, her face covered in some kind of sauce. "Say goodbye, Mila."

"I'll meet you in the car," my dad says, and skedaddles.

"Don't forget us," Babushka says. "College is important but so are your grandparents."

"She lives in Israel," Dedushka repeats. "Anna is the one who—"

"Ah. Yes, that's right," my grandma says nodding, still chewing on the chicken skin. "Masha lives in Israel, and never visits, that ungrateful girl."

"I'm Masha," I explain. "I'm here now."

She looks at me as if she hadn't noticed me there before. "Oh, okay." She folds her hands together on her lap and looks to my

279

grandpa. "Where does Masha live, Sasha? Italy?"

"*Israel*," he answers gruffly, sitting down on an armchair beside the couch. All the energy he had seems to have deflated

"Babushka, I'm visiting right now!" I explain, trying to keep myself from getting annoyed. Then I take a deep breath. It's not her fault, I remind myself. She'd always been easy to get annoyed with; my whole life she was judgmental and sort of mean, causing fights with anyone she could find to fight with, fights so intense that she no longer speaks with any of her living siblings or their kids. Usually I could laugh her judginess away. This, however, is no longer the case. Now that she is obviously sick, it's more sad than funny or annoying.

"Right," she says, nodding, staring into space. "Did you know my brother is trying to take my plot at the cemetery? My own brother!"

"Huh?" I say. "Can he even do that?"

"Enough, Mila. No one is taking your grave, for the hundredth time!" He shakes his head at me and apologizes for her. "I don't know where she gets this idea."

"It's okay. It's not your fault. It's not her fault either," I explain. But my grandpa doesn't believe this; I can tell from the expression in his eyes, which is still a little angry. He wrings his tiny, hairy hands together and closes them around each other. Sweat pools in the front of his white wifebeater tank top. Behind him, the radiator starts hissing. He stares at me, brows furrowed, serious now.

"Masha, I have to ask you: your sister's not in trouble, is she?"

"What have you heard?"

Dedushka looks towards the windows, which are covered in lace curtains and a layer of snow. They face a parking lot with several large Dumpsters in a row. An old woman is standing there waiting for a tiny white dog to relieve itself in the dead grass. "I gave her some money a few weeks ago, but since then I haven't been able to reach her. What happened to her phone?"

"Oh…I think it broke."

"Did she go on a trip? She wrote us a few letters."

"I think so."

"But she's okay?"

"She is totally fine. She had a fight with Papa." I really do believe now that she's okay. And if she's okay that means I can go home. I only wish I could take her with me. I can't stop thinking about how much better off we'd be if we'd never received that letter from the American embassy approving our refugee status; if we'd gone straight to Israel, like we'd originally planned. Israel is where we belong, that's as clear as day now. My parents chose America for financial purposes, and the cost of this was everything that had gone wrong. Money isn't enough, not the lack of it nor the surplus, to replace what you lose when you uproot an entire generation of people from their home. Money alone cannot take the place of community, culture, physical closeness. In Israel, it would have all been different. This would have never happened to Anna there. She wouldn't have needed it.

"I see," Dedushka says. From below, my dad beeps his horn in the parking lot. I know it's him because I can see his car from here. I stand to go, but my grandpa looks so miserable that I first have to give him another hug. He is even sweatier than he was earlier. My grandma, on the other hand, is covered now in two blankets and looks dry as a bone. I am filled with so much love for them it's like a balloon that could pop if I stand there any longer. "Well, as long as she is okay."

"See you soon, Dedushka," I say, blinking back tears. I hadn't realized till now how much I'd missed them being abroad all these years; how much I will miss them when I return. He doesn't ask me why I'm in town, which I'm grateful for. It occurs to me that he might not care why. Then he squeezes me so tight I can't breathe again.

"Oh, Mashinka, you and your sister are my life. Please come back more often. When are you flying home?"

I don't know the answer to this. My dad only bought me a one-way ticket. Possibly this was a hint, but I choose to believe it's because he doesn't know how long this might take. "I'll come say bye before I go, I promise."

I move to my grandma and give her another hug, too. A piece of food that is stuck to her cheek falls to the side of my sweater, and I quickly flick it off. "You tell my son Pavel I'm not dead yet and he better visit me soon. He's forgotten about me, his own mother!"

"He was just here, what are you talking about!" Dedushka yells.

"I'm a useless old lady now," Babushka laments. "Oy, you better hope you don't live this long, my granddaughter. Sixty, seventy, okay. But eighty? Put yourself out of your misery first."

"Mila, for God's sake!" my grandpa screams, getting angry again.

"It's not her fault," I explain again, patting my grandpa's shoulder. Because of the work I do in Israel, tutoring and helping new immigrants translate official documents, I've spent a lot of time around elderly Russians, and they seem to take dementia extra hard. It's probably because no one lived that long in Soviet Ukraine, so they never had a chance to witness what happens to people when they reach such an advanced age. Instead of being sad, they get angry, like the other person is merely trying to annoy them. "She's sick, Dedushka."

He continues to shake his head in bewilderment. "He was just here," he repeats, almost as if to himself.

"I know," I tell him, patting his shiny bald forehead like I used to do when I was little.

Once I'm outside again, my stomach aches with so many conflicting emotions I almost feel like I could throw up. I've only been gone a few years; in some ways, nothing has changed at all. But in others, it's like an entire lifetime has passed. My grandparents have always been old, in my mind. In some ways my grandma is right. Seventy is old. Eighty-three and eighty-five? Practically ancient. You can die from a cold. And that's if we even know their real ages. What if I never see them again?

How could I ever repay them for what they did for us? Can anyone really ever repay anyone?

I get into the car, squeezing the envelope in my fist. It's like a little bright star emanating from my pocket. Then I turn to Papa.

I try to take in the image of him, smoking a cigarette with his shoulders slumped, drinking his third espresso in a row. My father who is most certainly only going to get older, too, the longer I am away. I am already thinking about how I will remember this moment, how the trip will settle into my brain and feel less and less real the more days pass in Israel with David. And the more days pass, the more I will remember what I already spent so much time learning before and forgot: it's hard for me to be apart from my family—but it's harder to be *with* them. Not everyone is meant to share space. I prefer to love them all from afar. Because we are so different, it's the only way I can be myself.

I also want to forgive them. I've spent the last five years trying to ignore the shadow of guilt I feel every time I have a good conversation with David's parents instead of my own. I was so mad at them for being unable to accept me that sometimes I couldn't see straight. It felt like I could only see myself in opposition to them. This was, in part, why I'd left, and why I'd enjoyed Judaism, too. Sure, it has rules, but for the most part its followers can do as they please and believe in God as much as they choose. In contemporary Hebrew, Ba'al T'shuva describes a Jew from a secular background who becomes observant. T'shuva also means to atone for one's wrongdoings. So in a way, becoming religious in Israel is a process of also atoning for your past. In the month before Yom Kippur, rabbis preach T'shuva, or atonement, between people and personal relationships; on Yom Kippur, we seek reconciliation between us and God. If I'm being honest, I'd always skipped straight to the latter.

I'm seeing now that was a mistake. The two are eternally linked.

Without turning to face him, I tell my father, "You should have told me about Zoya."

He places his mug down into the cupholder with a thud. He doesn't appear to feel sorry; but I know it's not my responsibility to make him feel so. I can only control my own reactions, not his. "Why, so you can look at me how Anastasia looks at me now?" he asks. "What good would that have done?"

He's right. I can barely look at him. But it's not for the reasons he imagines. It's because he's a liar. It's because he's unable to look in a mirror and see himself. Everyone makes mistakes; even rabbis admit to them. It's how you choose to make up for these slipups that shows who you are. "Is Mama still in New Jersey?" I ask.

"I think so," he says. "Why?"

"Good," I say. "I need to tell her where to find Anna."

MARCH 2008

ANNA

CHAPTER THIRTY-SIX

I'm getting off the train at the corner of Neptune Ave. and Ocean, like I do every Tuesday and Thursday afternoon, when who do I see standing there at the bottom of the steps?

My mother, of all people.

I nearly fall down when I spot her distinct brown-and-cream fur coat. She surprises me by rushing forward and hugging me tight. That hug, or maybe the smell of her freshly washed hair, or maybe all of it—New York City, dust creased into my jeans, the uncertainty of tomorrow—sends a jolt of guilt through my whole body. And here I thought I'd left all that guilt behind in Wisconsin, along with the rest of my family.

"Privet, Anastasia," she says into my hair. The hot water is out at our Williamsburg apartment, and I haven't washed it in days, so I pity her nose, and feel slightly embarrassed too. Then that is replaced by a jittery nervousness. It's almost like seeing a stranger; at the same time, it's like looking into a mirror.

"Hi, Mom," I finally manage to choke out. I dig my dirty nails into my palm while she stands back and watches me like she is seeing a ghost. I can't look at her, so I turn my eyes towards a deli with giant pink sausages hanging in the windows, over various chunks of white cheese, pickled radishes, pickled onions, bright yellow signs advertising caviar and fish. My stomach starts grumbling. This is my main problem with working in Brighton Beach—or Brooklyn in general—everywhere I

287

go I just want to eat. But only a rich person can live that way, not a barista.

"What are you doing here?" I ask, finally. I look towards the café down the block, where I am due for a shift in less than fifteen minutes.

Mom turns to follow my glance, searching for the café, but being obstructed by too many Russian booths and stores in her way; unlike me, these places furrow her brow instead of making her smile. "What are *you* doing here?"

"I work down the block," I say. "But I am guessing you know that already."

"Yes, one of your roommates told me you work around here. His name was August, I think. Is he your boyfriend?"

"Oh my God, no, Mom," I tell him, my eyes bulged out in horror. "He's like my brother."

"Hmm," is all she says.

"Did Masha tell you where to go? I finally checked my UWM email at the library and saw a few emails from her." She doesn't answer but I can't help but frown a little. "I still don't understand why she was looking for me."

"Because we're family," Mama explains. "That's what we do. We find each other."

My stomach grumbles again, this time loudly. Because my mom is a mom she cannot ignore this and takes out some cash to buy me something from the table closest to us, which is selling piroshkies, a croissant-like pastry baked with farmer's cheese inside. The sign is advertising three for a dollar. I scarf one down instantly, then, seeing my mom's face, hold on to the other two in my hand.

"Thanks," I say, my mouth full.

Mom begins accepting change from the old woman at the table, doing the entire exchange in accented English as if she doesn't want anyone to know she's like *them*. I finish chewing and start walking, putting the other piroshki in a pocket on my bag meant for water bottles. Reluctantly, my mom follows me down the street, which is plastered in Russian businesses as far as the eye can see. We pass by bookstands filled with Cyrillic spines, tables with mounds and mounds of matryoshkas; we have at least three of them in their basement in Wisconsin, in a cupboard with many of the exact types of things being sold here on the street: shiny, plastic children's books, delicately painted china. Orange, polka-dotted metal pans. Tables filled with kitschy Soviet relics; cigarette cases and lighters with the hammer and sickle on them.

"God, this is depressing," Mom says in English.

"What do you mean?" I ask. "This is so cool."

My mom shakes her head. Her face is paler than usual, her freckles practically gone. She looks as if she's left someone's funeral. "It's like nothing has changed in twenty years," she says. "Like they all just came here and continued along as if this is the Soviet Union."

"They want to hold on to their culture," I say. "What's so wrong with that?"

"Because, they're not *in* the Soviet Union," my mom says. "Why even come to New York at all?"

"I think it's cool," I say. Whenever I'm in Brighton Beach I can't help but feel like we're with our people. There were so many like us who had come from the same place and now stood in the same place again—so many who'd made the same transition. For a moment I forget that I derailed my parents' marriage, left college, stole things, hurt my sister, and took a fifteen-hour train to New York City. That everything I own is sitting in a room no bigger than a closet. That I can't decide if it's freeing or incredibly depressing and maybe even stupid. No, that's not true. It's amazing. It's the poorest but also the happiest I've ever been.

I haven't done a single drug since I came here, because I no longer have to self-medicate myself into feeling alive, I just feel alive by living.

"Did you see all those old ladies selling fruit that's almost rotten? They're basically beggars," my mom complains. I don't even feel bothered by this; we clearly do not see home in the same way. The things that make her feel alive are not the same things that do so for me. "They could've stayed in the Soviet Union and been beggars there."

"I don't think they're like *beggars*, Mom. Come on. They're selling something. It's like any other store here."

"And who do you think buys rotten fruit?" Abruptly, Mom stops again and looks around. "I can't deal with this. Can we go somewhere else?"

I stop sorting through a pile of DVDs with Russian titles on them. *Brat* and *Brat 2. Night Watch* and *Day Watch*, an apocalyptic vampire series I have seen numerous times already, and follow her east towards the boardwalk, even though I have to be at work soon. I don't feel like I have much of a choice.

"Does your dad know where you are?" Mom finally asks me.

"I don't know," I answer. "Does he know where *you* are?"

The sidewalks are glistening, the trees dripping. It's cold, even under my sweater and leather coat. Not quite winter anymore, but not quite spring either. "Why don't you come back to New Jersey with me?" She turns to me, putting a hand on my shoulder, brows pointed with concern. "Sveta has plenty of space. You can share your cousin Olga's room."

"Why don't you go back to Milwaukee?" I ask, annoyed. She knows perfectly well that I can't stand my cousin Olga or New Jersey.

"Anastasia."

"What?" I ask, crossing my arms over my chest. The leather of my coat swishes and pulls. "Are you going to stay there forever? Have you moved in with them? What about work?"

"Not forever, no." She pauses, looks down at her manicured hands. "Until..."

"Until what? Dad goes back in time and doesn't sleep with his accountant?" I ask.

My mom looks like I've slapped her, and now I feel bad. It's not her fault. Why am I taking it out on her? Probably it's just guilt. I'd been expecting to be discovered at some point, but I thought it would most likely be Masha who found me, or maybe even my dad. Not my mom. I had no idea my mom wanted to see me after everything I put her through. Well, after everything that my dad put her through and that I maybe helped bring to light. "Sorry," I say softly.

We start walking again, and even though I can't hear it, I suddenly know my mother is crying.

"How did you find out anyway?" I ask, softly.

"I'm not blind," she says. "And your father can't ever remember to log out of his emails, which I'm sure you've noticed." She shakes her head and almost laughs.

"I see."

"Anyway, it's none of your concern."

"But did he...is she...?"

"We never heard from her again, if that's what you're asking." She looks at me sternly. "And let's keep it that way."

"All right. Whatever you want."

"I just don't understand what you're trying to prove. That you don't need us? Fine. Point taken," she says, her voice shaky. Her heels click against the pavement, and mine drag, one of the flaps of my boot coming loose. I feel embarrassed and yet defensive at the same time. We don't usually have these types of conversations—honest ones—and I can tell it's hard for her. I can't help but wonder, too, how much Masha told her about what I was up to. She doesn't mention it though, so neither do I.

"Isn't that the point *you're* trying to make?" I ask her. She stops and stares at me, her brows furrowed. Then, to my surprise, we both burst out laughing. I suppose it is funny in a way. Like we are leading some sort of parallel life, so different than the ones we had mere months ago.

"Can we sit?" she tells me more than asks. I follow her to a nearby bench on the boardwalk, where she sits, then takes off her heels and starts rubbing her feet. I don't dare to take my own shoes off, even though my feet are sore too. The smell would probably knock us both unconscious. Alternatively, I look out at the clear blue sky, the jagged skyline and smooth water reflecting it, calmness and chaos in equal parts. Like yin and yang; or me and my mom; or life in general, always balancing precariously on the precipice of that fragile line between. It's a beautiful image, and it fills me with a convoluted mess of emotions, which, as it often does, turns into an idea for a painting. I try to imprint the image in my brain to use later. I picture myself with my paintbrush, blocking in the shapes of our bodies on the bench, the line where sky meets water. One of those Russian couples walking past in the distance, next to a Russian mom pushing a carriage, like my mom used to push me. It could be my best piece ever. Something about the circle of life.

That I can never stop painting is basically all I've really learned from this little adventure that started with Zoya's absurd message. That, and that everybody lies, so you should do your best not to.

And that includes lying to yourself about what you need.

"How about this," Mom says. "I'll go back if you go back. We can go together."

"I just got here," I say. What I avoid explaining is how that is not an option right now. Liam wouldn't be the only one after me if I was to return.

"Okay, here's another option," Mom says. "Why don't you go to Israel with your sister?"

I groan. Somewhere I must have known this would come up. "Israel, again...why is everyone always trying to send me to Israel? I would rather go to art school."

"You want to go somewhere, that's somewhere. The flight is free if you go on Birthright first." My mom puts her heeled boots back on her feet. "You won't be alone, and living who knows where. You can stay with Masha or her boyfriend."

"What? Isn't her boyfriend a cop?" At the mere mention of a cop, my heart starts to race. Ever since what happened with Tristan, when I see a police car, I automatically look away even when I haven't done anything wrong. What if David could see just from looking at me all the terrible things I'd done?

"He works for the government," my mom explains. "He's not a cop. He doesn't arrest people for speeding."

"Well, that's *way* better. I definitely want to live with some government spy," I say. "Especially one who made my sister all religious out of nowhere. Have I mentioned how creepy that is?"

"Your sister isn't *that* religious, Anastasia. She celebrates a few holidays, maybe she goes to synagogue sometimes. She's happy, so what? Is the problem that you're not happy so you don't like seeing her happy?" My mom sighs again.

If I have a superpower at all, it's the number of times in one conversation I can make someone sigh.

"I don't understand how you can hate a place you've never even been. Do you have any idea how ignorant you sound? You're almost nineteen years old. It's not cute anymore."

I'm not sure how to answer this. I stare ahead, watching as a little blonde girl in a red dress chases her dog down the boardwalk. I wish I could be that girl, entertained so simply, with so many years still to figure everything out, everyone constantly singing your praises no matter what you do. When we're children, ninety percent of our lives consist of adults touching us and staring at us, most of the time telling us how cute and great we are. It's a miracle that, as adults, we're able to overcome all the constant devotion and learn to function without it.

Perhaps we never really do.

"I don't know," I admit. "It just...always gives me a bad feeling. I don't know why."

"I know why. It's because you're embarrassed to be Jewish."

"No, I'm not," I say, automatically.

How old do I have to get for my mother to stop telling me what it is that I think and know?

"Yes, you are," my mom says. "I get it, I do. We all have to struggle with being Jewish in our own way. And maybe it's our fault. Your dad and I didn't grow up with it. We didn't show you how to be Jewish because we didn't know how, either. But I always felt Jewish in my heart. Maybe I thought it was automatically a part of you, that we didn't have to do anything. But I was wrong; I see that now."

I can't remember my mother ever admitting to being wrong about something, and I am somewhat taken aback.

Am I embarrassed to be Jewish?

I certainly never offer up the information freely. Friends in Riverwest speak of Israel with such disgust I'd always avoided these conversations as if being associated with the place would beget disgust. I didn't know enough about it to get involved and honestly, none of them did, either, so there seemed no point in starting. It's not like being Jewish had ever felt natural to me, or relevant. Maybe my mom is right. On this point, anyway.

"When your sister was little, she fell in love with these red sandals that your great-aunt Vera brought from Israel." Mom shakes her head a little and starts to smile. She's watching the girl with the dog too, running back across the boardwalk, her bright blonde hair streaming behind her like a kite, her red shoes sparkling in the sun. "She kept walking around with them, even though they were way too big on her. She even started sleeping with them. Your father and I couldn't get the things away from her even to clean."

"Really? I can't see her doing that."

"We didn't have much in Ukraine, as you know. It was something new, something...exciting. A pair of shoes. Israel felt like the most magical place in the world to us then," she says, wistfully. "Anyway, I finally had to tell her that Babaika took them."

"Who's Babaika? Like Baba Yaga?"

"Sort of. She's an old fairy tale ghost who likes to steal stuff," Mom says. "All day long she was yelling 'Babaika, Babaika, give them back!' Bozhe moy." She starts laughing a little. "You should have seen how serious she was."

"I can't imagine her being so caught up with a pair of shoes," I find myself saying, but when I look over again, my mom is wiping her

294

eyes. I can't tell if it's from laughing or crying. Either way, I am so sorry about it I have to bite my lip and look out to the beach again. I know I'm not supposed to, but I feel this...spark of excitement every time I hear stories like that, stories from the Soviet Union. Maybe it's because, in a way, everyone else feels a little bit excited when they're telling me. It's probably easier after you've already lived through the scary, dangerous part, only to remember the high stakes, the action. Can you ever untangle nostalgia from real hardships? Is it your decision which truth to hold onto, the good or the bad, or does that decision get made without any input from you?

I clear my throat. "Do you ever...miss all that?" I ask my mom, once she has regained her composure. I'd never seen her cry and now twice in one day. She must really be losing it. I look back to the water to see that the girl is gone, replaced by a different dog, racing back and forth with a toy, followed by a man in jogging pants. The two of them stop at the water fountains outside the bathrooms and drink from it simultaneously. "The Soviet Union, I mean."

"No," Mom tells me, matter-of-factly. "I don't think you understand how stressful it is to think you could be jailed or killed at any moment. To be afraid to walk in the street because you happen to be Jewish. Someone once reported me for having 'capitalistic' jeans. I made them myself! How can that be capitalistic? It still makes me furious." She pauses. "I don't think I was able to relax until we were here almost a year. I kept thinking they would find something to send us back," my mom says. She pauses and takes a breath. "I thought it would be easier for you here, Anastasia. That you wouldn't even remember the place you were born. But, somehow...I don't know, for some reason you both insist on doing everything the hard way."

I let out a groan before I can stop myself. "Have you ever thought that maybe I don't want to do things the easy way?" I ask. "No one wants an easy life. They want a *meaningful* life. The two are pretty much mutually exclusive."

"Maybe you think you don't, but that's only because you haven't had to go through what we have. I didn't want you to have to be hungry or tired or stuck in a position you hate because you don't have another choice," my mom says, right on cue. If survival consumes your mind for so long, you don't get to see past it; you don't get to the part where necessity and need start to diverge. I know she won't understand, but I also know I need to explain. "I want what's best for you."

"Maybe instead of telling me what's good for me all the time you can let me try to figure out what's good for me," I say. "Isn't that the whole point of freedom? So every person can make their own decisions?"

For a moment I think I might be getting through to her—if I will ever get through to anyone it would be my mom—but then she goes and ruins it again. She looks pointedly at my clothes and says, "I wish I could do that, Anastasia, but I'm less and less sure every day that you're able to know what that is."

How they don't see the irony of constantly telling me what I know and what I need to do, after escaping a life under totalitarianism, is really beyond my understanding, so I do not even try to respond to this. But my silence only eggs her on.

"I just think whatever it is you're looking for, you can find it in Israel," she says. "Plus, they have tons of programs that support people like you. Probably art ones, too."

I move right past the 'people like you' comment and sigh. For a moment I try to picture it in my mind, but all I can imagine is camels and people with guns. A market full of hookahs and oriental rugs. Men praying to a giant wall. Donkeys in the street. Pictures my sister had shared.

"I'm not saying you should move there, honey. America is the greatest country in the world; I still believe that," she says. "But a few weeks in a different place... might give you some perspective, at least."

"If you like it so much why don't you go there?" I ask.

"Maybe I will. We can go together."

"You should go home, Mom."

Mom scowls, her eyes darting from mine. "Anastasia..."

"I want to stay here, Mom. I want to be an artist."

"I see," she says, gritting her teeth.

I don't look away. "I'm not asking for your help. I'm not asking you to understand. I'm just asking you not to hate me for it."

I expect her to argue more, but instead she stays silent. Then she puts her hand over mine, and, surrounded by the Russian language echoing in our ears, we sit and watch the birds for what feels like a lifetime, imagining the places we would go, the things we would do.

Because we are free, and we are American, the opportunities are endless.

ACKNOWLEDGMENTS

Biggest thanks to my editor, Chantelle Aimee Osman, without whom I would never have written this version of the book, and Polis/Agora for all the help and support throughout the publishing process.

Another big thanks to my husband, who is surprisingly good at editing for someone who doesn't write. Without his constant analyses and our long walks discussing all aspects of human existence, this book would also never have come to fruition.

A special acknowledgment to my daughter Alma, who has been my lucky charm since the day she was born! I always thought this book was my baby until I had her and realized: nope, not my baby.

Thanks to my dad Igor and my babushka Valentina and all of the courageous relatives who came before me and are no longer with us, including the ones I was never able to meet.

Lastly, thanks to my fabulous in-laws, Haya and Eran Talmon, for all their support.

About the Author

Zhanna was born in the former Soviet Union and moved to the Midwest in the early 1990s. She has a master's degree in Writing and Publishing from DePaul University, and has been published in many literary magazines, including *Ninth Letter, Bellevue Literary Review, Tusculum Review, Midwestern Gothic, Another Chicago Magazine*, and five times in *Michigan Quarterly Review*, one of which received an honorary mention in Best American Essays 2014. She and her husband, saxophonist for Jazz-Rock fusion band Marbin, recently relocated from Chicago to Milwaukee, where, besides writing, she is raising her newborn daughter.